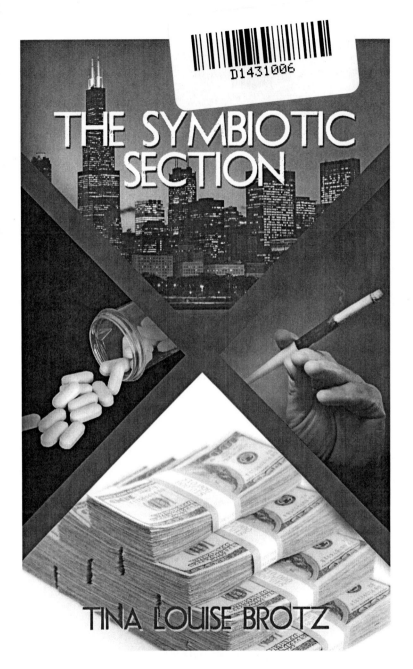

THE SYMBIOTIC SECTION

TINA LOUISE BROTZ

outskirtspress

DENVER, COLORADO

Outskirts Press, Inc.
http://www.outskirtspress.com

ISBN: 978-1-4787-0530-7

Library of Congress Control Number: 2013909471

Outskirts Press and the "OP" logo are trademarks belonging to Outskirts Press, Inc.

PRINTED IN THE UNITED STATES OF AMERICA

This book is dedicated to Frank, my best friend and hero who just happens to also be my husband.

Its creation would not have even been remotely possible without the support, love and patience you provide.

And for that, I thank you.

Live... Love... Laugh...

Prologue

The door to the secret chamber was locked behind him as he walked with a sense of purpose to the massive desk knowing that the task that lay in front of him tonight was a daunting one.

The business he wanted to purchase on the North side of the city was solid and the financials looked exceptionally strong. And although the wheels had been set in motion some time ago to acquire it and the preparation had been relatively smooth, there was just one problem, there was one person who had been vocally against him as the potential new owner, creating paper trails, roadblocks and red tape while trying to organize the workers to go on strike; and all the while, completely oblivious to the effect it would convey.

The phone's receiver was removed from its holder and the two-digit number was promptly speed-dialed.

"Tonight at eight o'clock there will be an unfortunate accident," was all that was said before the receiver was softly returned back to its original resting place.

Yes, he thought, *it was regrettable that an order for an execution had to be given, but it was necessary.*

Turning his attention to other matters, the hand that had promptly speed-dialed the number now reached for the over-sized accordion file, opened it and reaffirmed his closing arguments to present to the jury tomorrow morning.

Rubbing his chin, his steely eyes narrowed as they focused on the already memorized words staring back at him that were scrawled on the papers.

Either way, it didn't much matter, as far as he was concerned he had already won . . .

Chapter One

There was nothing else to do except to keep the child, who was playing in the next room, fed and comfortable while she sat and quietly waited. The ashtray, which now had at least a dozen cigarettes in it, was about to have one more added to the collection.

Elizabeth Dickerson looked up at the ceiling and then down at her hands that were clenching tissues that had been dampened with tears as she sighed. She thought about this newest affair, which she was certain her husband would swear was just a fling, just one of those things that just happened. After all, wasn't it *normal* to drive an inebriated woman home and then not only see her to the door but see her directly to her bedroom? Well this time things would be different and the tables would be turned on this egomaniac she had the misfortune of being married to.

How did things ever get so bad? she thought, as she took a drag on the cigarette, inhaling deeply. For the life of her, she just couldn't understand how someone could work such incredibly long hours, play rounds of golf, attend every marketing event in the city and yet, never go out of their way or allocate any time whatsoever for family.

But then, her husband wasn't just anybody. Oh no, to the world he was a great entrepreneur! Michael Dickerson, financial extraordinaire and marketing wizard, a modern-day legend in the banking world, but she knew the real man, had lived *his* story and had seen the filthy backside of his character; she knew he was filled with a thirst for power and driven to succeed; but at what cost? Apparently he had what her friends referred to as *cum-on-the-brain*, because even though he thought with one head, he was driven by the other!

Exhaling, she tilted her head back and watched as the smoke escaped from her mouth, while her hand smashed the lipstick stained butt in the ashtray until it finally stopped smoldering.

Now at a crossroads in her life, she was grateful for the photos that had been mailed to her by her brother, confirming all along what she had suspected these past few months. It had somehow made her decision even that more final, although it was unfortunate that it would not be less painful.

She heard the garage door open and took a deep breath as she sluggishly rose from the chair and grabbed her suitcase, listening as the footsteps came closer to the door that led into the house from the garage.

She was prepared.

"Where's Travis?" Michael said, walking right past her.

"A hello would be nice," she snipped then added, "he's in the playroom with his toys."

"Why is he in *there?*"

"Well that would be because he's *playing* Michael. That's why it's called a *playroom*," she said, annoyed with the very sight of him. *Who was he to question her?* she thought.

He went up the stairs, taking two at a time, as he shouted, "I've got to shower and then go back out for a dinner engagement. I just found out that Chris Swanson is in town and he's agreed to see me tonight. This may be the biggest account I've landed to date. Hey, I've got a great idea, why don't you, uh, call one of your friends from the country club to babysit Travis and join us?" he asked, as he continued upstairs. "You know Mary what's-her-name with the saggy boobs."

Undressing quickly, he stripped down to his underwear and walked through the master bathroom until he entered the adjacent closet where his eyes took in the vast array of suits, jeans and leisure slacks, all in different colors, styles and textures, making his selection choice somewhat difficult. He opened several drawers and compartments, slamming each one shut in search of the attire and accessories that would make the best impression for tonight's meeting. Irritated and unable to make a definite decision, he finally gave up and did what most men do given the exact same situation, he called out to his wife for assistance.

"Liz, I need some help up here!" he yelled, while looking at his watch. He waited for about a minute and then, upset that his needs weren't being met quick enough, he started with his daily barrage of insults.

"For the love of God, can you please get the lead out of your tired, stretched out pussy and hurry up, I'm on a schedule goddamn it!"

"I'm right here," she said, with coolness and dead

certainty in her voice, and then she added, "that's the problem, I've been right here the entire time but you never even noticed."

"Christ Almighty!" he exclaimed, stumbling back in surprise. He placed his left hand over his heart. "Are you trying to give me a heart attack?"

"No, I suppose I'm not trying to give you a heart attack Michael . . . since that would be too easy."

Dismissing her comment, he continued, "are you going to help me or not?" he said, looking at her with obvious irritation as he stood there with his arms crossed.

"What is it that you need *now?*"

"What is it that I *need?*" he asked sarcastically.

"Yes, I'm afraid the last time I looked, I didn't read minds," she said complacently as she held the opened envelope behind her back.

"What I *need* is a wife who helps me without me having to beg her all the time! What I *need* is somebody who wants to be with me! You know, like go to fund-raising events, dinners and charity balls. Instead, what do I get? I get some prissy-assed woman whose content to just go to her weekly bridge games, do volunteer work, which pays zilch, I might add, and spend a shit load of money on manicures and spa appointments and then when you come home you don't even look any better. Let's face it honey, you'll never make the cover of Vogue, not even close!" he spat.

"You ungrateful bastard!" she screamed. "What about me? Blah, blah, blah! You sound more like a hell-raising toddler than a grown man. It's always about you isn't it?

Always about being seen, always about the power play, always about another one of your *deals*!"

She positioned the hand with the opened envelope in front of her, looked down at it and then continued. This time, she was determined to say her piece, it was damn time, she thought.

"First of all, as for the fund-raising events, they're about as exciting as watching grass grow and the only thing they seem to *raise* is your hopes of finding some new slut to bed down with for those nights when you have your so-called long business meetings. Second of all, you know that I don't drink and as for your dinners . . . why on earth won't you just accept that I can't eat even half of that unpronounceable shit! And last of all, the charity balls that you seem to go out of your way for are pretentious, just like you. In fact, Michael, instead of *going* to the balls why don't you grow a pair and step up to the plate and be a man! Yeah, that's right, be a man to me *and* your son! That's all I ever needed and wanted!"

"Liz?" he said in a dismal tone of voice. "Are you getting your period *again?*"

"No Michael, no," she said with her head now bowed looking down at the envelope. Her hands were shaking, but in spite of that she removed the contents and held up one of the photos, this one was of her husband in a compromising position with another woman and then she stood there, solemnly waiting for his reaction.

"So what the hell am I supposed to say? You want an apology? Huh? Is that it?" he asked, with a defiant look on

be more humane. How can I look like I'm on the cover of Vogue when all I am is a goddamn slave! No! Not anymore! Today is the day I get my freedom from you and you can go get fucked, because now I realize that you're not even good enough for the sewer, yeah that's right, for the goddamn sewer!"

Michael's enragement, already at a high level, ignited into sheer fury, sending him over the edge as he walked over to his wife and punched her in the face, his eyes remaining fixed and hard as he watched his target fall back.

Staggering, she braced herself halfway up with her hands and then, looking up she saw Travis running towards her.

"Mommy, mommy, are you alright?" the child asked through tears.

Elizabeth, although dazed and in pain, made her move at that exact moment and swiftly pushed the young boy aside, grabbed her suitcase and ran outside, faster than she ever thought she could run. She screamed to the top of her lungs, "Help me! Somebody call the police! help!"

She ran and somehow managed to get to her car that was always parked in front of the house. Once inside, she opened the glove compartment and searched frantically for the keys, praying he wouldn't come out of the house. Her hand was shaking uncontrollably. Finding them, she nervously inserted the key into the ignition and took off, putting some much-needed distance between her and her abuser's dwelling.

Breathing heavily and feeling herself pumped up on

adrenaline, she glanced in the rearview mirror, actually seeing him open the front door to chase her, only to realize he was still in his designer underwear and he shut the door. She knew in her heart of hearts that she had done the right thing at just the right moment. Yes, she was now free and would have the kind of life she always wanted, always dreamed of and always deserved.

Still visibly shaken, she turned on the radio and blasted the volume. *Got to go faster*, she thought, *got to get away, got to survive!* She kept the accelerator floored and then . . . it happened; she noticed that the other cars on the road were all stopped. *Why are they all stopped?* she thought. *What's going on? What's happening? Oh my God!* . . .

But it was too late, Elizabeth's car was t-boned by an approaching fire truck, a fire truck she hadn't seen or even heard coming.

Perhaps it was because of the music on the radio that was blasting, or perhaps it was because she was driving in a state of delayed shock but regardless of the cause, she was ejected from her vehicle onto the pavement.

The sound of the car being totaled, her body hitting the street and the horrific scene sprawled out on the asphalt got the attention of many other drivers and made the onlookers who *did* look, cringe in horror.

Sometime later after what seemed like an eternity, as Elizabeth was strapped onto the gurney and wheeled into the ambulance, she finally regained a few moments of consciousness, just enough to answer the questions that the paramedic had put to her as he attended to dressing her wounds and numerous deep facial lacerations.

Yes, she thought. *I will survive. The doctors will certainly see to that.*

But there was another wound that manifested itself that day. A wound that couldn't be seen but was there, just beneath the surface.

Hate.

A hate festering inside of her. The kind of deep-seeded hate that motivates a person and essentially gives them the very will to live. Yes, she had decided she would not only go on with her life, a life which would never be the same again, but she would be driven to seek revenge on the one person who had caused her misfortune and changed her life forever.

Her eyelids were now droopy as the oxygen mask was placed over her face and the warm trickle of blood was wiped away -- the ambulance now in route to the hospital.

Her pain was agonizing as the excruciating feeling of broken bones and burned, torn flesh seeped into every part of her being. But just before she lost total consciousness, her lips slowly moved as she softly spoke two words, the two words that would now give her the necessary strength she needed to survive.

Saying them carefully and without hesitation, she whispered them in succession, "Michael Dickerson."

Chapter Two

Fifteen Years Later . . . . .

The coffee pot overflowed as the hot contents spilled onto the slab granite countertop and then onto the kitchen floor before it was finally discovered. "Oh Christ not again," Michael said with a defeated voice. Sighing, he walked over to the accident and pressed the illuminated orange button to the "off" position and unplugged the appliance. Grabbing a roll of paper towels, he tore off several sheets and allowed them to fall onto the puddle, moving his shoe in a circular motion to blot up the liquid.

"I'll have to deal with this later," he said out loud. "Come on Travis before we're late!" he yelled. Then he matter-of-factly poured coffee from the overly full pot into his extra large commuter thermos.

"Sorry dad, I guess I added too much water again," Travis said apologetically, "let me help you clean that up."

"No," his father replied solemnly through clenched teeth, "just get in the car."

Without a single word being spoken, father and son stepped into the vehicle, fastened their seatbelts and prepared for the trip that lay ahead of them. Adjusting the rearview mirror, Michael took one extra glance at his own reflection, and quite pleased with how he looked, he drove off.

The cars, buildings and scenery had all become blurred to Travis and were so similar to his fictitious relationship with his father. Looking in from the outside everything appeared normal. *What the hell was normal anyway?* he thought to himself.

"Ah, the torture and pain of silence. . ." Travis muttered softly to himself as he stared out of the window of the speeding vehicle. "Such a powerful weapon in the hands of someone so cold," but then, there was nothing warm or even normal about his father.

Michael Dickerson was the Chief Operating Officer and part owner of United Bank Marketing Incorporated, a large advertising agency, in the area deemed *The Magnificent Mile*, in Chicago that dealt with lending institutions, primarily banks. A highly specialized market, his job was to oversee the final stages of the production process in creating ads to generate more customers for the industry. The kind of ads that made customers feel warm inside and conveyed a feeling of trust so they would give you their hard-earned money even if the interest they received and the level of customer service were almost non-existent. More customers meant more profits and this meant late hours and being available to clients' twenty four/seven. Michael was driven by one thing and one thing only . . . the need to succeed and his success was the most important thing in his life. Now approaching forty with a seventeen-year old son, he would have to begin looking for someone to cheer on Travis at sporting events, host chic parties, prepare lavish meals, clean both his homes and, of course, service his every sexual whim on demand no matter how bizarre; yes, it was time to find wife number three!

In the car, Michael gulped his coffee, careful not to let any of the hot brew run down his expensive, freshly starched shirt and shifted his car into a higher gear. Taking a call on his cell phone, he swerved to avoid an oncoming bus, and then pressed down harder on the car's accelerator. Within five minutes he was in sight of his destination, Mercer High School.

Opening the door to exit the vehicle, Travis was barely able to grab his stained backpack before his father was driving off. "Drive like hell and you'll get there," he quietly whispered. He couldn't help but notice that his father never even looked back in the rear view mirror. Backpack in tow, he ran up the stairs to the main entrance of the school and made his way to his first period class, English.

Travis was bronzed, tall and lean with perfect teeth and just the right amount of muscle to make him an extremely good looking teenager. He hurried to Miss Young's class knowing he had two make-up tests to take today. He was grateful she had allowed him to do this since he had been ill off and on for the last couple of weeks. Winking at Kimberly, one of the cutest girls in the back of the room, he sat down at his desk and glanced at the thick exam packet before focusing on the ceiling. Then saying a small prayer, he took a deep breath, opened the packet and began.

Chapter Three

"Mr. Dickerson, line one. It's your ex-wife; I'm sorry sir, I don't know which one."

"It's okay Janice just put the call through," Michael replied with obvious irritation. He was on the phone for some length, mostly listening, when there was a knock on the door. Placing the call on hold, he looked up from his phone saying "What is the problem *now* Janice?"

"I'm so sorry sir, but it's Mr. Lindbloom on the phone and he says it's important," she stated with the wrinkles in her forehead more pronounced.

With an emotionless look on his face, he retrieved the receiver and noted the flashing button, realizing the call was in *hold* status. "Michelle, go ahead and check it out with your attorney since you insist and I'll have the papers to you by the end of the week," he said and hung up.

Slowly turning in his chair to face the window, he wondered what the hell was wrong with Black mothers. Why on earth did they have to give their offspring such weird names? If it was to show they were Black or African- American, as his ex wife had told him, he couldn't understand it. Hell, if they had named their kid John D. Rockefeller, people would still be able to *see* he was Black, at least *half* Black. He was glad he had insisted that their son be named Travis and not some strange African or ghetto-based derivative. At least something good came from *that* marriage.

Taking a deep breath he turned around, centered his chair in front of the desk and picked up the receiver. "Frank Lindbloom, what have I done to deserve this honor?"

The voice on the other end was rough and raspy saying, "Spare me the bullshit Michael. I've already reached my quota for the day. I want to know when I'll see a return on my investment." Pausing, the voice continued, "and I want you to audition a girl for me, Debra Morris, for a part in the next series of commercials for the Tollway-Arlington Bank. She's a personal friend of mine and this is important to me. She'll be at *Christopher's Bistro* tonight at five o'clock, that's all!" he ordered before the line went dead.

Quietly setting down the receiver, Michael thought about his life *before* Frank Lindbloom had entered it. He made his way over to the liquor cabinet and poured himself a generous portion of *Courvoisier,* a cognac he had grown accustomed to, and stared out of the floor-to-ceiling windows overlooking *The Magnificent Mile* on North Michigan Avenue. He ran his fingers through his thick sandy brown hair and looked down at the inhabitants of the sidewalk below as they frequented the high-end retail stores.

What had started out as an equal partnership had turned into an emotionally strained relationship over the years with Frank trying to have power over him and call all of the shots, orchestrating too many shady deals in the process to count. Unfortunately, he was still a partner and

and in Chicago, springtime meant really warm one day and freezing the next.

He couldn't stop thinking how different things were at this time last year when he was attending the Chicago Transitional Education Center or C.T.E.C. as it was referred to. He remembered how the students had left post-it notes on his locker telling him to *Black up or Black out* and how the words had stung.

Mercer High School had a more laid back vibe to it with kids of every ethnicity and every possible racial combination in attendance and he was easily accepted as being what he was, brilliant, beautiful and biracial. He was given the nickname Oreo, which would have been an insult to some, but Travis knew it was a term of endearment that only his friends used. Reaching his destination, he stood up, collected his backpack and waited for the bus to stop outside of the Windy City Gymnasium. He knew it would be a long day of practice but more importantly, he knew that his residence would be empty when he arrived home; with another long, lonely night ahead of him.

Chapter Five

Christopher's Bistro was extraordinarily busy this time of evening. The wait staff all wore black pants and off-white ruffled shirts. A red bow tie with an embroidered black "C" on it completed their look. It was deemed one of the nicest places to eat in the city because not only was it inside the John Hancock Building, it boasted a coveted East side location, which showcased incredible views of Lake Michigan. This was Michael's kind of place. He was truly in his element.

After work he had stopped by his home. He showered, shaved and threw on some beige slacks, a light blue shirt with white pinstripes, loafers with no socks and a custom-fitted navy sports jacket -- the perfect combination of dressy casual. As he drove to the restaurant, he tried not to think about how he was expected to audition this *personal friend* as Frank had referred to her, for the series of commercials to be shot in a few weeks. He hated to be ordered to do anything but he would have to swallow his pride on this since the Tollway-Arlington account was discovered, nurtured and cultivated by his partner. Just the price of doing business he kept telling himself. Hell, all he really wanted to do was get laid tonight and the sooner the better!

Arriving a few minutes ahead of schedule, he drove up to the curb, gave his car key to the valet and stepped inside. Michael went by the bar and collected his drink which was already waiting for him. As he entered, he noticed several female eyes watching him.

He instinctively knew which side was his good side, how to make his body appear even more appealing and how to carry himself in any given situation. He sipped his drink, smoothing his thumb over the ridges in the glass and instinctively knew that several hot-looking females were eyeing him at the bar. He ensured that his every movement was like watching a well-choreographed dance designed for maximum results, as he made direct eye contact with a few. Yes, he thought to himself, if his meeting with Debra Morris didn't go well, he might get laid tonight anyway.

Dispensing the necessary formalities, he nodded at the maître d and was escorted to his usual corner table booth. It was dimly lit and private so it suited him just fine.

Already seated at Michael's table was Debra Morris in an extremely low-cut, skin tight red dress, which left almost nothing to the imagination. *The newest flavor-of-the-month and wannabe,* he thought. He immediately recognized her and nodded. It seems after being in a couple of one minute tampon commercials; she felt she was ready for the big time. He sized her up in two seconds and determined that she was as bogus as the size 42DD retreads her bra now supported.

"Michael Dickerson at your service," he said, letting his eyes come to rest on what she was deliberately advertising.

"I believe you know my associate, Frank Lindbloom," he said extending his hand.

"Yes, he told me that you hadn't yet made a final decision for the female lead in the Tollway-Arlington Bank commercials. I believe I may be exactly what you are looking for," she replied.

"The casting is tomorrow morning at eight o' clock sharp; however I'll be glad to give you a private audition seeing that Mr. Lindbloom highly recommended you."

And so it went -- another dinner that he had to eat in autopilot mode. He knew that Frank Lindbloom was probably going to insist that she get the part even though she was wrong for it. If he was going to play along, then he damn sure was going to get something out of it. The conversation was strained during dinner on his part until he decided to just shut up, sit back, eat his meal and let Debra do all the talking.

Michael sat there, nodding and smiling but not really listening. He studied her closely as she rambled on, and she was completely oblivious of the fact that he was disengaged from her and decided to go on a quest to hunt for all the artificial things on Miss Morris' body.

Acrylic fingernails, veneers on her teeth, colored contact lenses, eyelash extensions, hair extensions that you could spot because of the unconcealed tracks, collagen-injected lips that were better suited for a baboon if she received one more treatment, wrong shade of concealer, two hole piercings in each earlobe and botoxed to the point that her eyebrows didn't move, he thought, noticing every single man-made accompaniment. *On the other hand,* he thought, *she was free of body odor, had nice teeth, no pimples, good posture, shaved her armpits, didn't have bad breath and, oh yeah, the most important part, she had tits and a pussy!*

Michael had ordered the filet mignon, twice baked potatoes with onion croutons, and broccoli in cheese sauce, fresh cranberries and dinner rolls with melted cinnamon butter. Miss Morris on the other hand ordered the lobster, crab, truffles, champagne and every other item on the menu that was particularly high-priced.

He took note of her as she talked non-stop about her looks, dreams and career aspirations. She was overly animated and her skin, although pimple-free, was dry which she tried to overcorrect with heavy, oily makeup.

Knowing a thing or two about jewelry, he noticed immediately that hers was costume; made to look like the real thing but in reality it was just a cheap, shitty-assed imitation, just like her. Christ! He was so tired of these women with champagne tastes and beer budgets. It seems they wanted permanent, lasting beauty but always had temporary, transitory funds in which to accomplish their goal. Hell, he was hard pressed to even find a woman without body piercing or a tattoo these days!

"I have a condo not far from here for late nights like this when I'm with clients, it's a special place. Why don't we go back there and you can audition for the part?"

Debra pursed her lips and did the proverbial hair flip that she was well known for, got up from her chair and left with Michael. She licked her lips while she checked in her compact's mirror for onlookers. She was hot and what's more, she put out, big time! A show they wanted so a show they would get. Two things she knew for sure; she was getting this part, no doubt about it, and she was great arm candy.

Chapter Six

Frank Lindbloom was feeling uneasy as he waited in the small receiving room to meet with Salvatore Rizzo because he knew exactly what this meeting was about. He took a deck of playing cards out of his pocket and nervously shuffled them back and forth in his hands; demonstrating his proficiency in this genre.

A small side door opened and he heard a voice tell him to enter. Walking into the semi-darkened room, Frank stood in front of the desk as he waited for the occupant of the chair to quickly turn around. Sadly, it did not happen.

As he waited, Frank noticed that there on the center of the desk was an ashtray made of Austrian borosilicate glass. Its top was formed in a shape that resembled a crown and was adorned with three distinct fine diamonds. Considering himself an aficionado because he knew a few things about expensive glassware and jewels, he determined its value had to be around seventy five hundred dollars by all conservative estimates. Frank's eyes widened as he stared at the ashtray. *It's only a goddamn ashtray!* he thought. *What an overstatement!*

This man had so much money he could probably wallpaper the walls of his estate with it and never miss a single hundred dollar bill. And yet, it should be me, Frank Lindbloom, on the other side of this desk telling people what to do. After all, haven't I paid my dues?

The occupant of the chair, which had still not turned around, was none other than Chicago's own, Salvatore Rizzo.

Salvatore Rizzo was first and foremost a Sicilian. To call him an Italian would have been a mistake and an insult! He was a man of tall stature who commanded the utmost respect and obedience when he entered a room. His mane of thick white hair was neatly coiffed with matching eyebrows and his bluish-gray eyes were as piercing as his smile was menacing. He was referred to in certain circles as *The Orange* since his family had settled in the small Sicilian town of Lentini, which was known for its orange groves. And just like an orange, he always squeezed until he got exactly what he wanted.

Salvatore lightly tapped the desk, avoiding eye contact as he inspected his well-manicured nails at length. Then, choosing his words carefully, he said, "One must lay the groundwork and always . . . always, prepare the work area for what may transpire, not only in one's personal life but especially in business. You know Frank; if you continue to ignore things they can get out of hand. Like fingernails, they serve a purpose but must be closely maintained to be of any *real* use and occasionally," he said rubbing his chin, "they must unfortunately be *cut* in order to maintain quality and harmony. You agree, no?" he asked.

Frank stood looking down at his shoes and answered, "Yes Mr. Rizzo."

"So we understand each other and we both know that the payment will be due in a relatively short amount of time. Let's just call this visit a social one although you can think of it as a pleasant reminder; from one friend to another. Let us further say that we, here and now, are preparing the work area, in a sense, for what is to come. I did you a good deed and loaned you the exact amount of funds for your various projects; without question I might add, and now you will return my unselfish act of kindness within the allotted time frame I have set for you."

Now he slowly and deliberately swiveled his chair around to have Frank Lindbloom in his full gaze. Salvatore Rizzo was a man that didn't miss much and he took personal pleasure in being able to read people, something he prided himself on. He could instinctively read that something was not right with the time frame.

"What is it? Speak up!" he commanded, his eyes cold and lifeless.

"I'm having some difficulty in obtaining the funds right now and I honestly think that since I've paid on time in the past that you might consider giving me a few extra weeks for an extension. Also . . ."

"Do you know who the fuck you are dealing with?" Rizzo asked. He then added, "opinions are like assholes, everybody's got one but you don't necessarily want there's in your face. We'll meet again in a few weeks and I hope you won't disappoint me, Frank . . . old friend."

Seeing the chair turn around in an about-face manner, Frank realized the meeting was over and was escorted out of the room. He walked quickly but as lightly as possible so as not to leave too many shoe impressions in the fibers of the carpet as he stepped on them.

Once outside, he took in several deep breaths and wiped the trickle of sweat drizzling from his temple. How he hated that pizza-making cocksucker for doing this to him!

His breathing was erratic and he had to walk slowly just to get through the parking lot. It was imperative that he remain calm just in case he was being observed. Staggering to his car, he unlocked it and sat down; his hands shaking and his skin was rather cold and clammy.

"Oh shit!" he muttered, as he immediately smelled something and realized there was no need to go to his proctologist appointment today. He looked in his lap, seeing the horrible stain on the driver's seat and knew that as far as he was concerned, he had just gone!

"Stop!" she cried, "I've never been fucked in the ass before! Never in my life, do you hear me! Stop, stop goddamn it . . . it hurts! Noooooooo! Noooooooo! You mother fucker! Get off me you son-of-a- bitch! You're splitting me wide open!"

"Everybody has a first time honey, so just consider this yours!" he said, with absolutely no regard to her objections. "Shut up!" he yelled back at her. "Just shut the fuck up, you gold-digger cunt!"

Now his appetite had become insatiable and he purposely applied added pressure as he rammed every single inch of himself into her tiny puckered asshole. Her screams continued but Michael didn't falter, he simply pressed her neck down, forcing her mouth into the pillow. "Bank on this!" he yelled as he pounded and hammered away.

His heart was pumping, the adrenaline was rushing, and the sensation was so overpowering that the pressure inside of him built up to a point where he thought he was going to burst but just before he let loose, he grunted saying, "Come on bitch, let's see if you can handle *this* deposit!" And with that, he let out a guttural sound as he exploded, completely relieving himself inside of her tight anal cavity.

Debra laid there on the bed, soaked in his sweat and shaking with her eyes wide and fixed on Michael. She cowered against the black leather headboard, her hands clenched tightly onto the bed sheets and she felt nauseous. The sharp burning pain in her now-inflamed rectum was almost unbearable. Blinking rapidly, she couldn't believe what had just happened.

THE SYMBIOTIC SECTION

"Stop looking at me that way!" Michael said casually sitting up in bed, "I just Ass--erted myself," he said laughing with a sneer on his face. Then he continued, "I'm not sure if you are adequate to meet the bank's needs at this time. But gee . . . thanks for playing the Who-Do-I Have-to-Fuck-to-Get-A-Job Game! Hope you enjoyed your parting gifts!"

Chapter Eight

The long line of female applicants reminded Janice of the candy necklaces she used to eat when she was a little girl. A string of candy with so many sweet pieces and so very many colors to choose from, she thought.

Janice Freedman had worked for Michael for the past ten years and, in that time, had learned all about her boss's idiosyncrasies and the refined art of discretion. Her maturity, tact and confidentiality were valued commodities that Michael immediately recognized and paid her handsomely for. Even though her hair was now gray, she used to be young and sweet like these women at one time in her life, but those days were now over and she would just have to accept it. Still, seeing these young women brought back a flood of memories and feelings, all of them good, and Janice smiled.

She was just putting the finishing touches on a letter to Debra Morris, thanking her for taking time to audition but that, unfortunately, the part had gone to someone else who, unfortunately, was more qualified. Next she carefully inserted a check, of a sizable dollar amount, and a hand-written note which read —

For medical expenses and to tide you over.
Thanks for the amazing ride . . .
"M."

Gradually sealing the packet, she was thankful Michael had taken her advice and allowed her to purchase the more expensive envelopes with the self-adhesive strips. Pressing the button on the phone she said, "I'll be sending this as a next day delivery right?" she asked.

"Better get a courier and have it delivered today. And, oh by the way, Janice could you send in the next applicant?" Not waiting for a response, he said, "thanks" and hung up.

The wrinkled script was practically shoved in her face and she was told she could either read from it or use the teleprompter. The production crew seemed preoccupied with her and some of them almost stumbled on the props as they stared openly. Lead to the desk and sitting down quietly, Ashley Taylor waited as the specialized group fussed over everything from lighting to camera placement. "When you're ready," the director said.

Ashley inhaled and bit her bottom lip as she looked at the teleprompter to begin her audition. She tried to make her words flow easily and appear effortless; as she neared the end of the audition the crew agreed that she sounded authentic and looked fantastic, the camera loved her. With her warm smile and calming demeanor, she was a natural. Aside from that, she was stunningly beautiful. She possessed the kind of beauty that didn't require hours of preparation in front of a mirror and she had a freshness about her that put everyone at ease, even the other females on the set; it was uncanny.

she said shrugging her shoulders.

Michael tried not to stare as he thought to himself; they were such pretty shoulders. Then, without thinking, he turned to her and said, "can I see you again?"

"Of course you'll see me again Mr. Dickerson. I'll be here next week, don't you remember?"

Snapping out of his momentary loss of thought, Michael replied, "right, right of course. I'll have wardrobe contact you and my secretary Janice, can put you in touch with some top notch agents that are credible and always hungry for work."

"Have you met Clarence, the director?"

"Oh yes," she smiled, "he's already given me permission to call him Casey."

"That *is* a good sign. He has his moments and he's very theatrical, but he's the best in the industry and we'd be hard-pressed to replace him."

Escorting her to the elevator, he smiled and turned away but not before he caught a final glimpse of her backside just as the steel doors closed.

Chapter Nine

The calendar on the enormous oak desk had a row of distinct X's on it. Scratching an imaginary beard, Salvatore Rizzo pondered what his next move would be. Sipping his morning cappuccino, he opened up the newspaper, written in his native language, to pass the time. He didn't have long to wait. One of his hired henchmen, always ready to do his bidding, appeared in the doorway.

"You may enter," he said. "What news do you have for me?" he asked.

"May I sit?" the man nervously asked, looking at the empty chair.

Salvatore slowly nodded but did not speak.

"We've been following Mr. Lindbloom as you ordered sir and we've discovered he's been asking a lot of questions about your affairs, way too many questions. He's making copies of things and paying for information from some of your business associates."

"You may continue," Salvatore said as he sipped his morning brew.

"Today he met with his accountant, stopped at a Lamborghini car dealership and then met with his attorney. Our sources tell us he was reviewing the articles of incorporation for UBMI. Oh yes," he added, "I almost forgot, he also purchased a large quantity of computer disks from an office supply store and then he made a trip to a landscaping outlet."

"That's all I have for now. Shall I continue with my assignment Mr. Rizzo?"

"Yes, but use caution. It is imperative that our good friend Mr. Lindbloom be made to feel comfortable so that he will move about freely without any restraint. I have a sixth sense about these things and believe I know what he is up to." Looking down at his desk he concluded, "you've done well Alfredo."

"Thank you Mr. Rizzo."

"Just one more thing . . . make sure that you are not discovered, otherwise you may find *yourself* lost. Now, please shut the door I have some business to attend to," he said with a hint of determination in his voice.

Alfredo met his boss's gaze straight on and nodded. He knew what the term *lost* implied and he was going to make damn sure he would not be one of the casualties because even after all these years, he always did as he was told.

Picking up the receiver, Salvatore deliberately took some time before he brought it up to his full lips. Accessing the speed dial feature on his phone, he pressed two buttons. A voice at the other end answered, "Yes Mr. Rizzo."

"Emilio," he began, "it seems we may have a problem with some undesirable trash by the name of Lindbloom. I may want you to be ready to dispose of the trash if it becomes necessary, on my order, of course."

"Capisce?" Salvatore asked.

"Capisco!"

Chapter Ten

"I can't believe you have time to go to a preliminary meet today!" Travis said with excitement. "It doesn't mean I'll definitely be on the team but at least you can watch me tryout. This is so rad dad!"

"What does r-a-d mean again Travis?" Michael asked, spelling out the letters.

"It means excellent," Travis said with a chuckle.

"We've got some time before we have to be there. Would you mind if we stop in the new coffee and sandwich shop just up the road? I think it's called *The Coffee Grind*."

"You're driving," Travis replied with a hint of sarcasm.

Standing in line was not one of Michael's favorite things to do. He wanted to be served and he wanted to be served now! What had it been, five minutes without so much as a millimeter of movement? He peered ahead in line at the good looking couple standing together that was having a difficult time deciding which pastries to buy with their coffee. He butted in their conversation, leaning forward and said, "excuse me; I heard that the key lime donuts with the coconut frosting are to die for this week. I buy them all the time," he lied.

"Thanks!" they said in unison and moved away from the display case.

Sighing, he turned to Travis and rolled his eyes mouthing the words *finally*.

Sitting down at the table, he listened as Travis began telling him about his teammates and the grueling schedule they had to keep. Laughing, he said, "I don't want this to sound weird or anything dad but I can only have one donut. I've got to weigh in when we get there."

"Hey, did I ever tell you that I used to run track at Ingleside High?"

"And what year was that?" Travis asked with his right eyebrow arched.

"Well," Michael answered, "that's top secret. I'd tell you but then, I'd have to kill you," he said jokingly.

Then he abruptly became silent and stared at the face that was now behind the counter. *She must have been in the backroom*, he thought. He couldn't believe it . . . it was the girl from the interview. It was Ashley Taylor.

"Dad? . . . Dad?" Travis repeated, "who are you staring at? Do you know her or something?"

"Hmmm? Oh, yes. Wait here," he whispered, "I'll just be a minute."

He walked up to the counter which now had a momentary break from the long line of customers that had converged on it just moments before. As he approached the display case, she looked up and smiled. She was absolutely gorgeous.

"Mr. Dickerson, hello! I didn't think you came to places like this."

Never at a loss for words, he responded with "Good

Morning Miss Taylor. He flashed his biggest, sure-to-get-results smile.

"Since you were signed for the commercials why are you working here?" he asked.

She leaned in closer to him and softly said, "because number one, this place pays the bills. I need something to put food on the table while I try to get my foot in the door. And, number two, that huge advance you gave me is gone."

"Advance? Your contract didn't include an advance," he stated.

"Yes, I know," she replied with a little giggle.

"Right," he uttered. He was familiar with the term *starving artist* and now he was feeling rather foolish for bringing this up. He should have remembered that she hadn't actually started shooting the commercials yet. It seemed he just couldn't take his eyes off of her and she continued to look at him. There was nervous laughter between them but their eyes never left each other.

"Well, sir . . . are you going to order?" she inquired.

"I've already ordered. Actually," he said quickly, "what time are you off today?"

"In about three minutes, and I can't wait," she answered. "I've been here since 5:30 this morning," she whispered. "And I can't wait to sit down, my feet are so tired."

Finally, he said, "I know this is last minute," he continued, "actually last second, but I was wondering if there is any way on God's green earth that you could join my son and I at a gymnastics meet today. He's sitting over there," he said as he pointed to Travis.

Travis gave a feeble wave and nodded before he returned to eating his donut. Out of the corner of his eye he looked at the two of them conversing and, judging from his father's body language, he knew his dad was interested, really interested.

"Oh, I didn't realize you were married and had a son who was that old. He's a good looking kid," she commented with a trace of sadness in her voice.

"I've been divorced for quite some time now and as for his good looks, you can tell him yourself when you join us." Then he waited and added, "go punch out or whatever it is you do and we'll be out front in the Silver Prius." This time he smiled but only with his eyes.

"Well, I suppose if it's okay with your son. I'll be there in a few minutes," she said looking at the clock behind her.

"Hey bro are you ordering, writing a book or gonna ask the girl out?" a voice from behind said. Pointing to the front door with his index finger, Michael turned to the impatient patron and said, "sorry, I didn't mean to hold up the line." He held up two twenty dollar bills, gave them to the new clerk that was just coming on duty, and said, "this should cover whatever *he* wants," he stated, pointing to the man who was complaining, then he left.

It was a great day to be alive and driving to the gymnastics meet with Ashley in the car made the day that much more enjoyable to Michael. He drove quickly so there would be extra warm-up time for Travis to stretch.

Looking into his rearview mirror, he could see that his son was bobbing his head back and forth, confirming that Travis' music on his headphones was playing.

"Are you okay? Too much wind for you?" he asked. "I can always put the windows up."

"Oh no, I love to feel the sun on my face and the wind in my hair," she said with a hint of laughter.

"Good, I'm glad."

They arrived in what seemed like no time at all and Travis grabbed his duffel bag and ran inside the gymnastics center, leaving his dad and Ashley to fend for themselves.

They talked very quietly while waiting for Travis to perform and they were not disappointed. His skill and artistry brought the crowd to its feet several times during his routine, even before he performed his dismount.

When the scores were shown on the electronic score board, the audience went wild with hysteria. The crowd began to chant, "we're number one!" over and over.

Pushing his way through the spectators who had now dispersed everywhere, Travis found his dad and yelled, "I'm going out with some of the guys so I won't need a ride home." Travis waved and then disappeared into the crowd but not before saying, "nice to meet you Miss Taylor. Thanks for coming dad."

"Well, can I drop you off somewhere?" Michael asked.

"Are you sure you don't mind? I can always walk or take the bus," she said waiting for his reaction.

"Where do you live?" he inquired.

"Marina City Apartments," she stated casually.

"Nice."

Finally outside the gymnasium, Michael opened the car door for her, lowered the sunglasses from his head and they drove off. He noticed that neither one of them could stop smiling. *Yes, indeed, it was a good day to be alive,* Michael thought.

Chapter Eleven

"Yes Mr. Rizzo, I am still very much aware of the date and I'll have a solution to what I owe you very soon." The conversation was nearing an end and Frank was viciously picking at his cuticles without being aware of what he was actually doing.

"Yes, Mr. Rizzo, I am glad that we spoke too."

"Just remember my friend, time stands still for no one."

"Frank," he continued, "you and I, we are cut from the same kind of cloth. Maybe one of us is checkered and the other has stripes. But regardless, we all have our vices and we all have our, shall we say, pleasures. That is why I hope you will not disappoint me. I make it my business to know *everything* that is going on around me." Then after a long pause he added, "do not forget, my friend that you and I are not so far off even though there are lines that I will not cross.

It would behoove you to practice some discretion, especially when it comes to the children for they cannot decide what path it is in life that they want to partake of. It is good to remember that, despite how one earns a living, one must still look after the children and ask yourself what is best for *them* even if it means a loss to your bank account.

Remember this in all matters that are connected with

your business and you will develop solid ethics. Yes, my friend, indeed, *We are exactly the same, but different.*"

Frank looked down at the tiny droplets of blood that stained his fingers and realized, once again, that he had let his nerves get the better of him.

"Imagine him telling me that my gambling, booze and broads has led to this. I'm Frank Lindbloom! Where the hell does he get off talking to me like that? Yes, I gamble every now and then . . . who doesn't? So I placed a few bets on horses that were losers. That's not *my* fault, I got bad tips! Yes, I like to drink, who doesn't? That's why I decided to go in on a deal with some friends of mine when they bought a club. It's not my fault that they didn't know jack shit about the restaurant or liquor industry. Sure I like women, but I have to have experienced, high class girls who specialize in what I require and everybody knows that costs big money. Does Rizzo actually think I'd stick my dick into *any* hole?" And so Frank Lindbloom continued his rage, talking to himself for quite some time.

He reached for the deck of cards on the table and flipped the cards over, one by one, to direct his train of thinking. Yes, that's it . . . he had to focus on the task at hand; he had to have total control.

The Articles of Incorporation for United Bank Marketing Incorporated were sprawled out onto the floor and Frank just stared at them. He took a longer than necessary mouthful of Jack Daniels, this time emptying the glass, as he continued to focus on the clause that stated that if Michael didn't have a beneficiary, all of the shares would revert back to the company, meaning him since he would make it his business to have the outstanding shares. Currently, Travis was Michael's sole beneficiary. So should anything happen to Travis. . . he imagined with a twisted leer on his face.

Then he conjured up a mental picture of Travis running the company and calling the shots and it made him ill. He instinctively reached for his trusted bottle of Jack Daniels "Old Friend," he muttered and poured himself another tall glassful. "That no good dog-ass half breed!" he said aloud. "But with Travis gone, it would only be a matter of time to arrange an accident for Michael," he continued. "Perhaps something as simple as a malfunction of his brakes, an unfortunate fire in his home or an understandable suicide due to his son's untimely death, or some other misfortune." He continued to ponder his options. "I could eventually sell off that prick's company piece by piece or, better yet, I could finally accept one of those sizeable offers from a rival company, the last one was for around twenty million."

Next he thought about Salvatore Rizzo and how he was closing in on him with iron-clad proof of his illegal activities. That Godfather mafia shit wasn't going to stand in his way. He'd drop that grape-stomping, bologna-faced goombah the way he dropped a stinking turd down the toilet. After all, this was *his* ass on the line! He couldn't wait to sing like a bird about Rizzo if he was forced to. He knew all the criminal reporters and knew they would fuck anybody and everybody twice over to get an exclusive like that!

He had heard stories of how some people had turned up with their throats cut from ear to ear, even after they had paid him on time. Those files and disks he had copied; that was *his* insurance, his ace in the hole that Rizzo would never taunt him again.

Step one; he would get the four hundred thousand dollars and maybe even a little extra. He had that planned out already. He would definitely pay Rizzo and be done with it. But if Rizzo ever even so much as attempted to put a contract out on him, he would ensure that the information he had on him would somehow be made public. After all, he had his reliable sources too.

Once law enforcement received concrete proof on Rizzo that they were never able to obtain themselves, Rizzo would be put away for a very, very long time. Step two; he'd continue to move forward with his long-term plan to take out Travis. Too bad it can't be a synchronized slaughter, if you will, but he would just have to bide his time. "Shit!" he cried out. "Salvatore Rizzo obviously doesn't know who the fuck *he's* dealing with."

He took out his pocketknife and once again began flipping over the cards in the deck until he found the card he had been searching for, the King of Hearts. Lowering his knife into the center of the card, he skewered it, scratching the wood on the floor underneath. "Hell yeah, I *am* one clever bastard! Michael and Rizzo, bring it on!"

Chapter Twelve

Over the next few weeks, Ashley, against her better judgment, began seeing Michael Dickerson socially. She was well aware of the effect office romances had on the other employees and the clause in her contract forbidding her to fraternize with the staff. She thought about the danger she might be getting herself into but there was something about this guy. She and Michael had what couples now referred to as a *connection*. Moreover, they had undeniable chemistry.

As she prepared for their date tonight, she was thinking about how she always arrived at the studio on time and was always prepared by knowing her lines and taking the advice that the director gave her, even when it was outrageous criticism. On her first day of work, she was told to appear with no makeup and, when she did, the director, Clarence Casey, had had a holy tirade demanding she remove her false eyelashes, cover stick, blush, mascara, eyeliner, lip pencil, foundation, beauty mark and colored contacts.

"This bitch looks better than I do and there can only be one queen bee around here and that's me!" Clarence had shouted.

When word had gotten back to Michael, he laughed for a good while then pulled Clarence off to the side in private and explained that that was exactly how Ashley looked *without* makeup. Stunned and remembering who signed his paychecks, he immediately apologized to the girl and sent her to the hair and makeup department to tone down her look. "Let's face it; the commercial has to be *believable*," Clarence had said, pursing his lips together. "You don't just go into a bank and happen to see a flawless supermodel in there!"

Sitting down in front of her lighted vanity mirror, she grinned and thought about Michael. He certainly knew his way around the boardroom and she suspected he also knew his way around the bedroom with no problem. She had determined that she would give him just enough encouragement to keep his interest but no further. She didn't want to tease him and, after all, she had no intention of being another notch on his *fuckbelt!*

The phone buzzed and she casually walked over to the intercom and checked the television monitor. *Yes, it was Michael,* she thought. Before depressing the buzzer, she spoke out, "I'm almost ready so you can fix yourself a drink. The doors open!"

Michael had a dozen long-stemmed roses for her, only one of the many gifts he had given. He had to be careful not to be too extravagant or appear too anxious even though it was his nature to do so where women were concerned. He wondered, as he got on the elevator, if he had lost his mind. Dating someone the *Fire and Ice Agency* had sent over was risky and he knew the rules, never mix business with pleasure except when he was with her, he honestly couldn't help himself and he couldn't even begin to remember when the last time he had felt like this. Michelle? No, he stopped himself, he had loved her but somehow this was much more intense. This was the real deal.

Stepping inside her apartment, he immediately smelled the assortment of scented candles that she always had lit, especially at night.

"I'm almost ready!" she called out from the other room.

Searching through her cabinets, he found a vase tall enough for the roses, added water and placed it on the counter.

Looking at the bar, he noticed she had it stocked with two new large bottles of *Courvoisier VSOP Napoleon 80,* his favorite cognac. He grinned and poured himself a drink, then stepped onto her balcony. He gazed out at the sky-line; there was something so electrifying about the view. He sipped his drink and stared.

"Three hundred North State Street. Isn't it beautiful?" the voice came from behind him.

When Michael turned around he saw her clad in blue jean Capri pants that were fitted but tasteful and a soft lime green knitted top, perfect for a Chicago spring night. He even noticed she had a small blue jean bow on each of her shoes.

He moved closer, his arms encircling her small waist.

"Whoa! Hold on there Michael. Don't you think you had better set your drink down?" she asked flirtingly.

He set his drink down on the ledge and looked deep into her eyes. She met his gaze and they kissed. A slow lingering kiss with just enough passion to ensure that there was something just beneath the surface.

Moving towards the railing she said, "we have a grocery store, two cocktail lounges, hotel, five restaurants and even a bowling alley in this one building. The quintessential way to live, if you like high-rises, that is."

He wondered how she could afford a place like this, on the fiftieth floor with unparalleled views of the Chicago River but right now the last thing he was concerned about was her bank account balance.

"And?" he teased her. "You forgot to mention the most important thing."

"The marina downstairs. Hmmm, do you think I'll need my jacket?" she asked throwing it across her arm.

"It's been unseasonably warm this week but, not to worry, the boat has a heater and you can always bring it just in case you get a bit chilly should you decide to go up on deck. Shall we go?" he asked as he touched a lock of her hair.

"Yes, let's."

Chapter Thirteen

The main door was locked but that didn't deter him. He had his electronic key at the ready and used it to enter. "Just as I thought," he mumbled. "No one is here yet." Peering down the hall he took notice that Greenberg's office was lit. "Just that smart guy, the numbers-crunching accountant," he muttered. He turned and continued walking, now a bit more rapidly.

Arriving in front of his private office, Frank unlocked the door and went inside. This was the day he thought; the day to get Rizzo off his ass and set a huge portion of his plan in motion. Sitting behind his desk, he opened the drawer on the lower left side and searched for the forms but there were none to be found. Frustrated and in a hurry, he would be unable to wait for Janice to get her old dried up ass in the office. He slammed the drawer closed and decided to walk down to the supply room. Once there, he found everything he needed and began filling out the check request form.

His pulse quickened although his hand was steady as he entered the amount; five hundred thousand dollars. Then he carefully forged Michael's name on the signature line. "Perfect," he whispered to himself. "I might as well get a little something extra for myself."

Walking around to the accountant's office he greeted him, "Morning Greenberg."

Continuing to add numbers on the calculator without looking up, the man acknowledged, "Good Morning Mr. Lindbloom. You're in awfully early aren't you?"

"Hey, I need a check cut right away. It's for a deal I'm putting together next week, something really big. Michaels' already signed the necessary paperwork." Pausing, he continued, "I'm just on my way out so I'll just be grabbing a few things and I'll be right back."

"No problem," the accountant answered, still engrossed in his numbers calculations.

Frank quickened his stride back to his office and called his bookie. "Yeah, it's Lindbloom; I'll set up a time to meet with you to pay what I owe you and, oh yeah, and I want five thousand dollars on Wolfthings in the third race to win," he said hastily and hung up.

Sufficiently satisfied that the check was done, he made his way back over to the accountant's office. Claiming his property, he opened the envelope and checked its contents. The corners of his mouth curved slightly upward as he turned abruptly and left. His steps now had a purpose; Frank Lindbloom was on a mission, yes indeed. *Funny*, he thought, as he stepped into the elevator, *I don't even know Greenberg's first name and it doesn't even matter.*

A new cigarette was placed in the silver holder by freshly manicured nails and after a relatively short length of time; smoke began to fill the dimly lit room. It was early but, as he had already anticipated, he didn't have long to wait. There was a knock at the door.

"Enter," the voice commanded.

"Mr. Rizzo, sir, we just received a call from our source in the Accounting Department, he's reliable. Lindbloom's got a check for five hundred thousand dollars and he's on his way to the Arlington Park Race Track where he placed a five thousand dollar bet on Wolfthings to win in the third race."

"So he is putting his plan in motion and keeping himself preoccupied. That's good . . . that's very good," Rizzo commented while nodding his head.

"Mr. Rizzo?"

"Yes Alfredo"

"What about Greenberg's brother being held for the next ten days at Cook County Jail? He says it's a fucking nightmare in there and his brother is scared shitless."

"Well, let us reciprocate Greenberg's goodwill towards us." Motioning with his hand, he said, "see that his brother is kept safe and out of harm's way . . . . for now."

Chapter Fourteen

"It's not every day a girl gets to go on a shopping spree!" Ashley said with playfulness in her voice. "I can't believe I got my first royalty check from my very first commercial! Isn't this mall amazing?" she asked the group of girlfriends accompanying her. "Two levels of luxury!" she added.

"I can't believe you live in Chicago and you've never been to Woodfield Mall," her best friend, Bianca announced. "Seriously, I am starving!" Then, without hesitation, all the other women expressed their hunger in one form or another, similar to a domino effect.

"Looks like I may have a mutiny on our hands if you girls don't eat, huh?" she said, looking at their faces.

Ashley walked behind the group of girls and couldn't help smiling and nodding her head from side to side while she looked at her best friend Bianca, who as usual, took charge of the group.

Bianca Lapicola and Ashley Taylor; what an unlikely pair, she thought. Young, smart and beautiful, they had decided to become allies at the prestigious Rothchilds Academy of Fine Arts almost ten years ago.

While Ashley poured herself into her academics and progressed on her good grades, Bianca had chosen a different more direct route and progressively slept her way to the top. With Bianca's voluptuous figure, pouty mouth and natural blonde hair, she was never at a loss for professors who taught her by day and screwed her until she was red in the face by night, all in secret of course; and all the while assisting her with her goal to be somebody in the world of high-fashion journalism. She used to say they were all on the PP, which of course stood for the pussy patrol. Surprisingly, each method had paid off big time for both women.

Ashley had begun in community theatre and was snatched up by a talent agency but their promises only added up to a few short lines in more bad movies than she cared to remember and she left them. Finally she got a recurring role as the love interest of Jerry Leonard on the hit soap opera, *Now is Forever*, until the leading lady became jealous of her popularity and threatened to walk off the show unless they killed off Ashley's character. But it was too late; with a highly-rated show, she had become noticeable with a small but solid fan base, even though she was written out of the show. Now with the bank commercials in play, she was finally being offered meatier roles in films and television and thanks to her representation with the new *Fire and Ice Agency,* she was becoming a household name. She had Michael to thank for that.

Bianca Lapicola had used her charms on some of the most powerful men in the industry to get what she wanted. She was always astute when it came to selecting her next victim and had a keen eye for who was going through male menopause, who was in a loveless marriage and who would be the most grateful and willing to reciprocate in the way of financial help and contacts. Her position as the youngest associate editor of *It's Strictly Personal Magazine* was no accident.

"You girls go on; I've got to go to the ladies room before I tinkle on myself," Ashley murmured. Looking intently, she made a mental note of what direction her friends went in so she would be able to find them at the table without anyone escorting her.

Once inside the bathroom stall, she overheard a conversation several women were having and she listened, hanging on every word.

"And do you think he's good looking?"

"Yes, but not as good looking as M.D."

"Who is M.D?"

"You don't know who M.D. is?"

"No."

"Oh honey he's the doctor and, you know women don't call him the doctor for nothing!"

"What does the M.D. stand for?"

"None other than Michael Dickerson!"

"Who is he?"

"Well, I'll tell you who he is!" A voice jumped in. "He's a great-looking, well-hung, two-timing, filthy rich, self-serving, cold-hearted, success driven, butt-fucking, kinky-assed, opinionated prick!"

"Yeah, but how do you *really* feel?"

"That's why he's called the doctor! Get it? M.D. . . for doctor."

"Servicing a girl's every need, huh?"

"Where did you two meet?"

"We met at a party a little over a month ago and he told me that we'd hookup again sometime this week when his schedule was finally clear. I put it on my calendar, but I haven't heard from him since."

"I can't wait for him to call me," another voice chimed in, "I've heard so much about that long, luscious tongue of his!"

"How long is it?"

"When you get your chance to fuck him you'll see."

"Have *you* ever fucked him?"

"Honey, the question is . . . who *hasn't* fucked him?"

As the group of females left, their laughter echoed throughout the small chamber and was deafening, Ashley felt as though she had just been bitch-slapped. She was totally numb inside as she cautiously opened the door to the stall. When she finally left the bathroom, she walked right by the restaurant, not even realizing that Bianca and the rest of her friends were still waiting there for her to arrive.

Chapter Fifteen

This time Frank Lindbloom walked with renewed confidence as soon as he was told to enter, this time his head was held high and he even made a weak attempt to suck in his gut. He squeezed the new deck of playing cards in his pocket and felt a sense of self-assurance and poise that he was obviously lacking on his last visit.

Walking in with a thick black leather satchel in hand, he saw that Salvatore was far away in the shadows and just finishing an afternoon drink. The side shutters were only partially open allowing just enough light to filter in, rendering it impossible to clearly see Salvatore Rizzo's face. He also noticed that the cigarette holder that was displayed on the desk today was made of jade and somehow couldn't take his eyes off of it.

"Ah, you have noticed the newest entry in my collection. Yes, you may admire it," he said with a slow movement of his hand. "This variety is just for cocktails so, of course, it's less than three inches. Now my friend, you are here to see me and so you shall. You may now begin," he said with a hint of expectancy in his demeanor.

"I have this package for you. I believe you'll find the contents are what I owe you Mr. Rizzo," Frank said. "All four hundred thousand dollars, in hundred dollar bills."

"And so you do," Salvatore replied calmly. He looked up from his desk and made eye contact with Alfredo who watched from a corner in the room. Taking his cue, Alfredo retrieved the satchel that Frank was extending.

"I'm sorry if I was agitated the last time I was here. I never meant to insult you by asking for an extension. I would never purposefully offend you in any way and again, I apologize for any misunderstanding that I alone might have caused," he whined.

Rizzo's bluish-gray eyes were piercing and at this moment he was using them to look at Frank Lindbloom; all the way into his soul. He leaned forward, clasping his hands together and said, "It was just a *Bel Niente!* As we say in the old country, it was just a beautiful nothing. The main thing is that you and I . . . we now have an understanding and can move forward from this point on. You agree, no?"

"Yes, of course, thank you for everything Mr. Rizzo, sir."

"Alfredo will see you out, until next time then?" he said as he got up from his desk.

While Alfredo escorted Frank out, Rizzo left through, yet another side door and under his breath, in an almost inaudible voice, Salvatore muttered, "Arrivederci Frank."

Chapter Sixteen

"Well, this is it dad, should I open it?" Travis asked as he stared at the odd shaped packet.

Michael smiled, "I don't see why not, it's got *your* name on it."

It was an envelope that Travis determined had to be a least a foot long. He noticed the return address in the upper left hand corner and his heart began to beat faster. *It's from them, I finally have a response*, he thought. With moist palms, he let out a deep breath and carefully opened it. Inside there was yet another envelope which displayed the words *Something Big Is About To Happen* on the outside in huge bold letters. Then a smile appeared on Travis' face, a smile that Michael had not seen in God knows how long. He ripped open this envelope and scanned the letter.

"This is it!" he shouted, "I've been accepted! Holy crap Dad! Ithaca College!" Travis yelled. "Woooo Hoooo!"

"Let me guess, this is the one you *really* want?" Michael asked with a touch of sarcasm. "Are you sure you don't want to go to M.I.T.?" he asked looking at the poster inside a confetti-filled tube on his son's bed. "And let's not forget the acceptance text message from Baylor University," he added. "They're all fine schools you know."

"No, this is it! Dad did you know that their gymnastics

team consistently finished in the top ten at the last national collegiate meet? They have an awesome facility and two of the guys on the team workout at the Windy City Gym with me in the summer. You know, Cody Jarrett and Justin Joseph. This is so rad!" Travis said. "The Ithaca College Bombers!"

"With your ability I can see why it's a good fit," Michael said. He couldn't help but feel a little excited for the boy himself, even though it was not the choice he had in mind for him. "So it's a full scholarship then?" he asked, already knowing the answer.

"Yeah, but I know I'll have to maintain my grades dad. No lectures please."

"Well, if this is what you want," Michael's voice trailed off. "But I have an idea," he said wryly, "since you aced your college exams and have kept your complaining to a minimum, I thought you might like this," Michael said.

Standing in the doorway of Travis' room, he reached behind his back and revealed a large envelope. Then he tossed it to him and waited for his reaction.

As he listened to his son trying to guess what its contents were, he took out his cell phone and called Ashley, this time he hoped he could reach her.

Hmmm, it went right to voicemail again, he thought. Irritated, he decided to text her. He made a mental note that it was the eighth time in two weeks without so much as a single response.

"A trip to Fort Lauderdale? Paris Island, a Caribbean cruise?" Travis guessed.

"No. I was thinking of something more permanent," he responded. He noted the time that he called and texted her and then replaced his cell phone. "Just open the damn thing Travis!"

Staring back at him was a car brochure. "A mustang convertible! This is so awesome! Oh my God!! Thanks dad!"Travis exclaimed as he hugged his father.

"Pretty rad, huh Travis? Now get your backpack and let's go before you make us both late," Michael said.

This time the drive was different, both father and son actually spoke to one another. They finally had something to discuss. Michael wanted to know more about the school but all Travis wanted to talk about was when he would get the car, his car, a car of his very own.

"I can't wait to tell the guys at school," he said. This is fucking unbelievable; Oh sorry dad!"

Pulling up to the curb in front of the school, Travis got out with his stained backpack in tow and shut the door. "Red is a cool color dad," he mentioned while winking.

"I'll see you later and, oh, don't forget I'll be staying over Mom's house tonight. She's making her famous, once a year, Cajun food. Laughing, he said, "she calls it her Cajun Invasion; gumbo, shrimp creole, greens, cornbread, fried okra in a cheese sauce and the best sweet potato pie in the universe. Sure you won't come?" he said, checking his watch.

"No. Not this time, but you can always bring me a doggie bag and tell your mother I said hi." And on that note, Michael drove off.

THE SYMBIOTIC SECTION

Stuck in traffic, Michael mentally rehearsed his presentation to the executives of Coleman Financial Services. He knew that their Chief Executive Officer was a hard ass and that he would have to have all his ducks in a row if he was going to make this deal a reality. "Stop and go, stop and go," he grumbled.

Looking at the steering wheel and then at the lighted display on the dashboard, he was at least thankful he had purchased a hybrid vehicle. Hell, he'd take fifty plus miles per gallon *any* day.

As soon as he was close to an exit, he turned off. Hybrid or no hybrid, he thought, time was still money! He made a sharp right turn and saw something that captured his attention. Distracted for a second, he set his sites back on the road and almost had a head on collision. He swerved just in time to avoid the oncoming vehicle. "Whew!" he exclaimed, "that was close!"

That was Ashley, he thought. *I'm almost sure of it.*

Wondering why she hadn't answered his text messages or returned a single one of his calls; he drove around the block, and decided to obstruct the bus stop area, while he waited for her to appear. "There," he unconsciously said. He leaned over and opened the passenger door from inside as she approached.

"Good Morning Miss Taylor, do you a need a lift?" he asked.

But there was no verbal response, not even an acknowledgment of any kind from her. Ashley stopped dead in her tracks and stared at him. The stare quickly became a glare and then, in a split second, she just kept walking. Michael dialed her cell phone but there was no response. "What the hell!" he said.

Puzzled and irritated, he slammed the car door closed and then gave the bus driver the finger when he heard its loud horn honking and it became obvious that he was in the way. "Go fuck yourself!" he yelled out and sped away.

He was already in a bad mood when he entered the building's reception area. Walking through the double glass doors, he failed to greet Janice as was his usual practice.

"Houston, I think we have a problem," Janice said out loud in a barely audible tone when she was positive that no one was around.

"Choose United Bank Marketing, Incorporated for all your financial needs, all the time. Remember, we're here, because you're there!"

The presentation had ended, the lights came on and a round of steady applause echoed throughout the room. Michael was now on his feet, smiling, shaking hands and giving assurances to the executive team of Coleman Financial Services. "Now if you'll excuse me, I have another appointment but my staff and the director, Clarence Casey, will give you the V.I.P. treatment which, of course, includes the studio tour and a fabulous lunch that I helped select myself. Gentlemen, I'll be in touch. Mr. Coleman, it's been a pleasure, sir," Michael said smiling.

He continued to make his way towards the door. He had to get to his office and find out what was happening with Ashley.

"You've hit another one out of the ballpark Michael," someone said to him as they gave him a congratulatory pat on the back.

Michael quickened his pace. *Got to get out of this god-damn arena,* he thought.

"Slam dunk, Michael!" another voice commented.

"Yeah, thanks," *blah, blah blah*, he thought, *and all I want to do is just get to the door!*

Finally inside his office, he glanced at his desk and found a note from Janice. "What's this?" he asked, already knowing full well of its intention.

"I can't explain it Mr. Dickerson," Janice remarked. "I thought she was satisfied working with UBMI. All I know is that her agency called this morning and said that Miss Taylor chose not to renew her contract for the Tollway-Arlington Bank commercials. So when it expires next month, she's done. Does she realize the bank wants her to do a two-year national campaign and the enormous amount of money she'd be passing up? She's young too. I wonder, is she really aware of what she's doing?" Janice asked.

"Yes, I believe she knows what she's doing," Michael answered dryly. He took out his cell phone, thought about calling and replaced it in his pocket before replying, "I don't know her reasons but believe me, she knows *exactly* what she is doing."

Chapter Seventeen

It was almost noon and the group of boys walked slowly down the stairs. "Hey, nice going Oreo! Ithaca College *and* a new car, you lucky son-of-a-bitch! You goin' to the gym today?" someone said.

"Nah, I'm goin' to my mom's house since it's only a half day of school. Then I'll stay over there to eat and spend the night," Travis replied.

"Yeah, that must suck having to split up your time like that between two parents. How long have they been divorced?" a friend asked.

"Oh, I don't know, since I was born I guess. I mean, I've always split my time up between the two of them so I grew up this way. It really doesn't suck. What sucks," he added, "is having to take the bus everywhere."

"Yeah, but not for long!"

"Okay, see ya," his friends said, as they began walking towards the student parking lot. "Do ya want a ride to the bus stop?"

"No, I think I'll just walk and then wait for the bus like I always do thanks anyway though," he answered as he held up the Mustang brochure, sporting a huge smile on his face. "But this time I'll actually have something to occupy my time."

Travis continued walking for a short time and, reaching his destination, he finally sat down on the bench. He opened his car brochure, soaking in every word he read when a white Lamborghini cruised up to the bench and stopped, immediately catching Travis' attention. When the window rolled down he smiled and his eyes popped. He recognized its occupant. "Hey Mr. Lindbloom, your car is so rad!"

"You like it Travis? I picked it up a little while ago. Isn't she a beauty? Are you getting in?" he asked as he pointed to the door. "It's not locked."

"Hell yeah, I'm getting in!" Travis exclaimed as he opened the door and sat down. "Ummm, I love that new car smell!" he said as they drove off.

"I just picked this up from the showroom this morning and I thought I'd break her in. Where are you on your way to? The gym?" he asked.

"No, I'm going over my mom's today. She's making her famous Cajun food tonight. Do you wanna come over and try some?" he asked.

"Oh no, not me. Always give a woman time to prepare and you'll live longer. Remember that Travis. I'll take you up on that another time after I've cleared it with Michelle though," he offered.

"Hey, are you thirsty Travis? Why don't I go to the convenience store over there," he said, pointing to the one up ahead. "Hey, let's see how fast this baby can change from a girl to a woman," he said barely pressing down on the accelerator, performing a one eighty turn. "Yeah! Now that's what I'm talking about!"

Parking the car he said, "You wait here and I'll go get us some drinks." He looked back over his shoulder, "you can sit in the driver's seat but don't go driving off anywhere," he added with a chuckle.

Once inside, Frank made his way to the rear of the store where the drink station was located and rapidly dispersed two fountain drinks. Setting the cups on the counter, he looked around, felt it was safe and removed a small plastic baggie from just inside his sport jacket pocket. He slowly emptied the entire contents into the smaller of the two drinks, using the straw like a spoon to stir the liquid and then returned to the front of the store to pay for his purchase.

"Wow, the line was so long with only one cashier," he stated. "Here's your drink," he said, holding out the smaller of the two drinks for the boy.

"Thanks Mr. Lindbloom."

The car seemed to move with jet rocket propulsion and they arrived in no time as it came to a halt in front of Michelle's house. "You've hardly had anything to drink," Frank laughingly admonished him.

"Oh, I'll finish it inside," Travis said, "thanks again for the ride Mr. Lindbloom."

"It's no problem," he said as he looked the other way being careful to not reveal the sinister look on his face. "It's no problem for me at all." And with that comment, he drove off just as rapidly as he had arrived.

THE SYMBIOTIC SECTION

Sometime later Frank Lindbloom stopped at an out of the way gas station. He removed his sport jacket and splashed cold water on his hands and face. He stared at himself in the smudged, cracked mirror, closing his eyes and thought about all the heartache and frustration that one man had caused his family. Yes, he had done what he had done but he knew he was justified and had a damn good reason.

Every man had his breaking point and Frank Lindbloom knew that he had reached his, where Michael Dickerson was concerned, and a long time ago. He leaned in closer to the mirror, fixated on his own reflection. Yes, the years had taken a toll on him. The drugs, the booze and his hit-and-miss lifestyle could be seen in every line that was permanently etched on his face. *Things were about to change,* he thought. "Now *you* will hurt the way that she was hurt all those years ago." Exhaling deeply, he whispered, "what goes around comes around Michael."

Chapter Eighteen

"He stopped at a convenience store and poured the contents of a small plastic baggie into the boy's drink and then took him to visit his mother and then stopped at a gas station. Now he's on his way to the Arlington Park Race Track in a brand new white Lamborghini. Two questions for you sir -- number one, we have the baggie, would you like us to keep it? And, number two, should we stay with him Mr. Rizzo?"

"Both answers are the same," there was a long pause on the phone, and then the answer came, "that will not be necessary Antonio. You and Alfredo are needed elsewhere; you have done well, *grazie.*"

"So, tell me about the school you've chosen," Michelle said, as she was plating their special meal.

"Ithaca College in New York! Mom, I can't believe this is happening. Did dad tell you? He's actually going to let me have a car!"

"Well, that *is* exciting," Michelle said, "I sure hope you're hungry," she said as she began serving up her culinary delight.

Travis eyed his mother in the kitchen and thought about

how talented and good looking she was and he wondered if she was lonely. "Are you seeing anybody right now mom?"

"Travis!" she answered, a bit taken aback by his question. "What kind of a question is that to be asking your mother?"

"But I'm not asking *anybody* mom . . . I'm asking *you*."

"I can *see* that!"

"I just don't want you to be alone. I mean you're so gorgeous and all."

"Travis!"

"All my friends think so. I know! If I could just conjure up one of my superhero characters for you everything would be perfect. He could save you from danger, be rich and do all the other stuff women like."

Michelle looked at her son and smiled. Almost a man but still reading comic books, still holding on to the little boy inside of him that she hoped he would never lose.

"Well," she answered, "I'm not in any sort of danger and, according to my accountant; I'm already rich, even though it doesn't feel like it to me. As for all the other stuff that women like; well you can't just conjure that up honey. There's got to be something there to begin with and build upon."

"Like what?"

"Well, like a friendship or something that attracts you to them in the first place. Maybe their body type, hair color or . . ." she thought for a moment before finishing, "their character and their heart, especially what's *in* their heart. And then, if you're lucky, there's a spark and then that spark develops into a flame. Notice I didn't say burst into a flame?"

"Why not burst?"

That's because those types of relationships always fizzle out, just like a shooting star. Long before it's reached the ground, it's burned itself out. Don't you worry about me Travis. I'll find my superhero . . . . or maybe he'll just have to find me. And now, Dr. Freud, this conversation is over, with a capital O!" she said, as they began eating.

Travis enjoyed these sleepover visits with his mom. They held a special place in his heart, especially since they were becoming fewer and far between. With his mom's work schedule and his gymnastics along with school, there wasn't much time for the super long visits they used to have.

"Travis don't smack!" she lightly chastised him.

"Mom, you outdid yourself this time, everything is sooooo hot and sooooo spicy good!" he commented while standing up. Grabbing his cup from the counter, he transferred it into a glass tumbler. "See mom, I remember your rules about no plastic cups or plastic silverware on the table," he mentioned proudly as he sat back down with the changed beverage container in hand.

And so the afternoon progressed with laughter, memories and a lot of catching up to do.

Sometime later, as they were playing Scrabble, Travis complained of a slight headache and laid down on the sofa. *Probably too much excitement for one day and way too much*

overeating, he thought.

"Mom, I'm feeling a bit warm, can you hand me the rest of my soda?"

"If you're warm, I think what you need is some good old-fashioned water," she said, frowning at his cup.

"Oh crap, not water!" he complained, "anything but that!"

"You kids today drink way too much soda. It makes your pee orange!" she admonished. And with one quick jerk of her hand, she picked up Travis' cup, walked over to the kitchen and emptied it into the sink.

Chapter Nineteen

"Okay, I won't come in, I just want to talk. Why can't I do that?" Michael asked, in an insistent tone.

"What if I don't feel like talking?" Ashley asked, as she spoke through the partially open door. "And how did you get past the doorman?" she inquired.

"He knows me; I've done business with his father," he replied.

"From what I understand, it appears you've done your business *with* everybody, *in* everybody and *on top of* everybody!" she retorted.

"So, that's what this is about. Hmmmm, I see," he said as he placed his thumb and index finger on his chin, pondering what he would say next.

"Since you're busy with that type of fun and games, why don't you get away from my door and go buy yourself some; if you can find some whores this time of day that are available. Oh, that's right," she added, "I heard you recycle don't you?" her voice was louder now.

That did it! Now he was beyond irritated, he was goddamn angry.

"You've either listened to some botoxed bitch-on-wheels that spends two hundred dollars a pop on manicures or you've overheard some cunt-on-crack that's frigid, frustrated and fuckless!" he snapped. "We *really* need to talk," he pleaded. "Ashley, knowing how busy I am, do you honestly think I would drop everything I'm working on at the office and come over here in the middle of the afternoon just to bullshit *you?*" he asked.

"Alright," she answered with hesitation as she slowly took the chain off the door and allowed him to enter although her arms were crossed and her jaw was rigid.

Having not seen her in weeks, he was cautious as he walked in; looking for tell-tale signs to indicate if another man had been or was still there in his absence. Convinced they were alone; he looked into her eyes, unbuttoned his jacket and sat on the sofa.

"No! Not so fast, not there!" she shouted. "If you want to stay, you'll have to sit on *that* side of the sofa and you can't move unless I say its okay," she warned while gesturing with her hand.

"What?" he quipped, "do you know how high-schoolish that is?"

Rolling his eyes, Michael knew it was pointless since he was not in a position to bargain. He stood up, poured himself a drink, and sat in the designated place she had chosen.

"I'm going to tell you a story. First and foremost, it's a true story," he said as he calmly sipped his drink; and then he began.

Michael told her how he was driven to succeed and how he had let nothing stand in his way. He briefly talked about the period when he was younger and how hard his family had to struggle just to pay the bills.

"Attending Ingleside High School was no easy task, especially once the dynamics changed and us White boys were in the minority. I got the shit kicked out of me almost on a daily basis. Then one day there was this girl that transferred into our Senior Business Administration class. Her name was Michelle Pierson, a Black girl."

"What kind of name is *that?* It sounds White."

Ignoring her comment, he continued, "she was unbelievably smart and sassy, very athletic and nobody in the entire school could touch her in the looks department, and I mean not a soul . . . . *nobody!*"

"You liked her? A *Black* girl?"

"Yes," he continued, "I was attracted to her right away and because she was friends with most of the local gang members, nobody gave it a second thought when they saw us walking in the halls or sitting together as a couple. It was a sign of respect I guess and I'd probably have been killed if she had wanted it. Anyway, we saw each other off and on throughout college even though she went to The University of Chicago and I went to Chicago State University."

He took another sip from his glass, this time longer, and set it on her coffee table.

"Uh, aren't you going to use a coaster for that glass?" she asked somewhat irritated.

"Sorry," he said.

"So what happened?"

"Well, we fell in love and I eventually asked her to marry me several times until one day she finally accepted." He paused and looked down at his shoes before continuing, "I thought it was a done deal."

"So what went wrong?" Ashley asked.

"She was driven to succeed and I was too young to realize that I wanted to try to make her into someone or something else. She had ideas and dreams and knew how to achieve her goals while I was still unsure of myself. When she found out she was pregnant, I was overjoyed but she wanted no part of it. I convinced her not to have an abortion, but after Travis was born, she grew cold and distant and mostly focused on her career, mostly," his voice trailed off.

Then he chuckled, "you know, she wanted to call him Travell. Have you ever heard of a name like that?"

"Go on, stop getting sidetracked!" Ashley instructed him harshly.

"Well, we divorced and she kept Travis," he stated. "She insisted, which I thought was weird but I didn't want to hold up the divorce and she didn't want spousal support, so I agreed."

"Then what?" Ashley's tone was just a bit softer now.

"Then I met Elizabeth at a charity event and, as it turned out, she was my business partner's sister."

"Frank Lindbloom's *sister?*" she asked.

"Yes. At that time she was a nurse. Unlike Michelle, she was more reserved and didn't enjoy the limelight, like I did," he added. "She was nice-looking and very supportive, but *always* behind the scenes. We eventually got married and my career took off on the fast track. I spent long hours at work to make a name for myself and eventually came up with the concept for a marketing firm catering to the needs of the financial community. All the heavy hitters jumped on the bandwagon and United Bank Marketing was born. Lindbloom and I thought it would be a good idea to incorporate even though we both equally held all the shares.

"So then it became UBMI, right?" Ashley asked.

"Right," Michael answered.

Slowly uncrossing her legs and smoothing her skirt, she said, "go on." Now Michael could see that she smiled with her eyes, but just a little.

"Well, I succumbed to the spoils of the success. I admit that I wasn't the best husband and, I hate to admit it, but I wasn't faithful either. To make matters worse," he added, "Michelle was an entrepreneur and had several successful enterprises. So one day she just dropped Travis off and she said . . . what was it? Oh yes, it's your turn now, you take care of him; and she left."

"She dropped him off at *your house?*" Ashley asked, astounded.

"Yeah, that's Michelle for you. She dropped him off with Elizabeth but the crazy thing is that Elizabeth adored Travis and took him everywhere. She eventually cut down her hours at the hospital to spend even more time at home with him. I thought things were going good; not great, but okay. Then one day when I came home there was Elizabeth confronting me about another one of my extramarital affairs."

"So what did you do?" she asked.

We argued and she said felt like a slave or something. That all she did was cook, clean and try, with no success, to please me. She said that she had lost herself and then she just snapped," he said.

"What do you mean *snapped?*"

"She got in the car after we had a really bad fight and drove like a demon on his way back to hell."

Then he hesitated for a moment and looked away before he continued. "She got into a terrible wreck that day and was laid up in the hospital for months. She had a broken pelvis and had to have her uterus removed so she would never be able to have children and the accident left horrible scars across her face. It was touch and go for a while but with a lot of operations and her incredible strength to live, she pulled through. "I sometimes wondered," he said, barely audible, "what gave her the will to go on." Then he continued, "the problem began when she was discharged from the hospital. She immediately divorced me and soon afterwards I heard she was taking massive doses of the painkillers the doctors had prescribed. Oh, she eventually married again and again and even for a fourth time, but she was badly addicted and with addiction, it's usually the addiction that wins out."

"Then what?" Ashley asked, wrinkling her brow.

"Well, I paid for some plastic surgery on her face and even for her to go to detox -- several times, but she was never able to complete any of the rehab programs. You see, my business partner blames *me* for her addiction, the failed marriage and for not treating his sister with respect. It caused a deep wedge between us; that's why you rarely see the two of us together at the office. And now he wants me to sell the whole company to the first buyer because he says he needs the money. He looks at offers from other companies but I just can't bring myself to do it. I've put my life's blood into UBMI, hell it cost me a goddamn marriage! I'm not going to just give it up or have some firm come in here and start making changes. What's next? Outsourcing? Layoffs? Not while I've still got both my balls," he added.

"Yeah, I'm a prick, I admit it. And I do frequent women that can take care of my baser needs with no involvement and no attachments. It's easier that way, I don't have to *feel* anything real for them or get into something that's complicated. These women, they *all* know exactly how I am and that's why no one gets hurt. But Ashley, I swear to you, on my son's life, that I've learned from my mistakes and I haven't been with anyone since I've been in a committed relationship . . . with us exclusively seeing each other."

"You see I've learned that a woman usually gets involved with a man hoping to change him; and he usually *never* does. A man gets involved with a woman hoping she'll *never* change, and she *always* does. I know that now," he said with finality.

"So what do you do now to satisfy your *baser* needs?" she asked, waiting for an answer.

"I do what every other male does who wants to remain faithful. I take a cold shower or I jerk off in a warm shower!" he declared with a chuckle. "But lately, I've just been too damn busy and too tired to even do that."

Taking all of this in, Ashley waited a moment saying, "wow, what a story. I suppose you can sit over here now," she said as she patted the empty sofa cushion next to her. Then she added, "so, what was that about a committed relationship?"

He sat beside her saying, "you have been absolutely wonderful and you're so damn beautiful that I would do anything, anything for you. That's why I've waited. I didn't want to rush things and I felt you weren't ready."

He leaned towards her and then she kissed him, inquisitively at first and then she let the kiss slowly build up and become passionate, igniting the flames of desire within both of them.

She undid his tie and unbuttoned the top button of his shirt, the entire time, her lips never leaving his. Next, she slowly let her hand come to rest on the huge, rock hard bulge that was visibly on display inside his pants. "Are you too tired *now*?" she softly whispered.

Oh Christ! He wanted to fuck her so badly! He began to loosen his belt and unzip his pants when suddenly and without warning, his cell phone began playing the song *American Woman* by the rock group, *The Guess Who*.

"What the hell is that?" Ashley asked.

"Shit! I've got to take this, it's important, it's Michelle's ringtone" he said with extreme irritation, "and she only calls my cell phone if there's something serious that can't wait."

Taking the call, he listened for a moment and stood bolt upright, practically knocking Ashley off of the sofa. "What! When? Where is he now?" Michael demanded. Then just as quickly as he was on the call, it was immediately over.

"I'm sorry Ashley, I've got to go!" he said zipping his pants and buckling his belt. "Travis is sick and Michelle's had to call an ambulance!"

Chapter Twenty

"**D**an, the man, you sonofabitch! I told you I'd be here and settle things didn't I?" Not waiting for a response, Frank Lindbloom shoved a fat bundle of money bound by a thick rubber band into his bookie's hand. "There, you can count it if you like," he said with a broad smile on his face.

"So, what happened, what's your secret?" Dan asked with a wide grin on his face as he looked at the wad of cash.

"No secret; just took care of some business and got real lucky at the track today," Frank replied. "I've got to go, I'll see you."

"Wait? Don't want to place a bet with me?"

"No way man! When I gave you my bet on Wolfthings that was the last bet you're *ever* going to get from me. I'm here at the track so I can place all my other bets from now on. I'm back in control now, the way it *should* be. Thanks anyway."

And on that note, Lindbloom walked over to the window and collected his winnings on all his prior races that day. Confident and empowered, he pushed through the crowd of patrons, elbowing some of them deliberately, and made his way back to his car.

"Unfucking-Believable! . . . I feel great!" he shouted,

looking in the car's rearview mirror. It would only be a matter of time before Travis was out of the picture, his bookie was now paid off, he'd won big at the track, he had a new car and next year at this time the company would probably be his to sell. Yeah, it was time to celebrate indeed!

He pulled out his cell phone and dialed a familiar number and, after several rings, the person at the other end answered.

"Who the fuck?"

"Elizabeth, it's Frank. Are you going to be home?" Not waiting for an answer, he continued, "I'm asking because I'm right in the area and I'd love to see your new place. I can be over in say five minutes," he said looking at his watch and hung up.

Driving down the narrow suburban side streets of Arlington Heights to his sister's house, he enjoyed the attention his new car received as he turned down the road and headed towards the cul-de-sac where her home was located.

Eyeing the outside, Frank couldn't help but immediately notice the lack of curb appeal. Tall weeds had sprouted in-between cracks in the sidewalk, all the shrubbery was overgrown and there were dozens of newspapers cluttering the driveway. He knocked several times and then began pressing the doorbell.

When Elizabeth didn't answer the door, Frank used his emergency key that he kept in his wallet, hoping nothing was wrong. Inserting the key into the tarnished lock, he slowly turned it and cautiously pushed the door open. He hadn't expected a palace by any means but he wasn't quite prepared for what he saw next.

A swarm of flies swirled around his head as he entered, some escaping to freedom, just as he gently closed the door. Frank gasped for air as an unpleasant smell invaded his nostrils and he decided it was best to leave the front door partially cracked. He stood there, in the middle of the foyer, taking in the ghastly scene, before his sheer will forced his legs to move forward. His lungs burned and longed for fresh air; the fresh air that could not be found in *this* house.

"Elizabeth it's Frank!" he yelled, but there was no answer. He thought he heard someone talking but he soon discovered that the television set was on a home shopping channel that ran twenty four hours a day with its volume blasting. He calmly walked over to the television and turned it off, removing his handkerchief and covering his nose and mouth in the process. Then as he turned around he discovered that his sister was on the sofa, dazed, partially dressed and reeking of body odor.

"My God!" he said out loud, "you look like shit! What the hell happened to you?" he cried, as he noticed she was wasting away to nothing.

Navigating through the maze of old magazines and the assortment of junk on the floor, he stepped onto opened, greasy, cardboard pizza boxes and made his way over to her.

"Frank?" she asked, questioning his identity, "is that *you,* Frank?"

"Yes, it's me Liz. It's your brother Frank."

"Oh good, can you get me the bowl on the floor over there? I've got to pee and I don't think I can make it," she said with a laugh. A moment later she was smiling and her glazed eyes closed again. He knew that in her present condition just talking to her was futile.

"Oh God," he whispered through tiny muffled gasps for fresh air. His sister was in the process of urinating on herself and there wasn't a damn thing he could do except watch in disgust as he saw a dark orangish-yellow stream gush down her thighs and seep into her sofa. Oh sure! He wanted to make her a pot of coffee or hold her or something but he couldn't get past the stench of her and the filth of her place.

He reached into his pocket and pulled out a few hundred dollar bills, five to be exact, and scribbled something on a pad of paper that was relatively clean that he found on the floor. Then moving to a nearby table, he cleared off a small section with his arm and left the note on top of the money for her to find when she was coherent. "So, it's come to this. You've sunk this low," he said with sadness in his voice.

He walked back over to his sister and gazed at her in her limp, decrepit state. He stared at the scars on her cheek and felt nothing but pity for her. The sister he had grown up with, counted on and protected was gone. Thanks to that ass wipe Michael Dickerson, this is what was left in her place. *Damn him!* He thought; he would pay. A life for a life!

All he could focus on now was getting out of this house and not touching the front door's crusty doorknob before the stench of the place permeated *his* clothes. He looked down, careful not to step on anything for fear it might move, and saw several pill bottles on the floor.

"Oxycontin," he said aloud. "She'll never miss *this* one," he whispered to himself as he placed the tall bottle in his pocket.

It had been a long tiring day with many stops and a great deal of business to take care of but now, thanks to his *solution*, that was about to change.

The inner peace he had searched for was finally creeping up on him as the room slowly swam out of focus. He smiled, lightheaded and carefree, before deciding to swallow even more of the pills he had taken from his sister's house. How many was that now? In how many hours? He thought long and hard but he couldn't remember and, best of all, he didn't care to remember. He was *finally* relaxed.

"Frank honey, all of us girls are waiting in here and right now it's my turn! Come on Frank, I'm ready to go!" the woman's voice said impatiently.

Frank supported his large frame with his hands on the wall as he staggered past a case of bottled water and went back towards the voice to continue with his celebration of sorts. The line of women was standing just outside the room and the one in front of the line stepped forward. She was of Asian descent with small perky breasts, narrow hips and a black, waist-length mane. She also had absolutely no pubic hair, something Frank always insisted upon.

Lowering herself, the girl spread her legs and squatted down on top of Frank, who was already in position. Then she asked seductively, "shall I make it rain for you?"

"Yes, Oh God yes, make it rain!"

"A *golden* shower of rain for you?" the girl asked, while puckering her lips.

"Yes, please . . . Oh God! Please, don't make me beg for it baby!" he pleaded as his arms encircled her tiny waist.

She held onto the sides of the empty jetted tub, gently swaying back and forth, and slowly began to urinate onto his belly, watching as his thick, limp penis instantly achieved a rock-solid erection.

Done with her task, she got out of the tub, dried her feet on a towel from a stack in the corner, and moved out of the way as the next woman in line now entered the bathtub.

Frank reveled in the warm sensation, arched his back and inhaled deeply as tears of joy came to his eyes. Yes, he was finally reaching the emotional and physical release he had craved and needed for days.

"Ahhhhhh! Drink more water, just keep drinking the goddamn water . . . Oh shit, this is heaven!" Frank mumbled incoherently.

Chapter Twenty One

Michael felt his heart was going to beat out of his chest while he was in the elevator. There were so many things running through his mind . . . *Why wasn't Michelle more clear with what was wrong? Was Travis okay? What had happened?* The thoughts just kept coming.

Rubbing his fingers back and forth on his dampened brow, he knew he had to stay focused and get control of the situation. He had to be able to maintain . . . to be able to at least drive.

Sitting down in his car, he fastened the seatbelt and listened as the click of the seatbelt brought images of a gurney transporting a body with bulky black straps to his mind. He suddenly felt a slight sense of panic but realized he had to get there for Travis; that was the goal now. Breathing faster, he undid his tie and started the car, listening to its engine purr for a moment, before he shifted into drive and rolled out of the parking garage.

Never one to falter, he passed cars and drove through numerous stop signs as he made his way to the expressway. Once there, he floored the accelerator and took off. He was a man with a purpose, even driving illegally on the shoulder when traffic stalled. Nothing in the world was going to keep him from seeing his son, his *only* son.

He placed his fist in his mouth and bit down hard while steering with his left hand. Right now Michael couldn't focus on anything else except getting to the hospital as quickly as possible. He felt so helpless and so out of his element. He didn't know what had happened, hell, he didn't know jack shit! *Got to keep breathing, got to maintain, and got to focus,* he kept thinking.

In Michael's mind it seemed to take forever to arrive at the hospital, "All this fucking traffic!" he growled, "why aren't these morons at work!" he screamed, as he maneuvered around a semi-truck. He could feel the sweat dripping down his armpits now and he felt as though his pounding head was going to explode, but he just kept driving.

His cell phone rang playing the ringtone, *The Girl from Ipanema,* and Michael knew right away that it was Ashley. He fumbled for a split second for his phone, taking his eyes off the road, and then remembered he had inserted his hands-free device into his ear; something he didn't remember doing. He depressed it in a swift movement saying, "Ashley, I'm sorry I had to leave so suddenly."

"Don't worry about me Michael, is your son alright?" she asked with genuine concern.

"I don't know. Right now I'm still on the road just trying to get there. I'll call you when I know something," he told her. Pausing, he added, "I'm here now," and hung up.

Next he called his office and explained to Janice the events that had taken place up until now. Still trying to focus, Michael parked in the pedestrian crosswalk area and slamming the car's door, he quickly ran inside the entrance to the emergency room making his way through the double glass doors to the front desk. He identified himself to the admittance person on duty and then waited. He didn't have long to wait.

Chapter Twenty Two

Michelle sat just outside the small private room, cup of cold coffee still in hand, as she waited for the doctor to return. She was totally exhausted from the ordeal of hearing Travis call out in pain and then finding him weak and unresponsive. She didn't know what else to do except dial 911 and do something she hadn't done in a long time, pray.

It had long been decided that she and Michael would have to have a united front when it came to their son. There was to be absolutely no bickering or using him as a weapon when it came to their differences. After all, with their schedules, neither one of them had time for those types of games.

She closed her eyes, holding back the tears and remembered when she had discovered she was pregnant and how she had wanted nothing to do with a child. Now she realized that her life, with all her money, success and material things meant nothing if she didn't have this child, *her* child, there to share them with. Perhaps she was being punished for even entertaining the thought of an abortion. Perhaps it was payback for dropping him off with Elizabeth, Michael's second wife. Regardless, it made no difference one way or the other. She had done a horrible thing and was dead wrong; and she knew it.

"How about a hot cup?" a familiar voice asked.

"Oh Michael!" she cried with arms outstretched.

Michelle stood up and hugged Michael before accepting the hot coffee he was offering. "I could sure use this! How long have you been standing there?" she asked as she walked over to the trash can and disposed of the cup of cold coffee she held in the other hand.

"I just got here," he answered, "now, what the hell happened?" Michael asked.

"I'm not really sure. I know that sounds crazy but we were playing Scrabble and talking and then it was time for lunch and we ate. . ."

"You both ate the *same* thing?" he interrupted.

"Yes, of course. The *exact* same thing," she began again. "Then Travis complained of being tired so he laid down and took a nap," she said, nodding. "I think I got busy, I don't know with what, and then the next thing I knew he called out to me and I heard him crying. I ran into the room," she said, then sipped her coffee, "and he was moaning and then he just collapsed." Sighing, she continued, "so he's in there," she said and motioned with her head towards the room behind her. "They said I'd have to wait here until the doctor . ." her voice trailed off.

"Alright," Michael stopped her in mid-sentence, "we'll wait, together," he said.

Repositioning his chair to be closer to hers, Michael gently took her hand in his and gently squeezed it. "It's going to be okay," he said comfortingly.

THE SYMBIOTIC SECTION

It seemed to take forever for Michael and Michelle to hear hurried footsteps in the hall coming towards their direction. They looked up to see a tall thin man, a little over six feet with a rugged face, five o'clock shadow, sporting a long blonde ponytail and in dire need of a haircut. He extended his arm. "Hi folks are you the parents? The Dickersons' right?" he asked, not waiting for a reply. "I'm Dr. Fulton, Dr. Reginald Fulton. I'm in charge of The Acute Special Medicine Management Division."

He saw that the parents were just about to stand when he mentioned, "please, don't get up. I'm going to sit down as well."

"Travis is resting quietly right now in the room behind us and we're waiting for the results of more of his tests to come back. He's in no immediate danger and we're treating him for his condition," he said.

"Which is?" his parents asked in unison.

"Oh, yes; for the arsenic, of course," the doctor stated matter-of-factly without bothering to look up from the medical chart he was now viewing.

"Arsenic! Oh my God!" Michelle said, barely able to catch her breath.

"Now, when did he first come in contact with it? I want you to think very carefully. A camping trip where he may have drank from an old well? Has he ever handled any poisons or chemicals in school or working in a garden?"

"Michelle?" Michael asked, careful to keep her focused, "on the weekend you have him has he ever helped you in the garden with any ant or weed killers, *ever?*"

"No, never," she answered while squeezing Michael's hand. "Arsenic? Oh my God!" she kept repeating.

"You two are divorced then I take it?"

"Yes, but what difference does *that* make? We're the boy's parents." Michael said.

"Hmmm, oh none, someone was asking me and I, ah, just wanted to get our records straight. You know how hospital's can mess up patient records."

Michael looked through the glass into the room to see his son resting with a variety of machines monitoring him. "Dr. Fulton, how do you know its arsenic? I mean, are you positive?"

Dr. Fulton finally set the chart down and looked at both parents. "Look folks, let me just say that in all my time here at the University of Chicago Medical Center, I've never seen such a clear cut case. We're just waiting for the urine tests to come back since they have to be administered within twenty four to forty eight hours for an acute exposure. I've also ordered tests on his hair and fingernails; that way we can determine the level of exposure over a six to twelve month period."

Michelle looked up at Michael and asked, "has Travis complained to you about feeling bad?"

"He had a brief period a while back where he missed a few days of school and had to take some makeup tests. Right around the time he took those college level entry exams but I thought it was just a virus or his nerves kicking in."

"Why didn't you tell me?" Michelle asked.

Then Michael responded, "he mentioned his joints hurt but Michelle I just chalked that up to his long hours of gymnastics practice at the gym. You can understand *that* can't you?"

Dr. Fulton stood up and walked over to the coffee machine near the nurse's station, pouring himself a large cup. Yawning, he said, "usually the victim will feel light-headed, have headaches, sleepiness or even complain of stomach or joint pain. In cases when the exposure is severe there will be convulsions and they'll be damage to the kidneys, heart and brain. But don't worry," he said, looking at their faces, "he doesn't have a severe exposure," he said smiling. A dose like that would have to be somewhere between seventy to two hundred milligrams for it to usually be lethal, and he's nowhere near that."

"So what do we do now Dr. Fulton?" Michelle asked, holding onto Michael's arm.

"You go home, get some rest and think about where and how he got exposed," Dr. Fulton assured them. "You can see him now, but just for a few minutes, he's been heavily sedated."

Keeping the noise to a minimum, Michael, Michelle and Dr. Fulton slowly entered the small private room. "Look at his fingernails," Dr. Fulton whispered.

"Oh my Lord!" Michelle softly exclaimed as she stared at the white lines on his fingernails. "Does that mean arsenic?" she asked with a hint of fear in her voice.

"Yes, that's one of the definite signs Miss Dickerson."

"It's Pierson, doctor."

Michael walked over and touched Travis' head with tenderness as he kissed his forehead. He fought long and hard to hold back the tears that he knew were welling up in his eyes.

"What's the line of treatment doctor?" Michael asked.

"Our best treatment is to start him up on Dimercaptosuccinic Acid. We call it dimercaprol for short."

Ignoring their puzzled looks, Dr. Fulton continued, "it's a chelating agent which sequesters the arsenic away from the blood proteins and it's a very common treatment for acute arsenic poisonings. Oh, excuse me, that's for me, I'm afraid I have to get this," he said viewing the screen on his cell phone and temporarily walked out of the room.

Michael put his arm around Michelle and knew he would have to be the strong one tonight, for her and for Travis. "We'll make it through this. Still my girl?" he asked with half a smile.

"I'm trying to be," she answered in a softer tone of voice.

Michelle stood near the bed and looked at her son. Then she broke down. "I never wanted him, remember? This is my payback for what I was going to do!" she said through her sobs.

"No. No, this is something else. God knows you've suffered enough," he said trying to relieve her guilt.

Embracing her in his arms, Michael kissed the top of her head and offered her his sleeve to wipe her nose on. She managed just a hint of a smile as they heard the doctor come back into the room.

"Anything else?" Dr. Fulton asked.

"Any side effects from the treatment?" Michael asked with hesitation.

"Yes, but nothing he can't handle. There may be some excessive salivation, mild hypertension but only in some cases, nausea, pain at the injection site and paresthesia, that's a tingling of the skin that can be treated with anti-itch cream," he stated while looking at his watch. "When he's home, make sure he takes iron pills every single day because he's going to be anemic for awhile. The bottom line is, he's young and strong so don't worry about his recovery. We've got to pinpoint the source and that's where I'll need your help so he doesn't end up in here again. I've got to be going now," he said as he extended his arm and motioned them out of the room.

"The best thing you two can do now is go home and get some rest! That's an order!" he commanded with a faint smile.

Following Michelle's car, Michael drove to her house and waited as she unlocked the door. "The spare bedroom is on the left and it has its own private bath. I sleep in on Fridays so no matter what you do, don't wake me up. I'll call you from the hospital tomorrow with updates on his progress," she said.

Making an about face, she looked into his eyes and said "Michael, thank you so much for being there."

He squeezed her hands and gently kissed her cheek before he opened the door to the spare bedroom and whispered, "no problem," before shutting it.

He was grateful that his ex-wife had made the offer for him to stay over her house since it was closer to his office but more importantly, closer to the hospital.

Showered and finally in bed, he remembered he had forgotten to call Ashley. *Tomorrow just has to be a better day,* he thought, as he drifted off to sleep.

Well past midnight, Dr. Fulton made his way to his office, locked the door and hit the redial button on his cell phone. He counted two rings before he heard the voice on the other end speak.

"Yes, what news do you have for me?"

"My shift is over and I'm leaving now. I should be there in less than an hour. I'll bring with me a list of all the meds he's on, all the tests we've administered along with the results we've received thus far and the preferred method of treatment."

"And the records, what do they indicate? Are they *both* his parents?"

"Yes. They're divorced but on very good terms though."

There was a longer than normal pause on the phone before Dr. Fulton continued, "I can't really discuss this in detail over the phone but since we're scheduled to meet at your home, I'll be there soon and we can . . ." his voice trailed off.

"Yes, I know that you will be straightforward and truthful with me, no?" the voice asked. "But I sense discontent. You are happy with the arrangement, no?"

"Of course, it's just that I'm worried about my upcoming DUI trial. I really fucked up this time buying some shit from an undercover officer. I just wanted something to give me an extra edge, with all the stress I've been under. Now I'm up all night losing sleep and shitting bricks that my wife will leave me and take the kids, I could lose my house and even my license to practice medicine if I'm convicted of the charges against me. They say they have dates, names and witnesses . . . that's it's an airtight case," he said with desperation in his voice.

"And of all these things that you could lose, what is the one that would tear you apart, make you lose hope and want to end *this* life? Think hard, for there can only be one right answer Dr. Fulton."

"I don't have to think about it because I already know what it would be. It would be losing my children. You see Mr. Rizzo, they mean more to me than life itself. They're my world and this . . . all of this, my wife, my career, the money, everything, it could all cease in a heartbeat and I could go on. But if I didn't have my children then I'd be ready to check out, right here and right now; that's how much I love them and that's why I'm so sorry."

The voice on the other end was calm; it was the voice of reason. "As I have said all along, I am not here to judge, I am here to offer you a solution. We all have our vices and we all have our, shall we say, pleasures. Don't worry my friend; I am a man who knows that relationships are a key element in life and that the most valuable commodity one can have is information. Good information. My sources tell me that *all* the witnesses have suddenly decided to recant their stories and the State's iron-clad case against you is being dropped. You will have confirmation of this tomorrow morning."

Dr. Fulton inserted his clenched fist into his mouth biting down hard to curtail his cries of joy as an emotional wave of relief flooded over his body and then exhaled deeply. It was all he could do to restrain himself.

"Thank you Mr. Rizzo," he managed to whisper into the phone.

"You are welcome, my friend, now don't keep me waiting!"

Chapter Twenty Three

Salvatore Rizzo still heard the resonating sound of clapping as he finally stood up and made his way towards the exit from his private box at the opera. He looked magnificent in his custom-made black tuxedo tonight, its tailored fit emphasizing his still-fit physique after all these years.

He picked up the black sequined wrap and draped it around Debra Morris' shoulders as he escorted her out. He eyed her backside as she walked slowly in front of him before quickening his pace and walking beside her.

Salvatore was sure of himself and made certain that everything around him fit into what he deemed -- his circle of convenience, that's why Debra Morris was going to be *very* convenient, at least for tonight. He smiled at her and when their eyes met, Debra and Salvatore had an unspoken understanding of what was expected of her this evening and also of what was to come. She was mesmerized and fascinated with powerful men and in the city of Chicago; Salvatore Rizzo was the ultimate power player.

As he walked through the crowd with only elbow room to spare, he thought about his humble beginnings in the small town of Lentini, a tiny agricultural community in Sicily, and how as a boy he had longed for more trips to Rome, Naples, Bologna and Tuscan even though they were few and far between. After years of struggling, his dreams finally became a reality when he attended law school thanks to his hard work and the efforts of his modest family.

Once there, his fellow classmates noticed many things and events taking place in the area but Salvatore saw something that the others had missed. Oh sure, he knew of the mafia, who didn't? He saw how people had to pay for protection and what the consequences were for those who went against the system. He also saw the drug dealers, pimps and prostitutes that were harassed by the police and by their own local government. But when he saw the same thing happening to the common people within several hardworking communities, he was determined to do something about it. Sure, there were attorneys but that was no guarantee that the results you got from them would be the results you desired. What you wanted and what you deserved were, in the eyes of the law, two *very* different things and he wanted to make a right come from a wrong, make it come to fruition.

Salvatore knew that after you paid the attorneys, it sometimes ended up being a crapshoot and you just had to lie down and accept *their* results. The average person had to incur all the risks because they had no one they could go to for protection. They had no *insurance*.

As far as Salvatore Rizzo was concerned, the police and government officials were no better than the mafia. So at the ripe old age of twenty-eight, he had come to America and become in his mind, a salesman, more or less. Working his way up the corporate ladder in some of the best legal offices, he slaved tirelessly and mastered his craft. He networked and made valuable contacts, always staying true to his goal, to simply offer a kind of *insurance* to make life easier for the average person.

In his mid-thirties, he married a lovely Sicilian girl, Gabriella Alisha, and they had a daughter together but she was stillborn and his wife, unable to deal with the loss of her child and her husband's demanding career, spiraled into a depression and soon afterwards, committed suicide. But instead of it hardening his heart, it softened it and allowed him to indulge in his craft even harder until he perfected it. In a sense, he worked through the loss and pain to find comfort and to *lose* himself but, because of his loyalty and dedication to his work, he realized that in time, he had *found* himself.

Race, creed, accent, background, country, color, heritage, religion? Whatever you wanted to call it, it was all bullshit to him. The heart and soul, those two things alone; those are what *really* mattered.

Now that he was fifty, he had established a name for himself not only in the legal community but within the entire city, giving back to the town of Chicago, no matter what the cost and letting his presence be known. Maintaining a lifestyle that was lavish and opulent, it was completely and utterly unattainable by his colleagues.

Although he never dealt in certain areas, such as child pornography and drugs, he had numerous contacts that jumped at the chance to do his bidding and remove individuals from society when the need arose. They paid him handsomely for a chance to work with him and perform these much-needed services; simply because in the end -- *he* delivered.

Yes, he was a force to be reckoned with and he had done it *his* way, with style and panache for he knew how to judge a person's heart and soul, and undeniably he had become a master of his own destiny.

Walking down the long staircase, he spotted Antonio standing just behind a marble column and his eyes took on a more serious gaze. He adjusted his bowtie and then turned to his date.

"Ah, I see a business associate of mine. Debra dear, why don't you visit the ladies room and I'll take care of this; I promise you I won't be long," he assured her.

With his date out of listening range, he made his way to an area behind a curtain that had been roped off. Eyeing the obstruction he simply unhooked it, removed the barrier, and motioned Antonio to follow him with his eyes before replacing it. They were both in a much quieter place now and, for the moment, in private.

Antonio removed a small red wallet-size note pad and began the task of briefing his superior on various events and activities, keeping his voice as low as possible.

Salvatore listened intently, smoothing an imaginary beard with his right hand and occasionally nodded.

"So that is what happened Mr. Rizzo, like I said before, a meeting was held and then something went wrong. It may have been the victim selling drugs to the defendant, but there is no proof of that. Anyway, the guy ended up shooting the other one in some sort of a struggle. He claims the gun went off accidentally and he panicked and fled the scene. Unfortunately, there are two witnesses who saw everything and are more than willing to testify against this . . . this Mr. Tyrone Robinson, and to make matters worse, he's a football star for the Chicago Bears."

"The man he killed, this Maurice Stevens, he was a detective, no?" Salvatore asked.

"Yes sir, he was working undercover, even though the department isn't confirming that one way or the other. But I know for a fact that he was a dirty cop."

"Yes, he was involved with child pornography, was he not?"

"Yes, Mr. Rizzo, not many people know that. Yes, he was heavily involved," Antonio answered, very impressed with his boss's knowledge on the subject matter.

"Well then," he said smiling, "the city smells better already, you agree, no?"

"Yes, it has become less polluted thanks to Mr. Robinson."

"And this Mr. Robinson, he is aware of my five hundred thousand dollar fee?" Salvatore asked.

"Yes Mr. Rizzo, I made sure that he is *fully* aware."

"Then, as we say in Sicily, we will show this Mr. Tyrone Robinson a *token della nostra fedelta,* a token of our loyalty, and lend him our support during this most difficult time. Contact our sources and see that I have a copy of the full transcript from his previous trial on my desk first thing tomorrow morning. I will also require complete files on the two eye-witnesses which need to include two photos. One photo needs to be a clear head shot and the other a full-length body shot. Furthermore, the file should also have everything from the time they were potty-trained to everyone they fucked last year and what they ate last night!"

"Anything else, sir?"

"Yes, send flowers to Tyrone's wife instructing her that detailed instructions will follow shortly and that she need not worry about her husband doing *any* prison time whatsoever. What was her name again, Jasmine?"

"Why, yes sir, but she spells it with a *z* not an *s*."

"Very well then, you have done me a first-rate service Antonio," he said, squeezing his shoulder. Now he focused his attention on his tuxedo and carefully removed a long, dark cigarette holder from just inside his breast pocket. He held it in front of him, admiring it at great length with a prolonged stare, and then turned again to Antonio.

"You see Antonio?" he said proudly, "this is the newest member of my collection. It just arrived yesterday, Turkish Block Meerschaum," he said. "Of course this one cost extra since it is opera length, a full twenty inches." Pausing, Salvatore stroked it from tip to end, almost entranced by the mere sight of the object.

"It is the equivalent of velvet and satin sheets being wrapped around the finest tobacco in the world, yes," he continued, "a velvety rich bath for the tobacco that makes it yield more pleasure and more intensity making it ultra smooth. They've been making them this way since just before the 1600's, and all hand carved."

Antonio knew about his employer's passion for many things and although he did not share his superior's passion, he completely respected it.

"You make it sound like chocolate or making love," then he remarked "I see this one has jewels in it."

"Ah, yes Antonio. I see you have acquired an eye for detail as I have. You'll notice the precious stones and special engravings I had carved into this one. One day, my friend, perhaps you will enjoy the simpler things in life as I do . . . a great wine, a fine woman and a good smoke."

Rizzo slowly walked with Antonio in front of him, studying his body language and almost intuitively he knew there was a contradiction of sorts within this man.

"I feel that you have some conflict because you are aware that this Mr. Robinson took the life of a policeman." He paused and then continued, "besides the fact that he was *not* one of Chicago's finest, you must never forget, Antonio that we are merely providing a service to Mr. Robinson, and, after all, he has given this opportunity to *us*. Keep in mind that Tyrone does not deal in matters where children are concerned and he has vowed to turn his life around. That is all that any man can hope for. You see Antonio, even football players make mistakes."

Their brief meeting over, they quietly made their way back to the theatre entrance and saw Debra making her way through the crowd towards Salvatore.

Antonio nodded, took his cue and disappeared into the crowd.

"Is your friend still here? Will he be joining us?" Debra asked.

"No my dear, what I have in mind for us this evening will be best carried out between only the two of us and we will be alone soon," he said calmly, as he openly admired her enormous bosom that was partially on display.

His limousine arrived curbside and after the door was opened for them, they were promptly escorted inside. Once they were settled, the black privacy screen separating the driver from the passenger compartments was immediately raised and Debra wasted no time in unbuckling her companion's belt and unzipping his pants. She bent down close to his crotch and licked her lips greedily in anticipation of the evenings opening festivities.

"Ahhhhhhh," Salvatore groaned under his breath, "let the games begin!"

Chapter Twenty Four

By now, Michelle knew most of the staff at the University of Chicago Medical Center since she made it a point to visit Travis every day since his arrival. It had been five days now and, with each day; she saw remarkable improvements in his coloring, appetite and strength.

Today she had a bag of Starburst chews, his favorite. No longer in the intensive care unit, she had no guilt whatsoever in smuggling these candies in to him on this day, his final full day. *Thank you Jesus he will be going home tomorrow morning,* she thought.

Arriving on his floor, she waved to the nurses at the duty station and pointed to the sign-in registry as she walked swiftly by; assuming someone on the staff would sign her in. "Thanks girls!" she said.

The television was tuned to a reality show and Travis was sitting up in bed applying more anti-itch cream as she entered his room. When he saw his mother, he sighed and smiled. "Thank God, you have saved me from a fate worse than death. Why do they show these programs for old people? How do people look at this garbage?"

"Well some of us old people over twenty-nine years of age actually enjoy a reality show every now and then. It takes our minds off of things," she answered, "like how our skin itches," she added, picking up his anti-itch cream and returning it to the bedside tray.

Michelle pulled up the chair that was in the corner of the room and positioned it as close to the bed as possible. Then she reached into her purse, unveiling a fresh deck of playing cards. "Tah dah!" she announced as she held them upwards just out of his reach.

"Hey, no fair!" Travis yelled, reaching for them.

Laughing, his mother handed the deck over to him and let him deal. They both loved playing cards and as Travis became older, it seemed this was one of the few ways they could still have a connection the way that men have a special connection to their sons with sports. No matter what was going on in his life, there were always cards.

"Have you had a chance to think about what you've been doing or where you've been going these past few weeks?" she asked. "The doctors said you've been exposed to arsenic for quite some time and, for the life of me, I just can't figure out how you came in contact with it."

He picked up a card, scratched his head, rearranged his hand and thought long and hard. "Your turn," he replied.

"Are you sure you want to discard *that* card?" she asked chuckling, as he laid it onto the pile.

"Oh no!" he exclaimed, as he watched his mother pick up his discarded card and lay down her remaining cards in sets and shout, "I'm out!"

"All I know is I didn't go to any landscaping place, gardening center, clean out your storage shed or pick up anything in the lab at school," he said out loud, contemplating his next move.

"Are you sure about the school, honey?"

"Mom, they lock all that stuff up because of the drug problems some of the kids have," he reminded her, "schools have to think about liability you know."

"Right, right," she answered. "Well, what about the day you got sick at my place? Did you sit next to someone on the bus or help somebody carry a package or something?"

"No mom!" he retorted. Then he squinted his eyes and said, "that was the day I didn't take the bus."

"Then how did you get there?" Michelle asked, puzzled and wrinkling her brow.

"I saw Mr. Lindbloom and he offered me a ride to your house."

"Oh really?" she asked in a surprised tone.

Travis picked up the deck and looked at his mother, "Your deal," he said. Then he grinned from ear to ear as he handed the deck to her while watching her remove the large bag of Starburst candy chews from her purse. "Mom you're sooooooo awesome!"

Shuffling the cards many times over, she began to dole out the exact number needed. Michelle had a unique rhythmic quality when she did things and dealing out the cards was an area where she made no exception. Picking up her stack, she continued questioning him. "So did you go with him?"

"Yeah, something wrong with that?" Then he blurted out, "mom you ought to see Mr. Lindbloom's car, he has a powder white Lamborghini and it's so awesome!" he cried.

Organizing her hand again, Michelle studied the cards that had been placed into the discarded pile before she pulled one off the top of the stack. "I'll bet you really enjoyed riding in that. Did you come straight to my house?" she inquired.

"Well," Travis said as he scratched his mass of thick sandy brown hair, "we did stop for a fountain drink but then we came right to your house."

"Frank Lindbloom bought the drinks?" she asked smiling.

"Yep. He usually gives me something to drink."

"Do you go in the store with him?" she asked, smoothly.

"No, he always buys it for me and brings it to me in the car. Is anything wrong mom?" his voice had a touch of curiosity in it.

"Hmmmm, oh no. Just wondering," she said softly. "

And so the card game went on for one more hour with mother and son laughing, relating to each other and really communicating, the entire time Michelle quizzed him about his whereabouts with such subtleness that he wasn't aware he was being pumped for information. She wanted to give the impression that she was deep in thought regarding the cards she had been dealt but in actuality Michelle Pierson had a gut feeling that something just wasn't quite right. And when Michelle Pierson had a gut feeling about something, there was no stopping her. She couldn't put her finger on it but she was going to make it her in-your-face-business to find out.

Chapter Twenty Five

Janice Freedman looked up from her computer as she heard the elevator doors open and smiled. "Welcome back Ashley, we're so glad you decided to return to help us in the next bank campaign commercials. Who are you here to see, Mr. Dickerson?"

"No, actually I'm here to see Clarence," she corrected her.

Without any hesitation, Janice was placing a call to the director and within a few minutes, Clarence Casey appeared in the reception area, tastefully attired in an expensive light gray suit and impeccably groomed, his neon orange tie, socks and handkerchief, making his usual strong fashion statement. "Hello Miss Ashley, we've all missed you but I must admit, I've missed you most of all," he stated eyeing her up and down. "You're gorgeous *and* delicious!" he commented, as he held both her hands and gently pulled her upwards, bringing her to her feet. "I want you to follow me back to my little love nest and we can sign the new contracts today. They were just delivered this morning by your *Fire and Ice Agency* and it was way too important to farm it out to one of my staff." Turning to look at Janice who was typing but listening to every word of the conversation, he winked and requested "hold all my calls dear," in a perfect falsetto voice.

"It's so good to be back Casey," Ashley said laughingly as she followed him down the long narrow hall.

"Had some trouble with the renewal amount offered, did we?" he chided in.

"No, it wasn't that at all Clarence; I mean Casey," she corrected herself, all the while following him.

Finally reaching his office, she sat down and viewed the assortment of artwork that covered a large portion of the walls, most of it weird by even Hollywood standards. *Welcome back to the love nest,* she thought, but then, this was just typical Clarence. Her eye came to rest on the corner of the massive desk where the contracts were stacked neatly.

Carefully retrieving the stack, she sat down again, smoothing her skirt and turned the pages. Ashley paused as Clarence appeared in front of her and handed her a pen, "Sign here. I've already got it highlighted for you," he said rather pleased with himself, "and in yellow too, your favorite color," he added.

Slyly eyeing him, she asked, "and just how do you know that yellow is my favorite color?"

"Oh, let's just say I have my sources; and it helps when you hear a certain somebody, that being your boss, ordering yellow roses from his cell phone every week," he answered, giggling.

"Casey, you wouldn't!" she chastised him, her eyebrows shooting up.

He looked deep into her eyes and then moved his hand

across his mouth, his thumb and index finger pinched together as he replied, "my lips are sealed sweetheart! Besides I wouldn't want you to lose any of the beauty sleep you get. You are a director's dream and we've just got to keep you remaining wrinkle-free."

Laughing, she replied, "it's all done with smoke and trick mirrors you know. Ready for my close up Mr. DeMille!" she said snickering. "By the way if I was blindfolded, I would think it was a woman I was talking to when I hear you talk that way. How do you make your voice go up that high like that?"

"I make it go up that high because . . . I can!"

After signing the contracts, she opened her handbag, removed a large clip and proceeded to pin up her hair. "Do you have some ideas for the new ads?" she asked.

"Well, I just happen to have a few ideas here and the second draft of what will probably be several before the script is finalized," he said wearily, as he picked up a huge stack of loose papers. "That's just the price some of us have to pay for creative genius," he affirmed, admiring his fingernails.

Ashley rolled up her sleeves, put on her reading glasses, smiled and softly said, "alright Casey, let's get to it then."

And so they read the script, line by line and word for word; it took well over two hours. Changes were inevitable so revisions were made. And just when it seemed they were getting their groove on, Clarence noticed that Ashley began to sneak a peek at her watch. "What's wrong?" Clarence asked, "you seem distracted all of sudden."

"Oh it's just that I have a million errands to run and my apartment is fit to be a crime scene. With everything that's happened I just don't have time to clean it," she said discouragingly.

"Tell you what. Why don't you use *my* service?" he asked. "They not only clean, but they go grocery shopping as long as you have a list, they'll wait in line for concert tickets, they'll do your laundry and they even iron and put it away! I have them make me special dinners on Friday evenings, my date night, so all I have to do is come home with a potential new boyfriend, reheat them and take all the credit," he said proudly as he twirled in a circle.

Ashley laughed at his antics but wasn't sure how she felt about someone being at her place. It was just an apartment but it was still her home. She narrowed her eyes and gave Clarence a weak grin. "Well, I suppose if you've used them before. I guess its okay," she said with a hint of trepidation.

"Alright," Clarence said, as he opened his wallet and removed a card, "done!"

Ashley read the name on the card, *"The Invisible Butler.* What a strange name."

"Not really, they're just like a butler but you rarely see them, if ever."

Reluctantly taking the card from his long buffed fingernails, Ashley slowly placed it inside her handbag. "I'll give them a call tomorrow. Do you mind if we call it a day?" she asked, feeling a yawn come on.

Clarence stood up, "hmmm, oh yes, you go ahead. Excuse me for not seeing you out baby girl."

After Ashley had left his office, Clarence thought about the card he had just given her. He placed his hand over his mouth and tried to stifle a giggle. He knew that Ashley was more than likely going to call the number on the card and he also knew that the owner would have to come out to view her apartment before submitting a proposal. What Ashley didn't know was that *The Invisible Butler* was just one of many lucrative business ventures that Michael's first wife, Michelle Pierson, had taken on.

He giggled again, as he walked to the mini fridge in his office and collected a bottle of water. Then he switched on his compact disc player, selecting a song from a familiar hip hop artist and sang along while he slipped off his shoes, laid on the corner sofa and wiggled his toes inside his neon orange socks.

Clarence smiled, wondering if there would be drama between the two women. But, what the hell, he thought; it's not as though one of them hadn't thought about the other. He yawned and then moved his head from side to side, popping the bones in his neck before singing to the music and changing the words in his best falsetto voice, "Because, baby girl, it's *always* about the drama!"

Chapter Twenty Six

"Yes, of course I have a moment," Michael said, looking up from reading his morning mail. He was grateful that Janice had pre-sorted the massive pile for him, placing them in stacks with color-coded labels on them. The red label indicated either urgent mail, a reply was needed or that it was date sensitive; yellow indicated it could be read at your leisure with no repercussions and blue was for ice cold, the back burner items. Michael had an uncanny ability to be able to go through mountains of paperwork in a short amount of time. It had given him a genuine advantage while attending Chicago State University and a leg up on other students when he was accepted into a coveted internship program at Channel Two – WBBM - T.V.

Marc Greenberg stood in the doorway for what seemed like an abnormal amount of time, even after Michael looked up at him. He was fidgety, something completely out of character, and the lines in his face showed an uneasiness that he rarely expressed.

Stepping inside, he gently closed the huge double doors and took a seat in one of the over-sized leather chairs, his right foot nervously bobbing up and down, and then he began. "Michael, I've finished processing all the mileage reimbursements and the expense accounts." Hesitating, he continued, "the monthly commissions were at a record high, but then again, so were the profits," he stated matter-of-factly before rambling on.

What in the holy hell! Has Greenberg lost his mind? Michael thought. *I've got a shit-load of work to do and he comes in here with some kind of juvenile work update, as though I don't know what the fuck is going on in my own company!*

"What is it exactly that I can do for you Marc?" Michael asked point blank, not trying to hide his annoyance.

"Well," he began and then cleared his throat, "I didn't want to remind you or anything like that but it seems I might have a very precarious situation," he said.

"And what situation is that?" Michael asked, careful not to instigate the man having a stroke in his office.

Greenberg leaned forward in the chair, two huge books in hand and looked at Michael straight on. "It seems that all I have to do now is begin the bi-weekly payroll and proceed with all the accounts payable items we have pending. As soon as you make the transfer to the appropriate accounts, I'll be able to do that sir."

Michael leaned forward, put down his pen and stared at the man, saying absolutely nothing. He summed up quite a few things in two seconds. First of all, Marc Greenberg never joked about money or anything else that was money related for that matter and; Number Two, Marc was very distressed and actually scared shitless about this turn of events. "What transfer is it that you are referring to?" Michael asked.

"I just need the funds transferred into the accounts to cover what was taken out so I can pay our creditors and pay the employees," he said with a hint of irritation in his voice. Then he added, "everything would have been alright except that when you authorized the check for five hundred thousand dollars, it kind of threw everything off, temporarily of course, so I waited for you to make the transfer, but now we're getting down to the wire and, you know me, I didn't want time to almost run out," he replied hastily, hoping he was making sense.

Michael, being a master of disguise, knew in a heartbeat what had happened. Now he realized how Lindbloom had secured the funding to purchase his precious new vehicle and pay off his bookies. Yes, Michael had his sources too, but with the Coleman Financial Services deal not finalized yet, Ashley refusing to see him for a while, and his son becoming hospitalized, he hadn't bothered to do the checks and balances that were part of the normal operating procedures. He had let that slip through the cracks like a fucking idiot! *That goddamn Lindbloom, that cocksucking bastard!* he thought.

Holding his emotions in check, Michael remembered that he was at the helm of his company and it was a role he had perfected. He took a stack of papers from his desk in disarray, shuffled them slowly and then returned them in a neat pile. "Why yes," he lied, "it seems I've been a real horse's ass Marc. With my son becoming ill, I completely forgot to transfer the funds. By the way, do you have a copy of the form that I authorized?" he asked nonchalantly.

"Right here," Marc said, holding it out for him to inspect.

Michael accepted the form, glimpsed at the signature line and confirmed in his own mind what he already knew, Frank Lindbloom had forged his signature. *Forgery and embezzlement. So it had come to this,* he thought.

"I'm glad you brought this to my attention Marc, I apologize for the oversight. The funds will be in the accounts you requested within the hour," he assured him. "Just leave the books here so I can peruse through everything," he said with a ring of finality in his tone.

Crisis averted! Greenberg thought, as he stood up and walked towards the double doors. "Everything okay with your son Michael?" he asked with genuine concern, before he left.

"I promise you that everything is going to be fine Marc," he said with dead seriousness, then he added, "without a doubt."

Chapter Twenty Seven

Travis had just finished his two eggs, prepared sunny side up, just the way he liked them. He swirled his fork ensuring the Canadian bacon came to rest in the last remnants of the egg yolk on his plate as he completed yet another of his mother's fabulous breakfasts.

"Are you finished Travis?" his mother called from the kitchen.

"Yeah, it was soooo good. Thanks mom," he replied while wiping his mouth on his pajama sleeve. "Is dad coming over today?" he asked, adjusting the pillows and repositioning himself in bed.

Walking into his room, Michelle straightened the bookcase items, and found a porn magazine hidden inside a comic book. *Well, I guess he is feeling better,* she thought smiling. "Here, let me take that tray honey. Your father is not only coming today, but he could be here at any minute," she answered while checking her watch.

"Relax mom!" Travis practically yelled, somewhat exasperated. "You don't have to clean *all* the time. I'm not an invalid!"

"Travis Dickerson, you need to lose the attitude or you may find yourself minus one very expensive car at graduation!" she chided. "Now you stay in that bed and do *your* thing and as your mother, your one and only mother I might add, I'll do *mine*," she reprimanded him further.

The doorbell chime began playing; abruptly ending their conversation and Michelle mouthed the words *I love you* to her son as she pointed to the iron pills on the nightstand. "Remember Dr. Fulton said you have to take these everyday," she nagged as she left the room.

Opening the door, she saw Michael standing there looking as good as ever. *It just wasn't fair,* she thought, *how men were sexier and got so much better with age.* But then again, it wasn't just luck. She had to take some of the credit for teaching him about calisthenics, nutrition and skin care while they were dating and now it had paid off, big time. *Too bad he had to go fuck it up,* she thought, *simply because his ego couldn't handle a woman who was more intelligent and successful than himself.*

"Hey," she said, lightly kissing his cheek, "why don't you say hello to Travis, he's in there," she added while pointing in the opposite direction to where Michael was heading. "You know Michael; I've got more than one guest room," she mentioned with a wide grin, all the while continuing to tidy up.

Michael walked into the bedroom and his heart melted. He went over to the bed, practically running, and hugged his son as he had never done before. "So what's this Travis? I hear you're feeling better!" he said with resounding enthusiasm. He tried hard not to show how choked up with emotion he actually was. Always having to hold himself in check, Michael realized he was still hugging his son and released him from his embrace before sitting on the edge of the bed.

"You know you gave your mother and I quite a scare," he said, while running his fingers through Travis' hair, messing up his son's sandy brown locks.

"Sorry dad," he replied with a sheepish grin.

The minutes flew by as Michael and Travis now conversed, more on the same level than ever before. They talked about the preparation for the new school in Ithaca, the approaching final gymnastics tournament, his upcoming graduation and, of course, the brand new Mustang which was just on the horizon.

With the soft knock on the door, Michael knew it was time for Travis to rest and for him to leave. "Hey, I'm glad you stopped by dad," he said.

"Me too Travis, me too."

With final goodbyes made and the last bit of tidying up done, Michelle left her house. She had absolutely no intention of discussing *any* of her suspicions regarding Frank Lindbloom within earshot of her son's remarkable hearing range.

Michael waited for her in his car, positioned in the driver's seat but looked more as though he was waiting at the helm of a large vessel. Michelle noticed this when she turned around from locking her front door and quickly had to look down at the sidewalk to hold back a snicker at her ex-husband's expression. *Why did this man have to pretend to be in control?* she thought.

Since they had divorced and she was back on the

market, she had learned during that time to make men *feel* as though they were in control; something she had to become accustomed to and constantly practice at, as this was not her nature. She often times wondered what it would be like to actually be with a man that was not only in control, but knew it. Then she wondered if she would even *want* to be with a man like that.

Opening the car door, she got in, fastened her seatbelt, and slammed the door closed. "Where to?" she asked with a just a hint of a smile, as she wiped the lipstick off her teeth in the vanity mirror.

"*Christopher's Bistro,*" Michael answered, as he pulled away from the curb. "It shouldn't be too crowded and..."

"Let me guess," Michelle finished his sentence for him, "they know you there."

"Is it alright then?" he posed the question to her.

"Yes Michael, its fine," she assured him.

Driving through the city, it brought back memories of their first few years together; some of the best years of Michael's life except, for the life of him, he just couldn't accept that her God-given beauty had been combined with street-smarts, above-average intelligence and a savvy mindset. At that time he was at a crossroads in his career and in his personal life while his wife was sure of herself, had set goals and knew exactly how to achieve them. *Major Fuck Up Number One,* he thought, *allowing her to leave me.*

Arriving at *Christopher's Bistro,* Michelle was escorted through the bar area to Michael's usual table and Michael, being attentive to a woman's needs, joined her a few moments later with two drinks in hand. He set them down on the table in front of him and hastily seated himself. "Vodka Gimlet, heavy on the vodka, a dash of fresh lime juice and a slice of lime right?" he asked, smiling.

"I can't believe you remembered," she said, sounding impressed, and I suppose you have your old standby, your Courvoisier?"

"Wouldn't want to disappoint you," he answered, looking at her beautiful profile.

"This place is packed to the max. Did they know you were coming?" she asked staring in disbelief at the large crowds. "I mean the way we were seated . . . ." her voice trailed off.

"Let's just say that rank has its privileges and it pays to be noticed. You of all people should know I try to always make it a point to make my presence known," he said smoothly as he sipped from his glass.

"Well, let's see," she said as she fumbled in her purse, "this ought to help you get the attention you desire," she said unveiling a tiny box with a red bow affixed to it. "Relax, it's from Travis," she said as she saw a momentary look of puzzlement on his face. "He got a part-time job as a tutor after school when he doesn't have gymnastics, strictly to pay for this," she said proudly.

Michael looked at the box, noting it was from *Tiffany & Company.* He opened it to reveal black onyx cufflinks with the letters MD on the front. "Holy shit Michelle! Why'd you have the boy get something this extravagant?" he asked with a bit of irritation in his voice.

"He insisted," she answered, nodding her head, "he adores you in case you haven't noticed."

There was momentary silence at the table as he admired the cufflinks but Michelle noticed that his glass was full and taller than it actually needed to be. *He looked tired, no; he was worried,* she thought. Wanting to address this, she decided to initiate a new direction of conversation.

"That's some drink Michael. What did you want to talk to me about?"

"Ladies first," he said winking at her.

"Come on," she said.

Now her hand slowly made its way over to reach his empty right hand that was resting on the table. "Please," she managed to say, as she softly squeezed it and looked into his eyes.

"I've got some trouble at the office," he stated, admiring her long dark hair, "it's Frank."

"Frank who? Frank Lindbloom?" she asked. "What's that bastard gone and done now?" Then with a worried look, "you've had problems with him for years, haven't you?"

Michael looked into her eyes and positioned himself very close to her face. Knowing, without hesitation, that he could completely trust his ex-wife, he whispered into her ear, "he's forged my signature on some documents and embezzled half a million dollars; probably more when I get the final figures."

"Oh my God!" Michelle gasped, "are you sure?"

"Shhhhh! Yes, although I'm not entirely shocked," he said with a serious tone in his voice. "You were right, our relationship has been strained and turbulent for quite some time now but I never knew he would stoop this low and that his contempt for me ran this deep."

"That shit with his sister again, huh? After *all* these years?" Michelle asked.

"Yeah, but its more than that."

"What about UBMI? Are you still solvent?" she asked, while signaling the wait staff for another drink.

"Yes, quite, but that's not the point Michelle. If he's *that* ruthless, then he's out of control and if he's *that* out of control, he's dangerous; and with a dangerous individual, there's no telling what they might do next."

Taking a long drink from his tall glass of cognac, he looked down at his thumbs as they rhythmically mirrored each other, stroking the sides of his glass and Michelle knew that he was contemplating what his next move would be.

"Are you going to contact the authorities?" she asked, as she accepted her second drink from the wait staff.

"What, and let everyone think that I didn't know what the fuck was going on in my *own* company? I'll lose credibility in the financial world and it'll kill any plans to take the company public in the future."

Michael rubbed his brow and with a final swig, finished off his drink. "Besides, it's a damn good forgery," he added, "it would even fool most of the experts I know."

With her eyebrows shooting up, Michelle exclaimed, "You've seen them? The forged documents, I mean?"

"Yeah and it looks *exactly* like my signature," he concluded.

This time he looked down at his empty glass and then into Michelle's brown eyes before continuing. "You see, the authorities aren't going to do anything! Most of them either have shit for brains or they're as crooked as a dog's hind legs. I don't have nearly enough shit to warrant a case that will stand up in court and I'd end up looking like a god-damn fool. Ultimately it's not *what* you know . . . it's what you can *prove*."

After that comment, there was an uncomfortable silence at their table and both of them could sense the other's anxiety. It was as though a big white elephant had entered the room and plopped down at their table, but they couldn't bring themselves to talk about it.

Genuinely concerned, Michelle was still digesting what Michael had just divulged to her as she brought her napkin to her lips and gently wiped the corners of her mouth, staining it with traces of her crimson lipstick. She was torn between trying to sit there and soothe her ex-husband's feelings or letting him know about her suspicions regarding his lowlife business partner. If ever there was a dichotomy, she was sure she would be listed in the dictionary as the poster child for it.

Taking a deep breath, she moved her lips close to Michael's ear and, keeping her voice extremely low, slowly began to tell him about how she felt their son received the arsenic poisoning over an extended period of time and who she felt was responsible.

Michael listened intently, the veins in his neck extending, as he gnashed his teeth and silently took it all in. Michelle, true to form, didn't hold anything back. She told him how she had gone to the Medical Center, under the guise of playing cards with Travis, and discovered that his partner, Frank Lindbloom, had not only given Travis a ride on that fateful day when she had to call 911, but that he had also shuttled him on several other occasions that included the Windy City Gymnasium. *Yes,* Michael thought, *it all correlated with the dates Travis had missed school and had to take make-up exams. His complaints of aching joints, headaches, etc. . . .*

More irritated than ever before, he was fuming by time she had reached the end of explaining her theory. So much so, that he could feel his heart thumping in his ears and his blood pressure rising exponentially.

"Goddamn motherfucking cocksucker!" he yelled out loud, unable to contain his rage any longer.

"Oh my God!" Michelle gasped, as she reached for a napkin.

Her eyes were frozen on the table, as she realized that Michael had been unaware of the fact that he had squeezed his empty glass so hard, it had broken in his hand.

Chapter Twenty Eight

The women all sat on the dark beige sectional with their feet resting on several of the ottomans that had been provided for them with their shoes removed, an ambiance of mischief was in the air.

There were definite waves of laughter coming from the other room as Bianca Lapicola hurriedly dried her hands on the towel and ran back into her greatroom. "Okay, I'm back," she said, out of breath, "did I miss anything?" she asked, as she seated herself in the center. No one answered her.

"Alright ladies!" the coordinator shouted above all the chatter, "our last item for tonight is The Tornado," she said loudly, as she reached into her silver briefcase.

The gasps and shrieks in the room were drowned out by applause as the woman conducting the event removed a black velvet bag, loosening the tie that held it shut, and revealed a massive red dildo.

"This one is our newest model, a full ten inches!" she said proudly, as she held it up for their viewing pleasure. "The red one comes with a heating device so it will continuously stay warm, which is great for those cold nights ladies," she said while winking. "It has a special spin button that mimics a tornado." Then she continued, "and by pressing the spin button twice, it even has a reverse feature, should you want to change direction in mid-stream."

"Can't expect a man to do *that!*" someone in the audience yelled, which yielded still more laughter.

"Does it come in any other colors?" Bianca asked.

"Why, yes. It's available in *Undercover Black* and *Pet Me Till I'm Pink*. Remember ladies that if you buy this tonight I'll throw in an assortment of love jelly and six edible panties from peach to chocolate to cherry for free, also if you buy two items tonight, you'll also receive the *Hot Licks Passion Fruit and Honey & Spice Flavored Body Lotion* and I'll even throw in some strawberry flavored douche."

"How much is The Tornado?" one of the guests asked over the noise of the other women.

"Tonight it's being offered as a show-stopper special for just one hundred ninety five dollars and ninety-five cents," the coordinator said as she passed the dildo around to the women before finishing up.

"I think we should all give a round of applause to Bianca, our hostess tonight, for agreeing to graciously host this event. Remember ladies, if you'd like to host a *Simple Pleasures Party* you can just contact me, Candace Hernandez. Call me Candy. My name, office number, fax, cell phone and website are inside each party favor bag and remember that each bag contains a set of complimentary bubble gum flavored condoms. Yes girls, I think that's all I've got for tonight, so in closing I'll just end the show with my motto: Remember that it can be both sweet *and* slippery!"

With the applause making it impossible for her to

continue, Bianca went to the coordinator, escorting her to the kitchen and helped to count up the orders.

"Wow that makes this show worth over five thousand dollars in sales!" Bianca said, "I can't believe all the free shit I'm going to get from hosting this. God, I can't wait!"

"Yes, I can't remember having this big a show, ever," Candace said, with a surprised look on her face.

"Really? Just imagine what sales would be like in a *good* economy," Bianca stated. "Would you like a glass of champagne?" she asked while offering the coordinator a libation before she could answer.

"Don't mind if I do," she replied, sitting down and finally taking her shoes off too. "God, that feels good. Now," she said, handing a huge color brochure to Bianca, "take a look at the hostess book I brought over for you."

When it was her turn for the inspection, Ashley held the red dildo in her hand and pressed the spin button once, watching its rotating motion; then twice as she watched it reversing direction. "Wow," she said, "look how *big* it is!" she remarked, with excitement.

"Are you getting one Ashley?" one of the guests asked.

"Oh yes, I'm getting the big black one!" she answered with uncontrollable laughter. "A girl has got to do what a girl is able to!" she quipped.

After all the guests had left, Ashley helped Bianca retrieve most of the wine glasses and the empty magnums of champagne strewn all over the room. "Wow, that was wild,"

Ashley said, "but look what all the guests have done to your greatroom."

"It's okay," Bianca said, "I'm not worried about it. I just keep telling myself it's just a greatroom and that's why I have parties in it," she said, trying to convince herself it was okay if the pillows were squashed and there were crumbs everywhere and the room was in a complete and total shambles.

"Ah, Bianca," Ashley began, "I wanted to thank you so much for letting me have the party at *your* place."

"Oh honey, don't even think about it. I know you must have your reasons for changing the venue at the last moment though. Who is he?" Bianca asked slyly.

"It's not what you think," Ashley corrected her. "I've got a cleaning service coming over in a few days and I'm going to be pretty much on location for some photo shoots. If I had hosted the party tonight, I wouldn't begin to have enough time to clean up my place. Don't want to scare off the people before they even get started," she explained. "Whew! Found another magnum of champagne under the sectional," she uttered.

"Say, if the cleaning service works out for you let me know. I could really use some help around here a couple of days a week," Bianca said, as she walked Ashley to the front door.

"Have fun tonight," Ashley said eyeing all the free sex toys on the table that Bianca had received for hosting the party.

"Oh honey," Bianca reminded her, "that's a given."

Chapter Twenty Nine

Elizabeth Lindbloom was alert today and functioning at her highest capacity, excellent for her but not so good for most people. She smoothed her hair down with the remaining water on her hand and then remembered to turn off the faucet. She stepped back from the sink and went over her checklist, "Shower, shave underarms, brush teeth . . ." she said aloud, reaffirming that she could handle things and was indeed going to have a productive day.

Looking through her closet, she found an outfit that she could still get into without it falling off of her and she wasted no time in dressing. Now it was back to the full-length mirror on the outside of her closet door. "One last look so I won't leave anything to chance," she said softly, as she admired her thin frame. "Yep, I can honestly say that I clean up pretty good," she said with a touch of arrogance.

She walked from the bathroom into her kitchen, checklist in hand, and enjoyed the floral scent that her plug-in air fresheners released. Turning towards the dinette set, she pulled out a chair and sat down, positioning herself near her once steaming hot cup of coffee. She felt herself smile with satisfaction as she gazed into the living room through the opening in the large plantation shutters that also doubled as room dividers.

After working non-stop for countless hours, everything was neat and in order, as it should be, she thought to herself. Hell, she had even killed all the flies that were laying eggs inside the pizza boxes so she had a lot to be proud of.

Singling out one of the last few items on her checklist, she set it down on the table, picked up the phone and dialed a number. She sipped her now lukewarm coffee as she waited for the familiar greeting on the other end.

"It's Strictly Personal Magazine, how may I help you?" a female voice asked.

"Yes, I want to change something in my subscription," Elizabeth said.

"Alright, are you cancelling or renewing it?" the girl asked.

"I'd like for you people to change my last name on my subscription label back to Lindbloom," she said with a touch of irritation.

"Oh, I see," the girl said knowingly. "You'll need the Corrections Department, and can you hold?" she asked, then immediately depressed the hold feature before receiving any type of response.

"Do I have a choice?" Elizabeth answered into a phone that played what she felt were the worst musical recordings she had ever heard.

"Corrections Department this is Marilyn."

"Yes, my name is Elizabeth, Elizabeth Lindbloom and I live in Arlington Heights at 3027 North Lake Shore Drive. I have a subscription with your magazine."

"What can we do for you today?"

"I just want to make a name change. You see on my address label it still lists my last name as Henderson and I haven't been Henderson for a while now. I went back to my maiden name of Lindbloom a few months ago," she stated.

"Alright Miss Lindbloom, I've got you on my screen now. Hmmm . . . let's see now. You went from Lindbloom to Dickerson to Starita to O'Neill to Henderson and now you say you're back to Lindbloom?" the woman asked.

"What the hell is wrong with you!" Elizabeth yelled. All I want is a name change, Christ Almighty! I don't need a goddamn history lesson!" she screamed, disciplining the woman on the other end.

"I've made that change for you. It's done now Miss Lindbloom and I apologize for any misunderstanding. Is there anything else I can do for you today?" the woman asked sweetly.

"Yeah, you can take your sweet voice along with that heartfelt apology and shove it up your sweet little ass, *without* Vaseline!" she screamed, slamming down the receiver.

Closing her eyes momentarily to compose herself, Elizabeth inhaled deeply and cracked her knuckles, before returning the coffee cup to her lips. Nothing was going to deter her from her outing today.

Grabbing her keys, she opened the garage door, stepped into her car and drove off. Yes, she was feeling good –- yes, she was feeling confident.

Her destination was the medical office of Dr. James

Whitman on *The Magnificent Mile*, located on North Michigan Avenue. It was one of the most prestigious medical offices in the city and Dr. Whitman was listed in the *Who's Who Journal* of Chicago physicians.

As she drove down the road, a sense of empowerment took over her. She was glad she had listened to her brother on one of his frequent visits and, with his assistance, had gotten herself back on track and agreed to see *his* doctor. Frank had gotten down on his knees and begged her to get her life together and get a physical and then, if she did that, he promised it would lead to a job with more things to come. Now for the last few weeks, she was only taking half her usual dose of Oxycontin, and hadn't done any illegal drugs for weeks. Though she still had frequent night sweats and some lingering skin ulcers, she knew her recovery was now imminent.

At this moment, she felt better than she had felt in years. Off to see the doctor to receive the results of her physical, she could hardly wait to see her brother tonight and tell him of the results. He would be so proud of her. Soon she would have a job, a new home and anything else she wanted.

She was trying, actually trying and, who knows, she might actually have a shot at luring her ex-husband back into her life. She couldn't hide the fact that every man she had ever been involved with or even married had always been compared to him. That's why all her past relationships had failed, she ascertained. He was the one true great love of her life and she knew that she would love him, with all of her heart and soul until the day when she didn't have the breath of life left in her body.

The underground parking lot appeared full and Elizabeth, not being a fan of walking, made the decision to park in one of the open handicapped spaces. And why not? It was close to the door and she had a feeling she wouldn't be long.

She eyed the powder blue convertible parked beside her car with its windows rolled down and, without hesitation, removed the dangling tag from the vehicle's rearview mirror that displayed a handicapped insignia, and threw it onto the dashboard inside of *her* car and then locked her car's door.

Humming a tune that she had just heard on the radio, she walked into the building, pushing aside the massive glass doors and walked the few steps that led directly to the elevators. Aside from her feet not being accustomed to walking in heels, she felt good as she waited in the lobby. Hearing the ding, she stepped inside the open doors and quickly pressed the number ten button.

Once inside Dr. Whitman's office, Elizabeth barely got a chance to sit down before being whisked off to a private waiting room. She sat down, picked up the latest copy of *It's Strictly Personal Magazine,* and thumbed through to page ninety nine, where she had left off in her own magazine which was setting at home on her kitchen table.

After a few moments, she heard approaching footsteps

along with whispering just outside the room she was in; then the footsteps grew fainter and there was silence. The door immediately opened and the assistant took her file from the counter and asked her to wait inside the doctor's private suite. "Dr. Whitman will be with you shortly. There's water in the fridge if you'd like some," the girl said smiling.

My, I'm sure getting the star treatment. It's about time someone realized my potential, she thought to herself, as she entered the doctor's private office. Once there, Elizabeth sat down and looked in amazement at the enormous size of the room. It had to be at least twelve hundred square feet! There was a fireplace, bar, library and even a small kitchen area. Her eye took in all the luxurious fabrics and materials that were used and she determined that it felt more like a high-end suite at a five-star luxury resort rather than a doctor's office. She wanted to sneak a peek at the bathroom setup when Dr. Whitman entered his office and walked quickly over to her.

"Elizabeth," he said without looking at her.

She noticed he wasn't smiling and felt he had bitten off more than he could chew with this fabulous, over-the-top practice. She was sure he was overworking himself just for status and to pay for all this.

"Alright Miss Lindbloom, I'll get right to it then," he said, as he opened her file that had been left in the center of his desk. "You're HIV-Positive," he said in a monotone, with a completely expressionless face.

Elizabeth froze in the once comfortable chair that had

now suddenly become rock hard. Her eyes began blinking rapidly as she sensed a burning sensation in her stomach and felt her throat begin to close. Leaning forward in the chair, she gasped for air with lungs that refused to inflate and then, after a feeble attempt at coughing, she stared blankly at the doctor.

Her body experienced a feeling of total numbness as she sat there motionless, with her heart pounding and her hands sweating profusely. This wasn't real, it just couldn't be happening, not to *her*.

She didn't hear Dr. Whitman's recommendations for immediate treatment or what her options were. All she could vaguely make out was his monotone voice ingrained in her brain and his total lack of compassion.

In that very instant Elizabeth realized that all her hopes and dreams had been destroyed and that her world, as she knew it, had once again been shattered.

Chapter Thirty

The phone buzzed, prompting Ashley to check the identity of her visitor on the television monitor and then walk over to the intercom to give them access. She ran to her fridge, opened it and ensured the items stored inside were all presentable and stacked just right. *After all, you only get one chance to make a first impression,* she thought to herself.

Opening her door, she stood in awe as she gazed at one of the most beautiful women she had ever seen. Moreover, it was shocking as the two women stared at each other, astonished at the unbelievable facial similarities they possessed, it was mind-boggling. "Won't you come in? My name is Ashley . . . Ashley Taylor."

"Thank you," she said, trying not to stare. "I'm Miss Pierson, but you may call me Michelle. I'm the owner of *The Invisible Butler,*" she responded with her right hand extended. "I'm glad to meet you and have the opportunity to give you a quote. Can I give you these brochures?" she asked.

"Why yes, thank you."

Ashley had a sudden intake of breath that she tried to hide, as she shook the woman's hand and then retreated into the kitchen.

"Can I get you anything? I'm having a slice of cheesecake

and a cup of coffee."

"Yes, that would be nice," she answered, "by the way, how did you hear about our service?"

"Oh, from a friend of mine at work. Clarence Casey, do you remember him?" she asked.

"Oh I could never forget Casey," Michelle commented, throwing her head back and laughing.

"How do you take your coffee Miss Pierson?"

"Just as long as it's hot and black, its okay with me," she replied.

Obviously, you don't take your men that way! Ashley thought. "It'll be just a few minutes, I've just put on a fresh pot but feel free to look around and check the place out. Oh, don't forget the wrap around balcony," she added.

So that is Miss Michelle Pierson, Michael's first wife, she thought to herself. *She looks almost like the spitting image of me, except in a café au lait version. Why we could be twin sisters!* She felt it was beyond creepy and with Michael, as with all things, this was no coincidence.

The slurping sound of the coffeemaker finished and she poured the hot brew into the two over-sized coffee mugs on her counter, noticing the rising steam and began to slice the cheesecake she had received from Clarence the night before.

Clarence Casey; who would have thought he would become such a good companion and confidante, escorting her to events, listening to the details of her day and knowledge-able about all the latest fashions and cosmetics. He was just like one of the girls.

She set up everything on the balcony to enjoy the spectacular view and get a close up look at the way Miss Pierson *really* looked, in broad daylight! Now all she had to do was wait.

"I'm just finishing up in the bedroom!" Michelle said, as she moved over to the floor-to-ceiling windows, noting their dimensions and the estimated length of time needed to clean each one.

Unexpectedly, Michelle stopped dead in her tracks as her eyes came to rest on a large pile of jewelry that was placed selectively on a silver tray. She walked towards the tray, picked it up and looked on the bottom to confirm that it was sterling silver.

As she set the tray back down to its original position, she noticed a pair of cufflinks intermingled with Miss Taylor's jewelry and upon closer inspection, she noticed that they were black onyx with the letters *MD* on the front. *It appears you've done quite well for yourself Miss Taylor,* she thought.

Not wanting to reveal her discovery, Michelle smiled and hurried off to find her potential new client on the balcony.

"Well, what do you think?" Ashley asked.

"Miss Taylor . . ." she began, "You have a lovely place. I've seen you on television a great deal lately. My you must work a lot, huh?"

I wonder just how much "work" she's had done, Ashley thought. *This woman had to be at least thirty seven years old and didn't look a day over twenty four,* she thought. "Call me Ashley," she insisted.

"Alright; Ashley I'll just have to do some final calculations and give you a written proposal by the end of today. But I'll need just a few more details," she added.

"Such as?" Ashley asked, as she sipped her coffee and tried to be cool about checking out this woman.

"Will there be any meal preparation or serving?" she asked.

"Hmmmm . . . possibly on Friday nights when my boyfriend comes over for a late night bite to eat. I always like to have something around that he can munch on."

I'll bet you do! Michelle thought but said, "Fridays are your busy day then?" she said pretending to write down details in her notebook.

"Why yes, I suppose you could say that, more or less."

"What marvelous cheesecake," Michelle commented before asking, "and shopping?"

"Thanks, Clarence picked it up at the *Cheesecake Factory* for me. And about the shopping," she added, "I usually have a few pieces of jewelry the studio's Wardrobe Department lends me that I have to return within forty eight hours. I'm such a scatter brain that if I don't set them on the silver tray in my bedroom, I'll forget and put them in my *own* jewelry box."

"Oh, so that's all the borrowed jewelry on the tray? From the studio I mean?" Michelle asked, checking out Ashley's fingernail polish. "I was admiring those pieces when I was in there I have to admit."

"Yes, it's all the studios' with the exception of my boyfriend's cufflinks. He always seems to leave them at the bar for some reason so I just set them aside for him," she said, as she finished her last bite of cheesecake.

"Are those the black onyx ones with the *MD* on them?" Michelle asked, taking a final sip of her coffee and staring directly at Ashley.

"Yes, that's right they're from Tiffany's . . . aren't they?" Ashley asked, meeting her stare.

The two women looked at each other for a long moment, without any provocation or as much as a hint of intimidation. Each woman's eyes searched the others for truth. A truth that they were well aware of and a truth that now had to be spoken.

"Michael's?" Michelle finally asked.

Without hesitation, Ashley simply answered, "yes."

"It seems that you *lost* him when he was in search of himself," Ashley said.

"Yes, and it seems that he now has you . . . now that he has *found* himself," Michelle added as she gradually stood up from the table.

Ashley slowly rose from her chair as well and methodically made her way to the front door, all the while knowing she was under the gaze of Michael's ex-wife.

"I'll have that proposal to you by the end of today if you're still interested and I hope to hear from you soon," Michelle said with a smile on her face as she stood near the front door.

"I'm still *very* interested," Ashley replied, also smiling.

Unlocking her front door, she stepped aside and allowed the other woman to exit her apartment.

From the hallway, Michelle looked at her for a few seconds longer than necessary before saying, "You know Ashley, he's not a bad guy and even though he may tell you differently, his heart is very fragile. You see, I still love him very much, but I'm not *in* love with him, I realize that now."

"Yes, I can see that," she answered, "don't worry, I'm in it for the long haul and I'm not out to break any hearts."

With the closing of her door, Ashley casually strolled back to her kitchen and poured herself another cup of coffee, taking it back out onto the balcony. She looked out at the morning skyline and enjoyed the warm feeling of the sun on her face and the slight breeze in her hair.

Closing her eyes and lightly sighing, she thought about the day's events that lie ahead; reshooting two bank commercial scenes, lunch with Bianca, and going in to read for a leading role in the soap opera *Now is Forever*, the same soap where her character was killed off some years ago thanks to some aging actress who was trying to reclaim her youth and felt that she was a threat.

Sipping her coffee, she chuckled at the thought of the producers of the show who were now willing to entertain the thought of introducing her as the new love interest of Jerry Leonard. Her star was rising and she had Michael in part to thank for her good fortune and, of course the *Fire and Ice Agency*.

Finishing only half of her coffee, she tidied up just a bit in the kitchen and waited for the studio's driver to arrive. *It seems that Michael's first wife has the looks and brains and determination to get anything she wants,* she thought. She truly hoped that since she also had almost the same looks, drive and determination, that Michael wouldn't try to make her into something she could never become, subservient and complacent.

The phone buzzed, indicating that the studio driver had arrived. "I'll be right down!" she acknowledged on the intercom.

Grabbing her purse and looking around for anything that was forgotten, she opened her front door. As she walked to the elevators, she thought long and hard about Michelle; Miss Michelle Pierson. What a name and what a woman! She knew she was definitely going to have some huge shoes to fill.

Stepping into the empty elevator, she smiled and softly laughed aloud as she pressed the button for the parking level. *"We are exactly the same, but different."*

Chapter Thirty One

Although it was 5:45 a.m., Michael had already been up since 4:00 a.m. that morning. "It going to be another long-ass day!" Michael groaned.

He had phoned Michelle at 5:00 a.m., partly to check up on Travis' progress, this being his first day back at school, and to schedule a time to meet with her. He disliked having to be penciled-in but had concluded he would have to grin and bear it, especially when a career woman was involved. It was just another of the life lessons that Michelle had taught him, among many other things.

Just driving up to the UBMI building, he cruised into his covered parking space, removed his tight driving gloves, and checked his new personal data assistant for today's itinerary. He had recently received it as a gift from Ashley and it had become a favorite tool in his arsenal of gadgets he had stockpiled at his home in the office, except this one was special. He pressed the buttons accordingly and, like magic, the screen displayed it was 6:00 a.m. in the morning. "Right on schedule," he muttered. Then he read the various notes he had made to himself, closed his car door and entered the building.

Just like clockwork, Janice Freedman was there waiting in the far corner of the lobby area, and to Michael's surprise, she was smoking a cigarette.

"I didn't know you smoked!" Michael said, somewhat alarmed as he gestured her to the executive elevator and they walked inside.

"I don't, Mr. Dickerson, but if I have to quit, it might as well be *after* today!" she said, following him quickly inside the elevator.

"Did you bring the master?" Michael asked, still checking his personal data assistant for his appointments.

"Yes," Janice whispered as she pulled it from her purse and displayed it proudly. "I just happened to see the locksmith leave the building when I was returning early from some errands one day and I knew since you hadn't ordered any of the locks changed . . . well, I just put two and two together," she declared. "That's when I gave him an additional fee and he gave me an additional master and a new code for the combination lock," she said in a hushed tone.

"Janice." Michael said, "why are you whispering?"

"Hell, I don't know Mr. Dickerson. This is so exciting like one of those stakeouts in the movies or something!" she gleefully stated.

"Alright Watson, I'll remember that, now let's hurry up since we don't have much time," he admonished her, "and put that damn cigarette out!"

"How's your hand?" she asked, noticing it was still bandaged.

"I'll live. It hurts the worst when I hold the steering wheel so I just wear gloves."

The elevator doors opened and they both exited together, keeping a heightened pace until they reached Frank

Lindbloom's office. Janice inserted her key into the shiny new lock and then pressed a series of numbers to the combination lock which was also newly installed.

Once inside, Michael made a beeline for the file cabinet while Janice performed a thorough search of the desk, not knowing exactly why her boss needed information in this way; but not really caring either, she knew who signed *her* paychecks. Besides, she had despised Lindbloom from day one when he had invited her out for drinks and Janice had asked about his wife only to hear his response of "My wife is married but *I'm* not!"

"Here!" she cried, "I think I've found something Mr. Dickerson."

"What," Michael said, "I don't see anything."

"It's not what you *see* Michael," she said as she picked up the blank notepad, "it's what you *don't* see," she said smiling with her eyes widening.

Setting the notepad on the desk, she took out an unsharpened pencil from the top drawer and using a nail file from her purse, she sharpened the pencil haphazardly until the lead in it was long and flat. Then she vigorously rubbed it across the blank note pad to reveal the indentation of the writing that had to have been made on the previous page before it was ripped from the notebook.

"You see," she said, "it's hard to read but if you turn it this way you can see it says:

Meet Melvin to get new intel — SR
Return overdue library book
Bring files home . . .

"Too bad I can't make out anymore, that asshole's got such bad handwriting," Janice remarked with pronounced irritation.

"That's alright Janice, you've done fine. Now let's fix things back the way they were and get the hell out of here," he said softly.

"Who's whispering *now* Sherlock?" she teased.

"Remind me to give you a raise," Michael said as he realigned a handful of files.

"It will be my pleasure," she answered chuckling.

The personal data assistant beeped loudly in Michael's pocket and Janice, startled and anxious, shut the top drawer on her finger. "Damn!" she exclaimed.

"You okay?" Michael asked, as he adjusted the files back in the cabinets.

"Yeah, I just broke a nail, that's all. What was that noise? It scared the living daylights out of me!"

"Just the computer voice screaming to make me aware it's 6:30 a.m. and that we're on schedule. Good girl," he said patting her on her shoulder and walking towards the door. "Let's go, *now!*" he urged.

With the office left exactly the way they had found it, they turned out the lights, locked the door and walked away, each in opposite directions as though nothing had happened.

It had already been a long morning, just part of this long-ass day, Michael thought, but he was looking forward to a quick bite to eat with his ex-wife. Waiting at *The Coffee Grind,* he couldn't help but think about how just a relatively short time ago, he had seen Ashley working behind the counter. In some ways, it seemed like a lifetime ago. He was comfortable with their relationship, no . . . he was committed and something more, he was in love for the first time in a *very* long time.

He took a sip of water and tried not to think about how he had restrained himself from going too far with her physically and how he had slowly allowed his true feelings to develop. This was new, unexplored territory for him and it was a voyage he was taking step by step. If she only knew how many times he wanted to just throw her down on her back and fuck the living shit out of her; and how many times at night he had been forced to jerk himself off just to get some kind of relief. He had never gone this long in his entire adult life without fucking somebody! At times he felt as though his balls were going to explode and it was absolutely agonizing!

Seeing a familiar face, he snapped out of his thoughts, "Miss Pierson," he said, flirting with her as he stood up. *God, she looks good enough to eat,* he thought.

"Mr. Dickerson, right?" Michelle laughingly answered, as she casually set down her laptop computer on the inside corner of their table, *Wow, I could do him right now,* she thought.

"I'm pressed for time so I ordered for us both already. It should be here soon," he said, holding up the single sheet that Janice had retrieved from the notepad.

"I hate it when you order for me," she annoyingly said. "What's that?" she asked, looking at the folded paper in his hand. "By the way, how's your hand doing?" she added.

"Why, are you going to do a karate chop on me?"

"No, and its kung fu. What's wrong with me taking martial arts classes? A girls' got to know how to defend herself these days. So? . . . . . how's your hand?"

"It's getting better but this is something I may need your help on," he said smoothly.

Their dual orders of chef salads and turkey sandwiches were placed on their table. "Looks good but I can't eat all this." Michelle complained.

"That's why someone invented this *thing.*" he said, pointing at an empty container. "I believe it's called a to-go box," Michael said, more than a little irritated with her.

"Ummmmm, at least it's good," she said biting into the sandwich. "What can I help you with?" she asked, as she opened her sandwich and rearranged its contents.

There's her ocd kicking in again, he thought. "I got this from Lindbloom's office and I need to know what you think it means; even the slightest thing that comes to your mind might help." He unfolded the paper that his secretary had given to him and slid it across the table.

Michelle looked down and saw the almost illegible scrawl. "No shit, you got this from Lindbloom's office? Let's see now," she said staring at the words. "Well, he's do-ing some kind of surveillance, that's what the 'intel'

means, with Melvin, whoever the hell that is, on some-body or something with the initials SR. Do you know anyone with those initials?" Rolling her eyes, she wrinkled her brow at not receiving an answer, and continued, "the overdue library books are an easy enough thing to check on."

"And the last thing that says *Bring the files home,* what do you make of that?" Michael asked.

"I honestly don't know, but we'll find that answer somewhere in his house," she offered.

"Can we have the check please?" she asked their waitress who walked by and ignored them.

She sipped her water and took out her cell phone dialing a number from memory.

"Yes, my son recently took out some books and I'm in his room cleaning and found some torn receipts. Could you please tell me if he has any outstanding books due? His name is Lindbloom, Frank Lindbloom. You see, if he does, I'd like to know how many books and whether to keep looking in his room or to just come in and settle his account today." She winked at Michael and took one last bite of her cherry tomato, purposely using her fingers instead of the fork.

"I see, and that was the *only* book not returned this morning? Alright, thank you for your time."

"Well?" Michael asked, raising his eyebrows.

"It seems that your business partner still has a book overdue with the title *Studies on Arsenic and other Poisons in the Human Body.*"

"Fuck me!" Michael said, almost inaudible, "so that was the plan all along? To kill our son?"

"Check please!" Michelle said, making eye contact with

their waitress. "I'm running late Michael but here's how we'll find out what's in his home office files." She opened her laptop computer and scrolled down to her client list. "I didn't realize it before but the names of last month's new accounts were accidently entered in an abbreviated format to save time and my new assistant forgot to re-enter them correctly. Look here, *L and Associates* is actually Lindbloom and Associates."

"What!" Michael exclaimed, "are you shitting me?"

"Can you believe it?" she cackled, "he's already a god-damn client!"

Michael pulled out the chair for her and they both gently tapped their hands together, fist to fist. "I'll find out who or what *SR* is," he said, as he shook his head disapprovingly at still no sign of any wait staff, and left a twenty dollar bill on the table. "Can't even get the goddamn check, what's it been ten minutes?"

"Yes, that's good and *The Invisible Butler* will be making a courtesy call to its newest client."

"Be careful," he said looking at her with genuine concern.

"I'm a big girl and you know I can handle myself," she confidently remarked, "besides . . ."

Walking over to their table, their waitress rudely interrupted their conversation and asked, "Don't you want your check?"

Both Michael and Michelle looked at the woman and in unison they both replied, "Do we look like we want the check bitch?"

Chapter Thirty Two

Quan Lee and Henry Chen shook hands and posed for a few extra photos for the newspaper reporters. It was a warmer than normal day with the temperature hovering in the upper 70's, the only saving grace was the overcast sky, a *Chicago Sky*, as many of the city's inhabitants referred to it.

Stepping up to the microphone, Mr. Chen cleared his throat and then realizing his lack in stature, he made an adjustment to the microphone in relation to his height. He smiled at the crowd that had gathered to reveal a set of large, worn, yellowish-brown teeth. Fumbling in his pockets, he pulled out a crumbled piece of paper, looked down at it, and began speaking.

"I would like to thank you all for coming here today to mark the opening of the new annexation of this building into our community. What was once a run down; abandoned warehouse has now been turned into a new school, complete with a new lunchroom facility."

The applause and cheers went on for several seconds before the crowd settled down and Mr. Chen was able to continue.

"We are thankful for the coordination it took for this massive undertaking. But now, we come to the main portion in our program," he paused and looked out into the crowd before continuing.

"We now reveal what will be the new shining jewel in our community and will become the cornerstone in the revitalization project for the Southern portion of Chinatown. It even contains an auditorium that will seat up to five thousand people!"

"I give you the Good Luck Cultural Center!" he said proudly just as the drop cloth-looking cover was yanked downward. As expected, the crowd went totally wild.

"But we have someone here today who has made the school and this cultural center a reality by providing the Chinese community with countless manpower hours and a bottomless pit of funds. And now it is with great pleasure and harmony and love that I introduce to you the sole benefactor of the Good Luck Cultural Center, Mister Salvatore Rizzo!"

There was applause, cheers and even banners being waved in unison as the crowd came to its feet in anticipation. Then a figure stepped out from the center of the crowd, with a scene mimicking the parting of the red sea, as the masses momentarily dispersed to allow him to pass and take the stage.

There was utter pandemonium and the crowd went into hysteria at the mere sight of him. He was their savior as far as they were concerned; the one who they knew they could count on when other city officials and government agencies had rejected their proposals and told them that the southern section of Chinatown was a lost cause and that it was dying.

The elusive and mysterious Salvatore Rizzo! He was for *their* cause and it didn't much matter that he was not Chinese. His genuineness and authentic kindness had long ago allowed him to overcome all racial, ethnic and cultural barriers, something not a single politician was able to accomplish. He had transcended into a Chicago icon and to some, worshipped as a God.

While the microphone was readjusted to accommodate his height of over six feet, he rubbed an imaginary beard with his thumb and forefinger and looked out into a sea of waving banners, smiling broadly.

The security for the event wondered if they would have to call for reinforcements should it turn into an unruly mob but they had to admit that this man not only had charisma, he had their undivided respect.

"Mr. Lee, Mr. Chen, honorable guests and to all my good friends in the Chinese Community, I want you to know that this has been a labor of love for me. Something very dear to my heart that I saw needed to be addressed a long time ago and I vowed to do something about it. I dedicate this cultural center to you, my good friends in the Chinese Community and my hope is that it will become a nucleus for cultural enrichment, entertainment and a hub for continued education not only here in Chinatown but throughout our lovely city. I pray that it will bring you all good luck! Thank you all for making this day a reality and for being a part of greatness!"

There was renewed applause, cheers and screaming

with even a few pieces of underwear thrown onto the stage.

Rizzo used this time to blow a few kisses at some of the babies in the audience and then he shook the hands of Mr. Lee and Mr. Chen posing for the photographers, before he exited the stage.

Mr. Chen was just finishing his conversation with Salvatore Rizzo in the soothing comfort of a limousine.

"Another drink, my friend?" he offered as he gestured towards the vehicle's amply stocked bar.

"Yes, thank you Mr. Rizzo," the small man said meekly, pouring himself another generous portion of his favorite liquor. Inspecting the glass, Mr. Chen remarked, "I have seen this kind of tumbler before, it's Baccarat Crystal, yes?" he asked, hoping he was right.

"That is correct, nothing but the finest for my good friends," Rizzo said as he studied this man. *So, he covets the crystal,* Rizzo thought.

Mr. Chen, proud of himself, was mentally adding up that this single glass he was holding was worth at least two thousand dollars and the decanter, a whopping seven thousand dollars! *All this for just a casual drink in the beginning of the afternoon!* he thought to himself.

"And so, there have been many continuances in the case against my client, Mr. Tyrone Robinson, the football star. Too many to count, and as such, the judge has disallowed any further delays in the case. So you see my friend, the lead prosecutors and the only two eye-witnesses have grown frustrated and tired." Salvatore said with positivity.

"Yes, *very* tired," Mr. Chen agreed as he greedily drank from his glass tumbler.

"I feel that the two eye-witnesses may *both* benefit from a much-needed vacation very soon to, shall we say, a place of enchantment where they can find peace. Someplace that is *far* away," he said arching his left eyebrow. "You will make the appropriate arrangements then, yes?" he asked as he handed a thick, sealed envelope to the man.

"Of course Mr. Rizzo, I fully understand," Mr. Chen replied as he accepted the envelope and placed it into the inside pocket of his jacket.

"I have something for you," he said as he looked at the package resting on the seat. "Inside there is a decanter set with six tumblers, already boxed and waiting for you. Why don't you take it as a token of my appreciation," Rizzo said, never letting his eyes leave the man's face. Now he was smiling widely.

With the meeting over, Henry Chen walked at break-neck speed to his office located just upstairs from the trendy *Black Pearl Chinese Restaurant* he owned. He took out his address book and began making a mental count of the number of calls he would have to make in order to achieve his goal. He knew he would have to surmount the enormous logistics problems involved in completing this almost impossible task that Rizzo had given him. But he also knew what would happen if it did not come to fruition. He shuddered and tried not to think about failing because he liked living too much.

Looking at the credenza just to the right of him, he smiled as he admired the crystal decanter and the six tumblers he had readily unpacked from the box.

Renewed and refocused with a purpose, Henry Chen picked up the phone and began the task of making his numerous calls. It would be time-consuming and probably take up a good portion of his day, but he had absolutely no intention of failing, not on *this* task.

Chapter Thirty Three

The nausea and vomiting had come in waves throughout the day and this morning was no exception. The queasiness that Elizabeth felt was overwhelming, so much so, that it had brought her to her knees, slumped over the ice-cold porcelain toilet in her master bathroom.

She rested her head on the side of it, momentarily enjoying the coolness on her sweaty brow. "Uggghhh!" she moaned and then leaned forward into the bowl. *These aren't dry heaves but it will be over soon,* she thought, as she held onto the bowl with one hand and flushed its stinking contents away with the other.

She reached up and turned on the bathroom's exhaust fan but found no relief from the rancid odor. Next, she exhaled from her mouth with caution, careful not to provoke another attack.

Staggering to her feet, she inhaled deeply, resting for a moment while she propped herself up against the wall; all the while tasting the sour remnants of last night's dinner on her tongue. *I can't go on like this,* she thought; this wasn't living, not in any real shape or form.

She would have to call the doctor today to once again have her prescription changed. The analog reverse transcriptase inhibitors, or AZT as Dr. Whitman had called it, was making her life a living hell. She knew it was a crap shot, since this type of medication was given in the early stages of the disease but she also knew that there were protease and fusion inhibitors that could be mixed with it to slow the progressiveness of the disease down.

She had been reading the brochures the doctor had mailed to her since she received the HIV-Positive diagnosis and was now ready to move forward with her treatment.

Lying to her brother, she had told him the results of her physical had gone well. Besides, the last thing she needed right now was her brother hovering over her and trying to run her life.

The night sweats she experienced left her sheets soaked and although she still had them, thanks to the medication, at least they were less frequent. The skin ulcers had lessened too, only her limbs were permanently scarred as a result of them. *What's another scar?* she thought. She was already scarred from that horrible day when she had that near fatal accident.

"There," she whispered, "the episode has finally passed."

Looking at herself in the mirror, she was thankful that Michael had paid for her to have the top plastic surgeons flown in to operate on her. But she knew it was only to ease his guilt-ridden conscience and that he could never have really cared about her to begin with. It had been many years since then but with the careful application of theatrical make-up and heavy concealers, her facial scars were a bit less noticeable.

Elizabeth made her way into the shower stall, picked

up her favorite body wash and relished the hot suds that ran down her unnaturally thin frame.

Feeling less queasy now, she wondered if she would be able to keep a glass of orange juice down and continued with her morning's routine. As she showered, she reflected on all the good times she had had in her life and all the men that had desired her in her life; hell, she had even had four men make the ultimate commitment to her and *marry* her!

It was unfortunate that her reckless lifestyle choices and numerous sexual encounters with men had led her to where she was now but she knew it was only temporary, and she knew she would get better, she just *had* to. After all, being HIV-positive was no longer a death sentence, right?

Finally dressed, she walked into the kitchen, picked up the remote control and turned on the small television set that was situated on the counter.

There was yet another of the sleazy tabloid-style shows on that probed into the Hollywood stars' personal lives. She poured herself a small portion of the orange juice she had been thinking about and tried to focus on the positive things in her life.

Michael Dickerson, now he was something positive, especially at the beginning of their marriage. If she had it to do over, perhaps she would have joined him in the limelight and been beside him in matters of importance where he needed her support; not playing a secondary role in the background as she had done. But would the result have been the same? She would never know.

"And now it's time to tune in to the stars, celebrities

and socialites right here in the Windy City. Yes, it's time for the *Made in Chicago* segment of our show," the announcer said. And then, suddenly and without warning, he was there. "Oh my God!" Elizabeth exclaimed, spilling a mouthful of juice down her blouse.

On the television screen, larger than life, was her ex-husband walking hand in hand with someone. Elizabeth leaned in closer to her television to get a better look. It was *that* girl, that girl who had waited on her in the coffee shop. "A waitress," she muttered. "Someone who serves burgers, slings hash and cleans the toilets? It would be downright comical if it wasn't so outrageously pathetic."

Automatically, she increased the volume. "That's right ladies; it looks like Chicago's most eligible bachelor is really tied up these days. Keeping him busy is Miss Ashley Taylor, the newest love interest of Jerry Leonard on the hit soap opera, *'Now is Forever'*. . ." the announcer continued.

Unable to contain herself, Elizabeth picked up her empty glass and proceeded to throw it at the television, shattering it and spewing shards of glass in every direction, in the process.

"That ungrateful cunt-chasing bastard!" she screamed. "I gave him the best years of my life and even raised his little ghetto hamster from that Black American Princess, who's always flaunting her money! And now you do this to me! Why don't you grow a set of balls and then burn them! Do you hear? Burn them you motherfucking son of a syphilitic bitch! And that waitress you're with . . ." she continued as she watched Michael and Ashley at a red carpet event, "we all know she's just skinny, scrawny, overly-tanned bird shit! Yeah, she's with you now but we both know it's just so she can have her little Ritz cracker lifestyle! Does *she* suck you off?" she said remembering that fateful day when he had said to her that he couldn't remember the last time she had performed this simple, *mandatory* service. "She must have a cunt big enough to drive a truck through if she can put up with your so-called love-making! I bet she takes it up the ass too!" she screamed, violently flailing her arms. "I hate you!"

Her emotional outburst continued for several minutes as she cursed his name and sobbed uncontrollably, her energy being sapped with every breath she took. She finally looked down at her napkin, only to discover that it was damp with her tears and shredded into several pieces. It was in that very moment that she felt a sudden sense of enlightenment and a leap of understanding, an epiphany of sorts, as she came to the realization that Michael would never want *her* or desire *her* again.

With a somber attitude and a face now devoid of all emotion, she walked with a zombie-like presence and opened a lower side cabinet door, exposing the lazy susan feature inside. She slowly turned it around and retrieved the phone directory that was on the top shelf. Sniffling and swallowing hard, she turned the pages until she found her desired heading and then moved her finger slowly down the page, picked up her phone and dialed the number.

She waited while the phone on the other end rang, fully aware that her anger had turned into rage and the rage had boiled over into the depths of obsession and madness.

"I'll have the last laugh!" she quietly said out loud.

"Clips, Etcetera, how can we help?"

"Yes, I'd like to know the procedures involved in buying something."

"Yes ma'am. What would you like to buy today?"

"I'd like to know how I can go about purchasing a gun."

Chapter Thirty Four

Janice Freedman was helping to coordinate one of the largest contracts she had ever worked on in her life. Just the sheer amount of administrative hours connected to this assignment was staggering. Michael must be so proud, she thought to herself, finally solidifying the Coleman Financial Services deal and bringing what they needed to the table.

Her boss was really something. She momentarily entertained the thought that if only she were twenty-five years younger with no gray hairs, no occasional arthritis and not in need of a minor neck lift, she would have snagged him for herself years ago. But her life had taken a completely different direction. At least she had her figure and thanks to her vegetarian diet and strict exercise routine; she had maintained her svelte size eight dress size.

Pressing down on the three-hole punch device, she pretended it was just another of her exercise routines. She had flat-out refused to use the automatic counterpart due to the paper adjustment time and, of course, the noise it made. *Manual was usually better,* she thought.

Now with only ten pages left to do, she heard footsteps approaching and felt pleased with herself, knowing that once she finished, she could turn over the next phase of the project to her relief worker and then take her turn on the switchboard, or as she referred to it, the *switch bored*.

The footsteps stopped in the doorway so she knew her relief was there but she was puzzled when she did not receive an audible greeting, so she looked up from her work.

Standing in the storage room's doorway with a cup of coffee in his hand was none other than Frank Lindbloom.

"What's that shit you're working on?" he asked in his usual rough and raspy voice.

"It's an important component of the final contractual agreement between UBMI and Coleman Financial Services."

"Give me a copy. I want to see it!" he ordered, as he tried to bully her with a penetrating stare.

Unfazed by his weak attempt to intimidate her, she answered, "my orders are to prepare these papers, place them in folders and then see that they get back to Mr. Dickerson," she said meeting his gaze.

"Looks like you're almost done. I'll be back in twenty minutes and I expect *my* copy to be ready. Do you understand me?"

"As I told you, my orders are to hand-deliver them to Michael, uh, Mr. Dickerson himself."

"Well isn't that sweet . . . you called him *Michael*. Now you listen to me, you dried up old goat! Stop telling me about your orders! Am I or am I not a partner in this firm?

"The firm's records indicate that you are indeed a partner Mr. Lindbloom."

"Well then you better start treating me like one," he said, raising his voice. "And you had better start treating me with some serious, goddamn respect or I'll make sure that no matter *who* you fuck, it won't save your little piss-ass job, Jew-Bitch! You Christ killers are all the same. God's *chosen* people . . . How self-righteous and sickening!"

"Mr. Dickerson signs my checks," she stated, "not some broken down loser who is obviously high on God knows what when you *are* here, which isn't even half the time," she hissed. "And if it was you that I *had* to fuck to keep my, what was that? My piss-ass job? Well then I'd just have to shave my head, tattoo the words eat-me on my forehead, slit my writs, disrobe and lay spread-eagle in the middle of North Michigan Avenue and take my chances, because no matter what happened it would be soooooo much better than *doing* you, you prick-faced bastard! Why don't you take all that money you have and go buy yourself a fucking personality? And by the way, for your information, I am a Jew! . . . and goddamn proud of it!"

Janice made her way towards the room's exit with her arms folded in an authoritative stance while Lindbloom sneered at her and held his ground.

"Everyone knows that you're only kept on here because you've brought in some heavy-hitting clients, but even that's dwindled down to a handful of brown-nosing ass-kissers like yourself. You don't even have the authority to fire me! Now get out of my way or I'll let Michael know how you disrespected me," she said through clenched teeth. Then with a swift motion, she shut and locked the door behind her. "You don't have a key to *this* room do you?" she said provokingly.

"Clit-sucking dyke!" he whispered, "but then, you're man enough for both of us, aren't you Miss Freed-Man? You claim to have balls but you're too fucking scared to come out of the closet and really be a *Freed Man,* aren't you?"

Realizing he didn't want to have a confrontation with his partner, whom he knew was in the conference room today, Lindbloom retreated to his office to collect some paperwork he had forgotten and collect his lucky writing pen along with a fresh deck of playing cards.

Once inside, he opened his desk drawer, searching towards the back and removed a small container of oxycontin. It had become his new best friend and with it, he felt invincible. He twisted off the cap, turned the bottle upside down and felt a sense of relief when several of the tablets spilled out into the palm of his hand. He leisurely put them all back into the bottle except for one of the tablets which he placed into his mouth. *Just enough to take the edge off, that's all,* he thought.

He reached for his coffee cup and took a small sip. "Ahhhh," he said and then belched loudly.

Replacing the cap, he returned the bottle back to its original hiding place and began searching for his lucky writing pen, moving mounds of paperclips, rubber bands and mounds of pushpins that obscured his view.

He found his pen but as he picked it up, he stopped dead in his tracks. His eye had noticed something. Lindbloom looked down at the tiny item that was in his drawer. It was the top of a fingernail. Not just *any* fingernail but a fingernail that was polished red and contained black polka dots.

"Just like the nail polish design that the Jew-bitch dyke wears," he murmured.

He collected the colorful fingernail and a deck of fresh playing cards, placed them each in his pocket, and then locked his office door though he now knew the locks that he had installed had been for nothing.

Stepping into the empty executive elevator, he looked at his watch as the doors closed and began talking to himself.

"Just a matter of time until you'll be sorry honey. Alright, Miss Freedman, you've hit the ball in my court and I hope you're ready because not very long from now it's going to be *my* serve!"

Chapter Thirty Five

"**D**r. James Whitman! Hey, good to see you again, I hope you don't mind us arriving so late. It seems with your new office comes more traffic, more hassles and more goddamn parking problems!"

After shaking the doctor's hand, Frank Lindbloom grinned and then stepped aside as his hired thug, Eric Hudson, entered the office reception area with the precious cargo.

"Well, Frank I guess it's just the cost of doing business these days, but don't worry, I'm up for the job, and I'm definitely your man. You can take the girls right back there and be sure they are undressed this time," he said, pointing Lindbloom towards the hall. "The examination rooms are in the back and they're all set up for you and ready to go. Besides," he said, as he eyed the patients being brought in, "the cover of darkness is to our advantage."

"Doc? What do you need from me?" Frank asked, eager to help.

"Ah, you can just tell me if they have been sedated, have they Frank?"

"Not yet. I thought you'd like the pleasure since you doctors seem to always have an arsenal of drugs."

"Oh, well, you can wash your hands and get a pair of

gloves from any of the drawers when we get in the rooms and you can meet me in the second room on the left. How many did you say there were this time?"

"We just have three girls this time, two who came with us voluntarily, at least at first, and one that we had to, shall we say, persuade."

"Oh, I see!" the doctor said, his eyebrows shooting up with interest. "So she wasn't a working girl or a runaway like some of the others?"

"Ohhhhh nooooo!" Lindbloom answered while chuckling loudly, "not *this* girl, she's primo – the crème de la crème! Yes indeed, she's the cream of the crop! She's seventeen so she's a little old but she doesn't have the mileage on her that the other seventeen year olds have. I've seen her around town but she's always chaperoned by somebody. She goes to a nice Catholic all girl school and she's really smart too. Doesn't try drugs and doesn't even drink," he said proudly. "I've had it confirmed from my sources around town."

Dr. Whitman and Lindbloom walked into the first examination room, where the first girl was being held but they still kept their conversation focused on the girl that wasn't like the others, mainly because the doctor found her case so fascinating.

The door was opened to reveal a young naked girl who appeared to be around fifteen years of age who was sitting on the examination table, frightened and shaking as she stared at the man in the nearby chair who had a gun aimed at her.

"That other girl sounds really intriguing, how did you manage to bring her here?" he asked, as he turned the water to the sink on and grabbed the disinfecting scrub.

"She was at the museum with her friends so when she went to the bathroom, well let's just say, she took too long. Actually I didn't have to *say* anything," he said, unbuttoning his sports jacket and revealing his gun. "I let my old *Smith and Wesson* here do the talking for me!"

"So you just *took* her? Just like that?" Dr. Whitman asked smiling widely.

"Well, there were some janitor uniforms we had to get and some people we had to pay to be out of their section for a few moments, but yeah, just like that. You know me doc; when I see something I want, I make it happen. A man has gotta make what a man is gonna take! Right doc?"

"I wouldn't know. You're the professional in *those* matters. What's her name?" he asked non-chalantly.

"Isabella," that's all I could find out.

"Got the gloves Frank? They're in the drawer over there," he said motioning with his head.

"I see them," Lindbloom answered.

Following Dr. Whitman to the examination table, Lindbloom stood near the door and nodded to Eric, the man who was holding the girl at gunpoint, indicating that he should go over to the doctor and provide assistance.

"As long as you cooperate, nothing is going to happen to you!" Lindbloom told the girl. "Don't forget that my friend over there," he said looking at Eric, "he's heavily armed and very dangerous. Don't speak or do *anything* to make him hurt you and when we're finished, you stay in here or he'll kill you!"

Now Lindbloom was able to sit comfortably and observe as Dr. Whitman and Eric took the straps, which were already attached at opposite ends of the examining table, and strap her arms down and then place the girl's legs inside the straps, one at a time, securing them in a spread eagle formation, with the doctor humming as he methodically went about this task. The young girl was not only scared to death, she was completely humiliated.

"Yes, she looks alright now. It appears the medicine has done its job. All the tests for diseases came back negative yesterday but one can never be too careful these days, that's why it's always a good idea to just go in and have a look-see."

He fastened an elastic band to his head that had a light on top and put his face closer to the girl, aiming the light into the area of interest. "There's no unpleasant odor and no sign of a discharge. I'd say she's ready to go Frank."

"And the procedure, did it . . . . . take?" Lindbloom asked hesitantly.

"Oh don't worry Frank, she's been sterilized alright. No chance of her *ever* getting pregnant. You want her left strapped down?" he asked.

"Yeah."

"You know my daughter turns eighteen tomorrow and thanks to this side job I've been able to put enough away to pay for her to go to college, have her take a trip to Greece as a graduation present, and even buy myself a retirement home on the island of St. Barts. Yeah, when I got this job years ago it was, and still is, a godsend. You have no idea," he said looking at the clock on the wall. "We're making great time! Where is the second girl?"

"Over here in this room," Lindbloom pointed as he walked in front of the doctor, anxious to move ahead with the examinations. "Eric, stuff one of those rags over there in the girl's mouth to gag her and then meet us in the next room. Oh, and be sure to keep your gun pointed at the next girl when you walk in, okay?"

"You got it boss."

Opening the door to the next room, the doctor said, "Oh yes, *this* one," he said with concern in his voice. "She's the one that had the case of Chlamydia."

Lindbloom took a step back and looked at the girl and then the doctor, "what the hell is cla…cla what?"

"Chlamydia. It's the new gonorrhea of the millennium. You know, one in five people have it and don't even know it," he said, as he smiled while looking at Lindbloom's zipper. "So many partners and so many productions these days. The trouble with today's young people is that if it feels good they just do it and don't even think about the consequences of their actions. It's such a nasty disease too. Well let's see now, where are those test results?" he said looking through the stack of files on the nearby desk. "Oh yes. Here they are. Looks like she's okay but I'm a bit of a worry wart so I'm going to give her an extra dose of azithromycin just to be on the cautious side just in case she's got a resilient booger."

Dr. Whitman washed his hands again and then looked

in a cabinet and took out a small package of pills. "Here Frank," he said, handing him the package, "make sure she takes these for five consecutive days in a row and try to have your customers not ride these girls *bareback* for Christ sake!"

As Eric entered the room, the young girl cringed and began to retreat into a fetal-like position, then had second thoughts when she saw the gun in Eric's hand, and fully co-operated, allowing her arms and legs to be strapped down.

"Don't speak," Eric said, as he pointed the gun directly towards her.

"Just a quick look-see, alright?" the doctor said, as he approached her, priding himself on using a reassuring voice. "Remember, my dear, we've done you an immense favor by clearing up a sexually transmitted disease that you had and we didn't even sterilize *you*. You'll be able to get pregnant and have a family one day when you're no longer needed."

Lindbloom looked at his watch and again he smiled. They were still way, way ahead of schedule. "Don't try to undo the straps or he'll kill you!" he warned the second girl, "Eric, don't forget to stuff a rag in her mouth and meet us in the next room for the last girl."

This time Lindbloom followed the doctor into the room at the very end of the hallway for the final examination of the last girl. He opened the door and, once again washed his hands and donned a fresh pair of gloves.

Unlike the other girls, this one was still in her panties, petrified beyond belief and began screaming even though Eric pointed the gun at her and told her to be quiet."

"Help me! Noooooooooooo! Get away from me!" she screamed as she kicked violently.

"Frank, you and your man need to hold her down, I've got something I can give her!" the doctor yelled, as he ran into another room.

The two men restrained her and did their best to avoid being kicked in their genital areas. The girl was strong and what's more, she was determined to not be examined or touched in any way by them or any other man.

In a few seconds the doctor retuned with a syringe and a small vial containing an unknown liquid. Carefully measuring the dose, he filled the syringe, squirted a small amount out, watching it make a small upward stream, and then quickly injected the mysterious substance into the girl.

"There, there now," he said, as he caressed the girl's cheek, "just breathe in deeply through your nose and then breathe out through your mouth."

"Whew! And not a moment too soon," Lindbloom said scratching his head.

"What was that shit you gave her?" Eric asked. "Hey doc, give me some!"

"Hmmm? Oh, Methohexital, its marketed under the name of Brevital. Not to worry though, it's just a powerful barbiturate that'll relax her. I like this one because it's super fast-acting and it'll probably start working in about three minutes or so," he said as he took great pleasure in watching the girl's rapid transformation from a combative victim to a more than willing subject.

With her eyelids becoming droopy and her breathing

now more relaxed, the men watched in silence as her body grew limp and her eyes, though still open, took on a blank stare.

"Eric, go unstrap the other two girls, have them get dressed in the same room so you can watch them both and then wait with them in the reception area," Lindbloom ordered. "Keep them gagged!"

"Okay boss, I'm all over it!"

"That's my point Eric," Lindbloom said, "I don't want you all over it, just *watching* it!"

Dr. Whitman took out a pair of scissors that were inside his doctor's coat and snipped at the sides of the thong underwear the girl was wearing, removing it in one swipe.

This time, Frank wasn't sitting down. He was up on his feet readily assisting the doctor with the straps that fastened the girl's arms down. "Bingo, look at that!" Lindbloom cried, "she's a natural blonde!"

"Yessiree that she is! You certainly don't find many of them these days in a world of Miss Clairol, but she's a natural blonde alright," the doctor said, playing with her curly pubic hair. "Is this the one from the museum?"

"Yeah, isn't she gorgeous?"

"Yes, I see what you mean. Well, let's get on with it Frank," he said as both men spread her legs apart and strapped them into the appropriate position.

Rummaging through the files, Dr. Whitman came across this new subject's records. He quickly reviewed them, nodded and then looked over at Lindbloom. "She's as clean as a whistle, probably never been touched."

"Really, how can you tell?"

"Well, it's hard nowadays with girls being so active. They usually end up breaking their hymens themselves with sports and all, but I'd put money on it that she's still a virgin Frank."

Lindbloom began to unstrap the girl's legs when Dr. Whitman placed a hand on his wrist, applying firm pressure as he spoke. "You know, I'll reduce my fee by *half* if you could do me a favor."

"Hey, you've helped me out of some real jams. What can I do for you?"

"Let me have this girl Frank, what do you say? I know that you'll still be able to command top dollar for her. It's just that she's nearly the same age as my own daughter and all. I won't take long. I — I just can't stop thinking about her. I really want this and you know at my age, I'd never be able to get a piece of ass like this. I *need* to be her first," he pleaded.

"How much sedation did you give her?" Lindbloom asked with concern.

"Enough to do what needs to be done, but she's young and strong. Oh, she'll have slurred speech and some mental confusion and even some drowsiness but she probably won't have any clear memory of this. Of course, there's a possibility that she may wake up in the middle of it but that's a chance I'll just have to take. Besides, I like it when they have some fire in them."

"You want to fuck her *that* bad?"

"I want her so bad I can almost taste it! What was her

name again?"

"Does it *really* matter doctor?"

"She's so much like my own daughter, my little girl."

"Her name is Isabella, okay?"

"My little Isabella," he said, "that's Italian isn't it?"

"Yes, her friends said she was Sicilian. Funny, I thought Sicilians were dark," Lindbloom commented as he touched one of the girl's nipples, bringing it to a state of erection.

"Apparently, not all of them. Remember there's always an exception to every rule Frank." Dr. Whitman informed him. "I don't have to tell you, that in the science of genetics there aren't *any* lifeguards watching over the gene pool."

"I see what you mean," Lindbloom said.

"What do you say Frank, I'll try not to be too rough so she won't bleed much, pleeeeaaaasssse!"

"Alright, don't beg man! I understand. Every now and then I've got to break one in myself." Lindbloom responded with an all-knowing look.

Against his better judgment, he walked down the hallway and into the reception area yelling, "Eric and I will be downstairs in the lobby with the other two girls," he said. "We'll get these two secured in the back of the van and maybe have some fun ourselves while we wait for you."

"Thank you, I really appreciate that.

"Hey, since we're way ahead of schedule, it's your lucky day doc, you've got a little over forty-five minutes."

Chapter Thirty Six

The pinkish neon light on the hotel sign flickered on and off as it made a strange buzzing sound, its aura, under normal circumstances might have been considered mystique, or even somewhat romantic, had it not been for the Pepto Bismol-like glow it radiated into the room. Or was it just that she needed some Pepto right now? As if *that* would help!

The nausea she felt was trying to get the better of her and the raindrops she heard outside, did nothing to calm her nerves or lessen the pounding of her splitting headache. This bizarre, dreamlike fantasy was too surreal for her. All she wanted was to be home with her parents, with her mother Angelica and her father Emilio, her champion.

Isabella lay on the bed with her eyes now open and, once again, she asserted herself in an all out attempt to sit up this time. At least the room wasn't spinning any longer, although she couldn't say the same for her stomach.

She waited and studied the room hoping to see how well her five senses were working. She noticed the peeling paint on the institutional gray-colored walls, the water stains on the ceiling and the drapes that looked as though they belonged in a Chiquita banana commercial. She had a terrible after taste in her mouth and her lips were covered with a crusty substance. The room smelled of tobacco, body odor and other smells she didn't even want to try to identify. Oh, and let's not forget the dripping faucet or the toilet tank that refused to stop filling up.

Yes, her senses were working alright and she was utterly miserable! The worst thing was not being able to remember clearly. No names, because she didn't know who did this to her; No dates, because she didn't know what day it was, and no memory of any kind that she could be one hundred percent sure of. She didn't even know where the hell she was! "Pain and suffering, suffering and pain," she moaned.

As she exhaled, she blew out; filling her cheeks with air while she emulated a whistling sound between her teeth. "What the holy hell happened to me?" she grumbled, as she finally sat straight up.

Closing the tattered bathrobe she was wearing, she thought about being gagged from behind in the bathroom of the museum and how she had seen and felt the gun lodged into her ribcage. Now she was inhaling a little deeper as she remembered more. "Let's see now. The ride in the car, or was it a van? And then there was the doctor's office with the man, or had there been more than one, and then a painful needle. She rubbed one of her buttocks that were sore and probably bruised, determining that it must have been the injection site, or had it? She wasn't sure because her arm also had an injection site, in fact, when she studied it, there were several. "Oh, I wish I could remember," she pleaded with herself, as she tried, with no results, to remember all the details of what had happened and how she had come to be here, wherever *here* was.

She gradually moved her legs around until both of her feet rested on the floor and that's when she made the awful discovery. "Oh God!"she gasped as, the searing pain in-between her legs took a hold of her, almost knocking her back down, and in that moment, she knew that she had been violated. Raped. Taken, not only without her consent, but without her knowledge. She placed her thumb sideways into her mouth and bit down hard, drawing blood. It was all she could do to keep from screaming and drawing unnecessary attention to herself.

Opening her bathrobe, she slowly spread her legs, looked down at herself and touched her most private area, ever so slightly. "Ouch!" she gasped, trying to catch her breath again. There was dried blood everywhere and she felt soiled and dirty. No. She felt beyond dirty, like something so polluted that it was actually foul and filthy. She leaned forward and managed to stand up but the intense pain and soreness never eased and the throbbing was so hard that it almost brought her down to her knees. "My God! What the hell did they use on me . . . a hammer and chisel followed by a red hot poker?"

With her lips quivering, she moved, very slowly, almost in a waddle-like fashion, and eventually, after a few minutes, made her way halfway across the room when the front door flew open.

"Hey sunshine, remember me? I guess not, huh? Well, let me introduce myself again, I'm Eric," the man said walking over to the bed and sitting down on it. "Hey," he said, "looks like you got broken in pretty good. But don't worry, the other girls tell me it'll eventually pass and then you just get used to doin' it."

"I was just on my way to the bathroom to try to wash off the blood. I was bleeding you know!" she said angrily but still didn't turn around.

"Well, hell honey, don't get mad at me! I'm not the one who popped your cherry. It was the doctor," he offered as he looked at the assortment of bloodstains on the sheets. "Shit, looks like he banged you pretty good. You know we gave him almost a full hour with you and when we came upstairs and finally picked you up, I heard him tell my boss that after the first go round, he rested for about fifteen minutes and then went on to have another session. Boy, he said that he rammed his cock into you so hard, he thought it was gonna come out your tonsils! Shit, he said he even jacked off twice and then started on your mouth! Whew! I wish I had been there. That ole man gettin' some action like that, I'm surprised he didn't die on top of you!"

"What doctor?" she asked, finally turning to look at him.

"Why, don't you know? Doctor Whitman, Dr. James Whitman. His name carries a lot of weight in the medical community. You couldn't have picked a more respected and refined gentleman like ole doc there. He's done you a big favor, being your first and all, yes sir, Dr. Whitman is quite a guy!"

Isabella looked at this man, this man who called himself Eric, and tried to take a photographic picture of him. Around five feet, eight inches, spiked blonde hair that was badly frosted, eyebrows that were actually tweezed and small brown eyes. And something else, he had a tongue piercing.

"What happens now, I mean when I get out of where ever I am?" she asked, a bit nicer as she purposefully made eye contact.

"Well, you'll be getting your tattoo later today; but don't worry it'll just be an identifying mark," he said, turning the palm of his hand face up and pointing to the inside of his wrist. "Right about here. I think yours will be L41 if my memory serves me correctly. The L stands for the first letter of my boss's last name and the number indicates how you will be identified to the clients. They'll never ask for Isabella, just L41. Smart, huh?"

"So I'm also a piece of property now, is that it?"

"Yeah, I guess you could say that. Girl, like it or not, you're now the property of Frank Lindbloom, he's my boss. Remember, that's what the L stands for. I'm not sure about the number forty-one though. He'll probably have his people work on you as far as grooming and fashion and stuff and then keep you just in reserves for his high rollers and for his best dealers when they deliver."

"I have a bra and some panties I picked up at a second hand store for you here," he said taking them out of his grease-stained pockets and throwing them on the bed. "They look reasonably clean, don't worry."

"Oh, so I'm a prize too, is that it?" she asked, letting her eyes focus on the paper sack he had in his hand.

"You're the ultimate prize! Hey, are you hungry?" he asked, plopping down the bag he had brought with him right onto the center of the bloodstained sheets. "Hope you like Mickey D's, that's McDonald's for short," he said, winking at her.

"What time is it?" she asked, completely ignoring his question.

"It's ten thirty."

"Ten thirty a.m. or p.m.?"

"It's morning! But it's hard to tell, huh? It's been raining all night with severe storm warnings but it'll clear up soon. Afraid of the rain, are we? Would you like me to stay with you a while honey?"

"No, I'm fine really, but I'd really like to be alone now Eric. Thank you for the breakfast. I'm assuming that's what McDonald's serves until ten thirty or so, right?" she said as she turned around and waddled towards the bathroom.

Eric instantly jumped up from the bed and practically ran in front of the bathroom, blocking the room's entrance and Isabella noticed that he had a pronounced limp with one of his legs being slightly shorter than the other one. She added that distinct feature to her mental portrait she had already painted of him in her mind.

He stretched both arms out and rested them on the door jams to the bathroom and looked at her, the lust he was experiencing, even in her state of disarray, was quite apparent. With his lips spread apart, he eyed the thin belt that held the tattered robe together and smiled broadly. "Come on girl, Isabella isn't it? One more won't *really* make a difference in the long run . . . will it?"

Isabella looked at him with such disgust and hatred that the revulsion she felt could clearly be seen on her face. Seething and furious, she adjusted the thin belt, tightening it as best she could, and through clenched teeth she hissed, "I'm on my way to take a shower, now get out of my way!"

Realizing he'd have to be more resourceful to get a piece of her, Eric stepped aside, letting her pass and then quietly stood there, giving her no ounce of dignity or shred of respect, as he watched her disrobe and enter the shower. "I'll be back in a bit and we'll talk then. You just remember," he said limping towards the exit, "Miss L41, you just need to keep in mind that . . . I like my girls to have just enough ass to keep their pussy off the sheets!"

Chapter Thirty Seven

Once Isabella heard the door close, she stepped out of the bathtub, grabbed her robe and turned the water on, engaging the shower feature. Tiptoeing to the front door, she grabbed the doorknob but there was no surprise there, it was locked. She stared at the lock that was on the door and noticed right away that it was a double key dead-bolt. She had seen this type of lock before and immediately knew that she would have to have a key just to unlock it from the *inside*.

The windows all had bars on them, but the bars on the bathroom window were a bit loose. She tried to pry the bar open, but it was no use since she didn't have a screwdriver or tool of any kind. Besides, if her counting was correct as she looked through the bars, she was on the fourth floor with no access to the outside and the bathroom window was extremely small, even for her. No luck there.

She looked around the room, somewhat hopeful that she would find a tool of some sort to pick this lock, but there was nothing. Her father, being a locksmith by trade, had taught her a thing or two about locks so she was feeling a tad bit hopeful in that area. She knew she would have to get out of wherever she was before that Eric person returned because she was in no condition to fend off an attack, not after the hell she had been through.

Waddling back to the bathroom, she grabbed a wash-cloth that felt more like sandpaper than cotton, and discarded her robe onto the floor and stepped inside the tub. The water was lukewarm, at best but, what the hell, water was water and at this point she was glad to just have the opportunity to scrub the stench, dried blood and crusty semen, and God knows what else, off of her bruised, banged up body. She took the rough washcloth and scrubbed fe-verishly, until her delicate skin turned bright red and then she closed her eyes and cried. "Why God, why?" she said through her sobs. And what if she was pregnant?

Sniffling, she would deal with that if she had to. Right now she knew she had to get a hold of herself; and it was going to be necessary for her to keep her emotions in check if she was going to get out of this place before any more damage was done to her. "Okay, okay, think Isabella, think!" she whispered as she closed her eyes. "I've got to get some-thing to pick the lock."

She opened her eyes for a moment to discover that she was standing in almost two inches of water. "So not only do I not get a hot shower, the damn drain is clogged on top of everything else!" she declared.

She kept the water running and used her big toe to try to unclog the drain, but it was a feeble attempt at best and to make matters worse, all she felt was hair. She rolled her eyes and positioned her face upwards to allow the running water to wash away the mucus that had congealed under her nose and then she took a deep breath and kneeled down in the tub but this time used her fingers to try to unclog the drain.

It was an absolute disgusting mess and Isabella couldn't figure out what would have been worse, performing this task or sticking her hand into an outhouse. Inserting her finger into the drain, she wiggled it around and felt the ghastly mess. There were slivers of soap, partially softened by the constant flow of water and, of course the hair, the hair that was twisted, intertwined and tangled into knots that formed a thick wad of gross, sour-smelling hair wool! She gagged and spit out a mouthful of vomit before giving the sickening glob a hard yank, releasing it from the hold it had on the circular drain. "Whew! Now we can add vomit to the drain as well," she managed to say, as she flung the wad across the tub as far away from her as she could and then turned off the water.

But in the process to remove the clog, she had heard something hit the partially tiled wall, it sounded like a metallic sound. She sighed as she saw the water began to quickly swirl down the drain and then promptly turned her attention to the source of the clog that was now stuck onto the wall.

Walking towards the nauseating gob, she picked it up with her index finger and thumb and stepped out of the bathtub. She squelched a muffled cry and took this hor-rible mass over to the sink and began to pick through it, suppressing her urge to vomit again. Bingo! Just as she had thought, there were two huge hairpins inside the matted clump. "Praise Jesus in heaven!" she whispered.

She dried herself off on the thin matching towel that, as she suspected, also felt like sandpaper, and then took it and used it to pick through the pile of disgusting stuff that was surrounding the hairpins. Still waddling, she walked over to the bed and put on the grease-stained bra and panties that Eric had bought for her. Christ! Two sizes too small, but it was better than the holey bathrobe that smelled of body odor. She looked down at her feet. *Bare feet,* she thought. *Hopefully, that won't present itself to be a problem.* Then she took the hairpin and went over to the front door.

She didn't move for a few seconds as she listened for any signs that someone might be standing there listening but after she felt the threat was gone, she inserted the hairpin into the lock and carefully and precisely moved it back and forth, just as her father had taught her. Damn, nothing! *Okay Isabella, you can do this,* she thought.

Her hands, damp with nervous sweat, were moved vigorously across the worn carpet in an effort to dry them since the single towel and washcloth in the room had been used and were now wet. Isabella regained her composure and once again placed the hairpin into the small opening for the key. This time, she progressively turned it in an upward motion, until finally her expert handiwork ended with the sound of a small click as the pins moved and the lock opened!

After a sudden intake of breath, she placed her hand on the knob, said a prayer, and slowly opened the door until it was ajar and looked out. Shit! There was a man down the hall! Had he had seen her? She wasn't sure. He looked

Latino, not that it mattered, and he was wheeling a huge cart full of what looked like towels and sheets down the hall, stopping by each room, one by one. She thought about the gravity of her situation and she realized that this is one of those times where she would just have to go with her gut.

Creeping out of her room, she made eye contact with the janitor. Alarmed, he stopped dead in his tracks. Isabella placed her index finger gently against her lips. "Shhhhhhh!" was all she could think of to say.

"Do you understand me? Do you understand English?" she asked, "my name is Isabella," she whispered. "There are men holding me here against my will. I need to get to a phone, a telephone. Can you help me . . . please?"

The man looked at her for a moment, glancing at this beautiful young woman in her skimpy bra and panties, a sight he hadn't come across very often in all his years of janitorial work.

"You need the help señorita? Sí, my name is Ramiro. I speak the English. What you need?" he asked.

"Do you have a phone?" she whispered.

"No," he said, shaking his head, "I am sorry but I have no phone here."

"Where am I? What is this place?

"You are at the Stanford Court of Arms Hotel. It is old and has been here for many, many years. There is no one here right now but they will return in twenty minutes, always on time, he said, looking at his watch."

"Ramiro, can you help me escape?" she asked, looking

around suspiciously.

The janitor looked at her and thought about his own daughter. He had heard rumors about what really went on in the hotel but had always tried to push the rumors to the back of his mind. After all, he was poor and didn't possess a formal education so he knew it was best not to make waves or cause trouble. But as he looked into her eyes he felt something, there was an innocence and kindness about this girl that allowed him to care and he realized that what he was feeling for her was compassion. He looked around and then glanced at his watch, before he addressed her.

"Señorita, get in the cart, hurry! There is not much time!"

Then without so much as blinking, Ramiro ran into the room he had just seen her exit from and went inside. He stood just inside the doorway and looked around the room where his eyes were immediately drawn to the blood-stained sheets on the bed. His eyes moved back and forth and his pulse quickened as he was thinking. "Got to help the señorita but not get in the trouble," he said quietly.

Walking into the bathroom, he raised the window all the way up and noticed that the screws were loose at the top. Ramiro looked back in the direction of his linen cart and without hesitation; he made the decision to take a calculated risk. He knew he didn't have to, but something inside of him let him know that he had to.

With his heart beating rapidly, he carefully removed the screwdriver from his rear pocket and quickly began to undo the screws that were holding the bars in place against the window. He stepped back for a moment and thought how he could complete the illusion of a bathroom escape. "Yes!" he said, as he ran back into the bedroom. He looked around, snapping his fingers to try to mentally prompt his mind to think faster and then he stopped when he looked at the bed. Then he took the top flat sheet off and tied it to the fitted bottom sheet, knotting it every few inches to create a sort of rope, if you will, and then he secured it in a haphazard fashion to the window. It looked like just the kind of thing a young woman would concoct if she were to escape, if left to her own devices.

Satisfied, he shut the door and ran to his linen cart. Looking down in the bottom, he gave Isabella the thumbs up sign, rearranged the soiled towels and sheets over her crouched body and then pushed his cart to the elevator in anticipation of it arriving.

Hearing her speak, Ramiro lifted some of the towels off of her face and asked her, "I cannot hear what you are saying señorita with the towels on your face. What are you saying?"

"I'm just praying that we can make it out of this alright," she said. "Don't you believe in God, Ramiro?"

Señorita my family does and that is fine but as for me, I believe in the here and now. And right *now*, the elevator is *here!*"

The doors opened and he carefully maneuvered the cart inside. "Almost there señorita," he whispered as they approached the first floor. "You no get off here. Wait, okay?" he asked.

Isabella, was about to have a heart attack right there in the linen cart. *Was this guy crazy? Why wasn't he letting her out? It was the first floor, wasn't it? Or was he in on the deal too and just setting her up?* she thought.

She began to think and then rethink when suddenly the doors opened and several men stepped inside. Isabella froze. She dare not breathe because now she was beyond terrified. She recognized that voice! It had a hoarse, raspy sound as though the man was either on the verge of contracting laryngitis or a heavy smoker. She couldn't remember his face but she knew she had heard the voice in the doctor's office, and it made her almost wet on herself. This wasn't good.

"Come on Eric, we can't hold the elevator forever!" a voice said.

"So, what do you say Mr. Lindbloom? Can I be next?" another voice asked.

"What makes you think she'll do it with *you?*"

"I should be next in line!" another voice interrupted.

"Let's not fight boys, there's plenty to go around, besides we've got to get her used to the heroine in really small doses. That way, she'll be begging to be fucked just to get her fix."

Eric finally entered the elevator, limping as usual. "Finally," he remarked, "thanks for waiting."

"Where are *you* going?" Lindbloom asked, finally noticing the Latino man.

"To the basement, señor. I go to the bottom," he answered, keeping his eyes downward.

"Rightfully so!" Lindlbloom chuckled. "You heard the man, Eric. Let's get him to the bottom, where he *belongs!*" There was an outbreak of laughter in the elevator and Ramiro, not wanting to express his true feelings, laughed with them until the elevator reached its destination and he wheeled out his cart.

As the doors closed, the laughter grew silent but Ramiro continued to wheel the cart full speed ahead into the laundry area before he came to a stop. Breathing heavily, he removed some of the towels and sheets from on top of the girl. "It is okay now, señorita. Here take these," he said, handing her a gray uniform that was too big.

"I'm going to need a miracle to get out of here, God help us!" she said.

"So God, he helps *you?*" he asked.

"Yes, but how do you know he doesn't exist?"

"I am not sure señorita but never mind that now. You can change into the uniform right here and then you can go to the bus stop over there but you will be in the open and will risk being seen." Then, seeing the look on her face, he countered with, "or you can stay hidden and trust me a little longer and be loaded into the back of my service van. You will have to continue to hide in the back, but you will be able to use my phone."

Confused, Isabella said "I asked you upstairs if you had a phone and you said that you didn't have a phone here."

"Sí, señorita. I did not have a phone there, because my phone is *here*," he said, taking his cell phone out of his locker and smiling. "You do understand English, don't you señorita?" he asked, laughing at her.

"Yes Ramiro. I understand now," she said, taking his cell phone and getting down even deeper into the laundry cart. "I'll trust you as long as you need me to."

"I take all the linens to be cleaned off-site this month since the water, it does not get hot enough and the pipes, they leak so the bed bugs do not go away!" Rearranging the linens on top of her one more time, he said, "now get down!"

Then, without further words being spoken, Ramiro simply wheeled his linen cart out of the service entrance and into the back of his van, quickly closing the doors and starting the vehicle's engine.

"Ramiro, I want you to write down your full name and address for me and give it to me before you drop me off to a safe place."

"Sí. Where is the safe place at señorita?"

"Just keep driving, I've got to make a phone call and then when I get off the phone, I'll tell you where it is," she said.

"Sí."

As Ramiro drove away, he looked into his rearview mirror and saw the sheets he had knotted together, blowing in the wind and then realized that the rain had stopped and the sun was finally beginning to come out.

Isabella dialed her father's cell phone and waited.

"Ahhhh!" she heard Ramiro shout.

"What is it? Are we being followed?" she asked, as she began to feel uneasy.

"No, señorita, you finally can relax now. It is just a double rainbow in the sky. It is a sign of good fortune!"

Isabella smiled and listened as the voice on the other end of the phone answered. "Papa, it's Isabella! Oh papa, I'm okay!" she exclaimed.

Chapter Thirty Eight

"Dinner was great Ashley, did you make that?" Michael asked, knowing full well that the Chinese meal they had just eaten could never have been prepared by either of them.

"Michael you know there is no way in the world that I could have made that. Why are you being so silly tonight?"

"What was the name of that place again?" he asked, playing with several of her long strands of hair. "Yum, your hair smells good enough to eat."

"The Black Pearl Restaurant, silly."

"Sorry?" he said, snuggling close to her on the sofa. "I need to get closer so that I don't miss a single word."

Michael sat there on the sofa, looking at Ashley for the longest time and thought about how their relationship had developed over these last few months. He wanted to tell her that he loved her and that he was finally ready for an all out serious relationship, even if she wanted it to include marriage.

He smiled at her, gently caressing her cheek with his hand and then pulled her nearer to him and she had only to look into his eyes to feel the conflict that had been within her finally subside. She would have to trust her feelings and hope he felt the same way.

He took the opportunity to move his mouth over hers in an unhurried motion, with a barely-there brush of the lips at first; followed by a long warm sensuous kiss, all the while his hands searched for and cupped her soft, ample breasts.

Her mouth, warm and sweet, responded to his in kind, to match his eagerness as her tongue playfully mingled with his.

Pulled yet even closer, she was now lying down on top of him, locked in a full embrace with every nerve in her body tingling and pulsating. She could feel his warm hands beneath her dress, well aware of where they expertly came to rest.

Rising up on her elbows she grinned sideways and bit her bottom lip, "is there anything I can do for you sir?" she asked doing her best Asian accent.

"Yes, I'd like to know what is on the menu for tonight?" he asked, being a willing participant in her game.

"Oh, we have many things on the menu and tonight we would like to offer you our special," she continued in her pseudo-Asian voice.

She unpinned her hair, letting her blonde locks cascade well below her shoulders.

Michael looked at her, with a bit of amusement and then with deep desire. He reached up to cup the back of her head and held her on top of him for some time before releasing her, his longing desire growing more visibly apparent in his pants.

She sprang up from him and walked quickly into the

bedroom, looking forward to his arrival. As she lay on her bed, she smiled as, moments later, Michael crossed the threshold of the bedroom with two scented candles in hand. Setting the candles on the nightstand, the dark room took on a warm glow and the ambiance it created was picture perfect.

"Will I receive an appetizer with my dinner?" he asked as he took off his shoes and sat on the edge of the bed.

Bowing gracefully, she replied "Oh yes, we not only have a special dinner for you, we have a wonderful appetizer for you, our favorite customer, that we know you will enjoy."

"What is the name of the appetizer?" he asked.

"The name of the appetizer is *Help You To Forget*," she said.

"What?" Well then, what is the name of the main course?"

"Oh, that name is *Help You To Remember*," she said seriously.

He came closer to her and they kissed passionately and without hesitation, with her hand resting on the outline of the huge bulge inside his pants.

They both slowly undressed each other, taking in every curve, every angle and every muscle of their bodies as their flickering shadows appeared larger than life on her bedroom walls. Their kissing took on a life of its own.

"I want something," he said, in a husky voice.

"And what is that?"

"I'd like you to help me to forget *and* to help me to remember."

THE SYMBIOTIC SECTION

Unable to contain himself or his desire any longer, Michael repositioned himself with Ashley thoroughly enjoying the weight of his body on top of hers and they excitedly joined together in a feverous uniting of their flesh. *It felt so goddamn good to finally be inside of her,* he thought as he took all the love that she so eagerly and willingly gave. He adjusted himself to ensure maximum penetration as he skillfully thrust every inch of himself inside of her, never holding back; not for a second!

"Oh shit!" Ashley gasped. She hadn't expected *all* that!

She arched her back and completely gave in to the overpowering feeling without any shame or uncertainty, all her inhibitions melting away, and it felt right. She moved with him in unison while her body was flooded with waves of intense pleasure she had never experienced before, not on this level; God, how she yearned for him and ached for him in this moment! He was not just a want . . . he had now become part of her . . . he was a goddamn *need!*

Michael felt the sudden sting of her fingernails dig into his back, all the while he kept moving as hard and as deep as he possibly could, vigorously thrusting as he hit his target every time. He couldn't believe how rigid he was and how the searing heat from in-between her legs enveloped him; cloaking him in her wetness and in the intensity of her desires. God, they were both in the moment!

Unable to stop, they were both swept away in a tempest of pure unadulterated pleasure and raw ecstasy and with every fiber of Ashley's being, she savored every pulsating inch of him. "Oh Michael!" she whispered.

And so they continued on, escalating into a frenzy until their passions exploded into a red hot crescendo, leaving them both in a state of near collapse in each other's arms.

"Oh! . . . fuck me!" she said breathing heavily.

"I just did," he said smiling while trying to catch his breath.

"You're quite a wildcat I see," he said playing with one of her nipples. "Next time I may not be so gentle," he warned.

"I'm a lady in the boardroom and a straight-up, stone freak in the bedroom; whatever it is, I'm ready, bring it on!" she said with an arched eyebrow.

She sat up in bed and looked at him whispering, "Oooops! Michael, you're not going to believe this but guess what I forgot to do?"

"What?" he said with a look of puzzlement on his face.

"Close the curtains!" she laughed.

"That's okay," he said as, as he kissed her cheek and then pulled a few strands of hair away from her eyes. "If you really love me, you'll sleep in the wet spot!"

Chapter Thirty Nine

"The plane was airborne for just under fourteen hours and traveled a distance of some ten thousand six hundred thirty one kilometers and according to my calculations that is a little over six thousand miles!" Quan Lee said.

Henry Chen smiled and nodded repeatedly as he heard the detailed update from his business associate. He rubbed his hands together, hardly able to contain his excitement; his plan had been set in motion and now all he had to do was give an update to Salvatore Rizzo, whom he knew would be pleased.

Herbert and Paige MacNamera were both in their late-thirties, married and owners of the small boutique; *Paige's Place,* an upscale resale shop in the small village of Long Grove, a Northern suburb of Chicago that was predominately upper middle class, which was known for its specialty and antique shops. Its covered wooden bridge, rolling hills, gigantic colonial homes and pristine, duck-filled ponds made it a candidate for a Norman Rockwell painting.

Deciding to work late one evening, they had seen two

men in the dimly lit parking lot just as they were locking up for the night. Within seconds, they saw a flash and heard a shot as one of the men crumpled to the ground but not before the killer's face was revealed when he had stepped directly under the old-fashioned street light, before exiting the crime scene.

Shaken up but not deterred, they immediately knew they would have to become involved and ultimately identify the person responsible for the murder of another human being.

Frustrated with the timing, they still resolved to take their dream vacation and planned to leave the country directly after the court proceedings were over.

Although the trial had been pushed back and the monthly continuances were countless, the couple was now ready for the task that lay at hand in court, ready and willing to give their testimony against Tyrone Robinson, the football star, and they hoped that this would all be over soon.

Two days before their scheduled court appearance, they walked into their garage, noticing that the lights didn't work and were shocked when something was placed over their faces with a pungent, sweet-smelling odor that they could not identify. It was the last thing that they had a clear memory of.

Groggy and a bit dazed, they both awoke at relatively the same time and they were both in a state of confusion. Dumbfounded, the couple gasped as they realized they were in a strange place with their bodies situated on a king-sized bed in the middle of a room. Mrs. MacNamera was outwardly upset when she realized she had on a change of clothing.

After a short while, a small Asian man entered their room; a tray of hot tea with an assortment of pastries was in his hands. Setting the tray down before them on a mobile cart, he wheeled it close to the bed, nodded and then quickly left, ignoring their pleas for answers and explanations.

"Ah, welcome," a male voice said from behind them. "Oh, did I startle you? I didn't mean to. Let me introduce myself. My name is Mister Quan Lee.

Don't bother with the staff here; you may bring all your concerns, no matter how trivial, to me. I am the only one here who understands and speaks the English language. I trust your accommodations are sufficient. You are Americans, yes?"

Paige wanted to speak, however her husband squeezed her hand to indicate that he would speak for the both of them. She was staring at the tray that had been set before them and even in her state of befuddlement; she had to admit that she was starving.

"Yes, we are Americans," Herbert answered, "where are we and what's happened to us?"

"You are in Ziketan Town, a small village in the Qinghai Province in the People's Republic of China."

He waited while that information sunk in before he continued. "We are about thirteen hours from Beijing and far removed from the big city life. Here, it is peaceful and most things are the way they have been for many, many centuries."

Mr. Lee noticed that the woman was eyeing the tray of food and he smiled and bowed towards her. "Ah, I see that the absence of nourishment denotes an increase in your appetite. Please eat. We have prepared for you some banana rolls, egg tarts, steamed yam cakes and delightful pillow puffs, but we have made them with a touch of Western influence, instead of the usual way. I hope you will enjoy them," he said, never taking his eyes off of Paige.

Mr. MacNamera took a bite of one of the pastries, nodded at the man and then proceeded to pour his wife a cup of tea before he poured one for himself.

Satisfied that they were now eating, Quan Lee continued, "I will tell you a story. You have been brought here as part of an exchange. We have taken the liberty of removing your passports . . ."

"What!"

"Please, Mr. MacNamera. I do not wish to be interrupted again!" he said narrowing his eyes but not blinking.

"Now, back to my story, we are all merely pawns in an important game, think of it as a game of chance if you like. So the two of you have been moved here in order to allow the key player, Mr. Robinson, to score and move freely about the board. You see, by *not* appearing in court there will be no real case because the State will be unable to produce their two star witnesses, that being the two of you."

Mr. Lee smiled and clapped his hands and the same small Asian man that had brought them the tray of appetizers, now appeared with a wooden chair for Mr. Lee. Speaking in his native tongue to the man, he sat down in the chair and the small man quickly left the room.

"We have your passports so that you will be able to get back into your country so when the time comes that will not be a problem. The problem for us was to have it appear that you left the country of your own free will so we hired two people who are similar in height and build and bone structure to use *your* passports and then get on a commercial plane to China. That way, if anyone wants to check, they can just review your departure with the video at airport security. The real witnesses, which are the two of you, were drugged and secretly taken to this remote village on a private plane. And as you know Mr. MacNamera, there are no mandatory flight plans or security checks when a private plane is involved. So the look-alikes arrived in Beijing China on a commercial flight, gave us your passports and will return back to the States upon our authorization, but in a private jet. It will just be assumed that you decided to take your vacation early, a trip that, according to our sources, you have been planning anyway. They'll just think that due to, shall we say, all the stress associated with the delays of the trial, that you bumped it up a few days."

"You two were not being subpoenaed to testify so you have broken no laws. You just had a, shall we say, change of heart in order to better Mr. Robinson's chances in the game. It is all legal and very ingenious," he said proudly, making eye contact with Paige.

"Accept for the kidnapping part," Mr. MacNamera

said, stating the obvious.

"Well, yes that *is* a problem, isn't it? But rest assured you will be treated with the utmost respect. Think of yourselves as our guests," he said eyeing Paige. "Do you workout?" he asked. "You have stupendous muscle tone and a gorgeous figure for a woman your age. I noticed it right away as you were being undressed."

"What the fuck! . . ."

"Be very careful Mr. MacNamera," he said giving him a warning glance before he continued. "Tai chi can be of great benefit to you in your life, and especially during our stay with us. It will offer you fitness, harmony and inner peace without the strenuous, sweaty routines you probably now do. I promise you that you will be less stressed and be more energized. It will open up a whole new world for you. I will see that you receive personal instruction during your lengthy stay with us where you will be taken to many sights with our photographer to document your trip."

"Lengthy stay? Are you out of your Kung-Fu-Ping-Pong-Fucking-Mind!" Mr. MacNamera screamed.

"Are we able to use a phone? To call our kids, I mean?" Mrs. MacNamera asked politely.

Slowly standing up from his wooden chair, Mr. Lee replied, "may I call you Paige?"

"Yes, I suppose it's alright, I'd like that very much."

"Paige that will be a problem since the nearest phone is about twenty miles away. But don't worry, we have already sent e-mails and telegrams from you to your loved ones and to the defense attorney letting them know you are safe and enjoying a much-needed *early* vacation.

We have limited electricity here in the village so we must conserve it, so for tonight you will have candles. There is also no running water but don't let that bother you. We have plenty of bottled water in the other room over there," he said pointing in the general direction. "The well is a good one and Huang Cho, whom you have already met, will be at your beckon call to fetch well water for your bathing and I will ensure he boils it first. He will also bring you your meals and should you need me, he will know how to reach me."

"What about transportation, to the sights I mean?" Paige asked with half a smile.

"What the fuck are you doing smiling at him!" Herbert demanded.

"Keeping us alive you asshole!" she hissed thorough clenched teeth as she continued to smile.

"We have a bus that brings us supplies once a week and as luck would have it, the bus arrives tomorrow morning. We have your luggage with us since you had already packed for this trip and we added a few incidentals to make your stay more comfortable along with a great deal of cash. So when the bus arrives tomorrow morning at seven o'clock, please be ready. It will take you to the nearest town and from there you will be re-routed to all the sites you wanted to see and stay in the finest hotels that you desired in the first place. Huang Cho will have a small staff with him in order to assist you along with the photographer. Think of it as a free trip to China."

"So we are being paid for our silence?" Herbert asked.

"Paid to play the game Mr. MacNamera, paid to play the game; nothing more and nothing less."

"Anything else?" Herbert asked in a smug tone of voice.

"I hope I will not have to think about ruining your vacation with news that perhaps your son or daughter are missing or that some harm has befallen someone in your family. That would truly be unfortunate for everyone involved in this game. My advice to you is to forget about how you arrived here, forget about using a phone in any of the hotels and proceed to make the best of your situation and truly enjoy your first-class all expense paid vacation that starts tomorrow morning. Any monies you have left-over will of course be converted to U.S. dollars and given to you just before your departure."

Paige stood up and shook Mr. Lee's hand, grasping it a bit longer than was actually necessary, to the chagrin of her husband.

"Don't worry," she said looking back at her husband with a frown on her face, "we'll both remember to smile for the camera."

Chapter Forty

It had been another exhausting week at the office not only due to the recent altercation with Lindbloom, but with all the extra work involved in completing the Coleman Financial Services deal, Janice really needed this little pick me up at the end of her day.

Checking her fingernail polish, she ensured it was dry to the touch and went to the front counter at the White Lotus Nail Salon. "I'll be back next week at the same time," she said smiling.

She was still tired but at least she felt a little better. Now came the tricky part, getting her car door open without damaging her expensive manicure. With keys in hand, she began walking to her car which she dreaded.

It was parked all the way at the other end of the lot which, of course, was now almost empty. *What was that sound?* she thought, and then dismissed it since she was really tired.

And then it happened; without a warning or an impending sign of any kind, she was face to face in the embrace of danger.

She didn't have time to react as she saw what she thought was an older model car racing towards her. Then at the last instant she recognized the face behind the wheel just before the point of impact. She reacted just as planned, just like a deer caught in headlights; she was totally stunned.

Janice didn't have time to think or call out for help or to even scream, even as the car revved up its engine and sped towards her with its gas pedal floored. Unfortunately, she also didn't have time to run!

Chapter Forty One

The air was thick and heavy, weighted down with moisture; moisture that could be detected with hardly any effort just by inhaling, but still, on this day, the rain had not come and the cool, strong wind had started up again, making the town's name of The Windy City, aptly earned.

Antonio stood just outside of the limousine, adjusting the maroon checkered scarf around his neck and squeezed his gloved hands together in an effort to keep them warm. He looked down the cobblestone trail just a bit, noticing a squirrel that was prancing on the neatly manicured lawns and wondered how much longer he would be at the cemetery waiting for his boss.

Salvatore Rizzo was deep in thought as he sat in the lawn chair that had been provided for him. His head slightly bowed, he made no attempt to fix his windblown hair or adjust his loosened scarf, blowing in the wind, as he focused on the gravestones before him. Anyone who could have seen his face would have instantly known that here was a man, who appeared troubled and saddened yet, even in his grief, somehow profoundly strong.

He narrowed his eyes, keeping his gaze focused and then, after a brief moment, he brought his hands in front of him, placing them in his lap, both in clenched fists.

There was no trademark cigarette holder to be held today. No, none. For he knew that the only thing that was to be held here, in this place, were memories, memories of a life that was gone too soon for one, and over before it even began, for another.

His beloved wife, Gabriella Alisha, and their unnamed child were here, taken from him in the cruelest of ways.

If he could go back to that awful day, *if* he could have just been there, *if* his work had not kept him . . . *if* . . . always the same . . . *if* . . .

He slowly turned his head and looked out at the water. Yes, Lake Michigan was so beautiful at this time of year and summer would be just around the corner. He thought about how he had selected Calvary Catholic Cemetery in the nearby suburb of Evanston, located directly on lakefront property and how, on a windy day such as today, it almost mimicked the ocean with recurring waves and strong tides. Reaching down, he picked up the flowers that had been resting on the ground next to his lawn chair and finally stood up, walking just a few steps. Then with a solemn face, he placed them at the foot of his wife's grave, securing them with a large rock that he found nearby. He had brought red peonies today, her favorite.

"It is time Gabriella, it is time," he softly whispered. "No more ifs and whys; not any more." After that he took a handwritten note out of his pants pocket and stared at it. No. He stared *through* it, his face becoming slightly contorted as he exhaled deeply through clenched teeth, with raw emotion and intense pain, and finally, silently, Salvatore

THE SYMBIOTIC SECTION

Rizzo wept.

He took the note and placed it under the rock that was holding down the flowers and then gently kissed both gravestones, making the sign of the cross as he slowly began to walk away from the gravesites.

Emotionally drained, he lifted his hand and Antonio, always at the ready, heeded the signal and promptly opened the door upon Salvatore's return.

"There's a pre-heated blanket and a container of hot sake for you sir," Antonio offered.

Salvatore nodded and engaged the darkened divider shutting off the passenger compartment from the driver's side. It had felt good to let go of this part of his life, to finally have closure and allow the past to dwell in the *past*. But, knowing himself as he did, he also knew that there were feelings he now possessed that were growing and couldn't be denied much longer. Yes, he had met someone but he wondered, as he situated himself under the blanket, if he could take a chance again and open himself up to being in love again. He would wait he decided, for now was not the right time. His heart and soul, the two things that really mattered, they would tell him when.

Shutting the door of the limousine, Antonio quickly ran down the narrow cobblestone path to retrieve the lawn chair he had placed there for his boss. But before he walked back with it, he looked down at the larger of the two gravestones, the one that displayed the name Gabriella Alisha - My beloved, with the dates nineteen seventy – nineteen ninety five engraved on it. He saw the secured piece of paper blowing in the wind and read the note before he left the area. The note read:

The things we cherish are the things we love;
Their warmth and radiance truly set them above.
Yet we all have flaws, which make us the same;
So rest here now my love, for your life was not in vain!
Gabriella, my beloved -- I now set you free and I hope
that you can forgive me as I now, can finally forgive you.

The air was still thick and heavy as the limousine un-ceremoniously rolled out of the cemetery but now the moisture in the clouds gave way and the rain that had not come all day . . . finally began to fall.

Chapter Forty Two

In the judge's chambers, the conversation was finally drawing to a close. Steven Powell, the young assistant district attorney and Darryl Black, the defense attorney, were trying to make sense of the MacNamera's failure to appear in court and what it meant for the State's case.

"Well your honor, I don't exactly know *what* happened. You see, I was just talking with the MacNamera's a couple of days ago and we had even gone over their testimony over the phone. They felt comfortable and confident."

"Obviously Mr. Powell they were not confident enough!" Mr. Black said looking directly at his adversary. "Last night I received this e-mail along with a telegram informing me that they were not one hundred percent confident that they could correctly identify my client and instead of being pressured into something they would regret, they apparently decided to just go on vacation," the defense attorney stated, as he held up the printout of their e-mail transmission along with the telegram for the prosecutor's perusal.

Steven Powell took the papers being offered to him and read them with an unbelievable look on his face. "Your honor, I suspect that something is wrong here, terribly wrong and I'd like to request a continuance until such time that my witnesses can be located and I can have the opportunity to talk to them personally regarding this case."

The papers made their way to the judge's desk, who quickly glanced at them before looking up at the two men and speaking. "I've got a packed schedule for today and my docket isn't going to get any better six months from now. Mr. Powell, do your witnesses know the penalty for failing to appear once they were issued a subpoena?"

The prosecutor looked down at his shoes and straightened the imaginary crease in his pants before answering. "I didn't have them subpoenaed because they came forward and seemed anxious to testify. It wasn't as though I was working with hostile witnesses."

"Well, I'm afraid that in this case since we've had numerous continuances over the course of several months that I'm not going to grant another one. Mr. Powell, you'll go out there and try this case today! I'm sick of you guys coming in here with your chests puffed out to here and your balls so big you can hardly walk and you expect me to bend over backwards so you can make a name for yourself. I'm not wasting a second more of my time or a penny more of the taxpayer's money. It's an election year gentlemen and I don't know about you but I damn well plan to be here next year!"

"But your honor! . . ." the prosecutor pleaded.

"Good day gentleman," the judge said blandly, as he stood up and walked out.

Darryl Black walked towards the door to exit the

judge's chambers, glanced back at his rival and smiled. "Don't be so hard on yourself there Steven, it's a classic rookie mistake."

"Fuck you Darryl!"

With no key witnesses to call throughout the entire length of the trial and the case imploding all around them, the District Attorney's office was unable to make a solid case against Tyrone Robinson.

After all the evidence at the trial was presented by the State, the jury took a cool forty-five minutes to deliberate and brought back a not guilty verdict for Tyrone Robinson, music to his wife Jazmine's ears.

Shaking his defense attorney's hand, Mr. Robinson walked to his wife and embraced her. "Let's go home baby," he whispered in her ear. Moving past the reporters that congregated on the courthouse steps, the only statement Tyrone gave was something about justice had prevailed or some other bullshit line he had heard on an old Perry Mason episode.

They walked with hurried footsteps, as far away from the press as possible. Hand in hand with his wife, Tyrone and Jazmine were led to the open door of an awaiting vehicle and ushered inside before it took off.

Night had already fallen by the time the limousine parked in an alleyway. Its window was closed while its occupant was waiting patiently for his visitor.

Walking up to the car, Darryl Black stood just outside

and watched as the window moved downward just enough to create room for the end of the thin silver cigarette holder that protruded slightly from it gave way to a barrage of smoke.

"Good evening, I have the package," he said as he held up a large manila envelope that had a thick rubber band holding it shut. Mr. Black readily handed the envelope over to the occupant in the passenger compartment of the limousine. "It's all there; all five hundred thousand dollars, you can count it if you wish. My client and I wanted to thank you for all you've done."

"If ever I can be of service again, please do not hesitate to call on me," the voice from inside the vehicle answered.

The window was slowly raised almost to the top and Mr. Black walked away into the darkness of the night.

"Another happy ending Antonio, you agree, no?"

"Yes, Mr. Rizzo. Thanks to you . . . a very happy ending."

Chapter Forty Three

It was six thirty a.m. at *The John Hancock Center* located at 875 North Michigan Avenue and this was listed as the very first stop on today's agenda and Michelle, being true to form, was ready for the challenge.

First, she knew that she had to gain access into Frank Lindbloom's condominium and look for the information that was on the note that Michael obtained from Lindbloom's office. Secondly, she had decided that she would take matters into her own hands and not wait for Michael. She would just have to take control and find out about the SR in the note and why Melvin, whoever the hell that was, was performing surveillance on SR. And lastly, she had to try to find receipts or a connection of any kind that would tie Lindbloom to the arsenic poisoning of her son.

Feeling yet another pothole in the road, she was jolted back to reality and thought about the task that lay at hand, making her inwardly wonder about the wisdom of wearing dangly earrings that continued to catch on her lace collar; that being said, the earrings were cute so she knew she could live with the inconvenience. Hell, in the past she had even worn shoes that had made her feet bleed, all in the name of fashion.

Today, she had the aid of one of her newest employees at *The Invisible Butler* to help her search his condo, only she was doing this under the guise that she would be watching the woman work and grading her on not only how well she cleaned, but how *fast* she cleaned.

Getting out of the colorfully painted van, they walked into the building and made their way to the elevators, each woman on a separate mission. The employee was mesmerized by all the retail outlets in the building and Michelle, noticing this, guided her over to the building's directory.

"See over here Lucinda, they have a post office, bank, office supply store, dry cleaners, travel agency and even a shoe repair place. The list is endless! You've never been here before?"

"No Miss Michelle, never."

"Well this is it; you're on *The Magnificent Mile*! All the offices, condos and stores between Oak Street and Grand Avenue make the real estate in this area as valued as Fifth Avenue is in New York. Come on Lucinda let's go to work."

The elevator came to rest on the forty-fourth floor in what seemed like two seconds. Michelle and her employee stepped out and were greeted immediately by the security guard at the desk who was attempting to solve numerous crossword puzzles at the same time.

"We are here to perform a cleaning service for L & Associates on the seventy-ninth floor." Michelle stated, as her eyes caught a glimpse of all the candy wrappers under the counter.

"I.D.'s please and, oh yeah, you'll have to sign in," the

guard said. "By the way, this here notation on the clipboard says there is usually only one of you and the cleaning is usually done on a different day. Why the change?" he asked, gnawing on his pencil and waiting for a response.

"Oh that's easy," she whispered. "Mr. Lindbloom is having today's service free of charge for being a new full-service client. You see he just recently signed his contract with us and we wanted to surprise him so it would be all neat and fresh for him when he came home tonight to get ready for his cocktail party. You see we don't have much time but with the two of us it won't be a problem. Of course if you'd like us to come back on our regularly scheduled day next week . . ." her voice trailed off.

"Naw, that's okay," he said returning to his crossword puzzles. "I guess you already know he's in Unit 7942. Don't forget to check back here when you leave."

"Now what Miss Michelle?" the woman asked.

"Now we have to go up in the special elevators that will take us to where the residences are in this building. All the residences are from this floor all the way to the ninety-second floor." Michelle said.

"Yes, I understand Miss Michelle."

They stepped into the elevator and, within seconds, they were stepping out and walking along the hallway of the seventy-ninth floor. Finally reaching their destination, Lucinda used her master key, and they entered.

Lucinda pushed her lime green cleaning cart into the unit and switched on every light before unloading it. Michelle always thought the cleaning carts looked like fifty five gallon drums on wheels but they were relatively inexpensive and she was able to use them for some of her other business ventures as well.

"Is something wrong?" the woman asked.

"Oh, it's just this one earring that keeps catching on the lace of my collar," she said with a hint of annoyance.

"Alright Lucinda, you may begin but remember that under no circumstances does the client want the closet touched."

"Yes Miss Michelle, I understand."

Michelle watched as her employee scrubbed floors, fluffed pillows and straightened at break-neck speed all the while never stopping or even slowing down. With Lucinda busy, she took the opportunity to go into the bedroom area and begin opening the numerous built-in dresser drawers, careful not to leave the contents noticeably disturbed. She had to give this slimy prick credit as she looked around the room; he didn't have any class but he at least had a class act decorator.

Now in the master bathroom, she was amazed at the size of the shower. She removed her shoes, stepped inside and quickly determined it had to be at least eight by eight feet. *Absolute overkill*, she thought. Looking at the gadgets, she quickly realized it was a steam shower that boasted a rainfall showerhead, waterproof speakers, a dozen body jets and LED lighting. Christ Almighty, where was Lindbloom getting the money to live like this?

She stepped out of the shower and went to find where her employee was, grabbing her clipboard in the process, to keep up the charade.

Watching the woman, she nodded at her and then slowly walked backwards, retreating to the master bedroom closet. *Holy shit!* she thought, this closet was bigger than her master bedroom and bathroom combined and the hardwood floors were the darkest Brazilian walnut she had ever come across. Polished to perfection, they took on a deep blackish sheen.

Michelle set her stylish overnight bag that was doubling as a purse, down on one of the shelves and pulled out a pair of surgical gloves. Satisfied that the fit was nice and snug, she checked each ledge, nook and cranny of the closet's massive shelving unit.

Exhausted, she rested on the floor. "Nothing, not even so much as a crumb," she whispered to herself. Then she thought about how some clients hid things in their shoes, perhaps the number to a combination or a key! She got down on all fours and crawled along the floor of the closet with her knees killing her on the hardwood floors. Her goal was to check each of the shoes on the built-in customized shoe racks, well over a hundred pairs, by the looks of them.

She rocked back and forth as she performed this painstaking task, until she heard a dreaded familiar sound and instinctively reached up to grab her bare earlobe and immediately looked down. "Oh shit! I knew that would happen!" she muttered. Looking around she was glad there was egress lighting installed along the baseboards. "Ah ha!" she said out loud as she found her earring stuck in the tongue and groove feature of the floor.

"Did you call for me Miss Michelle?" the employee asked from the other room.

"No, its okay Lucinda, you're doing fine!"

And then it happened -- as she was grasping her earring trying to pull it free from the grooved floor, her hand pressed down against one of the floorboards and it wobbled! She got down closer to the floor to inspect it and pressed down; again the slight wobble. She looked behind her at the rows of pants obstructing her view and felt for any wires or alarm devices that might be installed. Then on a leap of faith, she pried apart the dusty boards, lifted them and held her breath.

There beneath the floorboards were two black satchels with silver clasps. "That motherfucking cocksucker!" she exclaimed.

She put her hand over her mouth to prevent herself from screaming and then picked each one up from its hidden chamber. She realized the weight was quite considerable. "Whew!" she gasped as she lifted it and set it on a nearby chair.

Good, she's cleaning the final three bedrooms, she thought as she heard the vacuum cleaner being turned on. *The woman was absolutely amazing.*

Michelle wasted no time in opening the first satchel and hastily rummaged through its contents. She not only had to be quick, she also had to be meticulous. Nothing in the way of receipts for any type of poison so she struck out there, just an extensive list of real estate that SR owned, whoever the hell that was. *Had to keep looking though,* she told herself; not much time. She decided to close the first satchel and open up the second one.

"Hmmmm, what's this?" she said as she noticed two thick white pouches inside.

Hastily undoing a clasp to one of the pouches, she discovered a medium-sized notebook, several disks and several envelopes containing cash. "Lord have mercy!" she gasped as she looked inside the envelopes, each one contained a tightly waded cluster of money, all hundred dollar bills.

Next she scanned the notebook's contents. It used dividers to section off different items. There were dividers for many topics but the one that caught Michelle's eyes rested on the dividers labeled for human trafficking, drug deals and child pornography. No wonder this prick was never in the office. So this is how Lindbloom could afford this over the top lifestyle. *Michael wanted this asshole out of his company and this is just the ticket I need to get him out of there,* she thought.

Then she undid the clasp on the second pouch. *More disks and a lot of papers,* she thought.

Leafing through some of the papers at arms length, she drew nearer as she quickly understood that they appeared to link Salvatore Rizzo to extortion, bribes, jury tampering and secret payoffs. Her astonishment continued. There were names, dates and payoff amounts. So the S.R. stood for Salvatore Rizzo! *Sweet Jesus! This guy was more connected than AT & T!* she thought, as she recognized the list of politicians, dignitaries and government officials, worthy of a black-tie celebrity event. According to this, Salvatore

Rizzo was heavily involved in running the city like a well-oiled machine and had a host of V.I.P.'s and public figures indebted to him in one way or another.

"And I thought my lawyer was just another rich guy with a law degree . . . motherfucking shame on me!"

She made the decision to keep the second black satchel with the thick white pouches containing the cash with her. After all, the floorboards had been dusty so he obviously hadn't gone in to check its contents in quite some time. Yes, she would take a chance and confiscate the entire satchel to carefully go through it. Copies? Perhaps, but she would have to go through everything first. Examining the outside of the satchel, she concluded it was a very generic one. Yes, she would come up with a plan to replace it later.

Checking her watch, she carefully returned the first satchel to its hidden chamber and returned the floorboards back to their original position. She looked around to ensure that nothing appeared disturbed and inserted the second satchel into her oversized overnight bag that was still resting on the closet shelf. Next, she walked casually back into the master bathroom and retrieved her shoes.

"Lucinda are you done?" she asked, as she removed her surgical gloves from behind her back and threw them in her bag.

"Yes, Miss Michelle, is everything okay for you?"

"Yes, you've done exceptionally well. The next stop is the forty-fourth floor, don't forget to lock up."

Signing out at the desk, both women picked up their identification and returned to the first floor lobby, the green cleaning cart squeaking just a little.

"Remember to get that fixed before your next appointment Lucinda. I won't be traveling along with you any more today. I'll be catching a cab and taking care of a few things then I'll catch up with you later this morning. I'll go over the results of your review at the end of the month."

"Is there anything wrong Miss Michelle?"

Michelle turned around and felt the pouch in her purse before she answered the woman. "No Lucinda. Everything finally feels just right."

Chapter Forty Four

Nothing had completely worked; none of the pills and none of the treatments and God only knew how many she had actually been through.

Elizabeth sat on the edge of the bed and brought the straw up to her nostril, sniffing the white powder as fast as she could. With her face now flushed, she shook her head and swallowed hard as she snorted a few times making a grunting sound in the process.

The test was still negative for AIDS and most of the time she even felt better. But just the thought of knowing she was HIV-Positive, gnawed at her belly. These things happen for a reason, Dr. Whitmore had told her. *With proper diet and treatment she might expect to live many, many years before it turned into full blown AIDS.* Shit! So easy for him to say! Just to hear the news that she wasn't *normal* had been as though she had been issued a death sentence as far as she was concerned. She didn't know when she would leave this world but she knew what would take her; it would be AIDS and the thought was terrifying to her.

The occasional snort of cocaine, the pills and booze had done more for her these last few weeks than any of the traditional treatments that any of the so-called doctors had tried. Fuck the treatments and fuck the doctors! It was *her* life, what there was left of it, and she knew what was best.

Coked up and enjoying a feeling of exhilaration, she looked at the small twenty-two caliber handgun on her kitchen island that she had recently purchased from a friend of a friend and smiled. Thanks to an old drug conviction, she had been unable to pass the check that all gun dealers were required to perform. Besides, given her circumstances why should she have to wait the mandatory ten days? She wanted what she wanted and now she had it.

Perhaps she would only do Michael or perhaps just Ashley or both of them at once but she couldn't decide because her thoughts were not crisp. She would just have to make it to the bathroom and get some oxycontin. *Yes, that would take the edge off,* she thought.

She had a hatred inside of her that was growing like a cancer every day. Her hate had once again become the driving force that was keeping her alive and healthy. And soon, very soon from now, Michael and that girlfriend of his with her dysfunctional cunt would be sorry.

Chapter Forty Five

It was early morning and Clarence Casey had tears in his eyes as he sat in the corner of the room looking at Janice. One of his favorite co-workers had not only been hurt, she had been reduced to this. It was a hit and run incident the six o'clock news had said and to make matters worse, the driver was still at large. *Who does this kind of shit to other people?* he thought. He removed a turquoise handkerchief from his pocket and wiped away his tears before he turned the page of the latest issue of *People Magazine* and began reading to her again.

He had heard that some coma victims could actually hear in their unconscious state and regardless of whether or not it was true, it made him feel better. *It must be a slow news week;* he thought to himself as he thumbed through the pages, *here they are digging up more stuff on Michael Jackson and Jackie Onassis. Gees, let folks rest in peace* he thought, shaking his head.

He made a few sighs and decided to go sit in the bathroom to compose himself. Maybe take a few deep breaths and say a prayer while he was in there. He closed the door but left just a sliver of it open, just enough to peek out and see her in the bed.

Lowering the toilet lid he sat there trying to make

some sense of everything that had happened. Everything happened for a reason . . . he knew that, but it still didn't help him. After all, Janice was one of the first people that had befriended him when he began working at UBMI and over the years he had sometimes come to look upon her more as a maternal figure to him than his own mother. Then came the silent flood of tears again and out came the turquoise handkerchief to stop them.

Wait! What was that! He sat bolt upright on the toilet and peered out through the small crack in the door. There was someone else that had just entered the room. *Frank Lindbloom? Are you shitting me?*

Clarence didn't think he could have promised the male nurse a date as he had done in order to get into Janice's hospital room since he wasn't family either, so that would mean he probably snuck in somehow.

He dared not move as he watched Lindbloom come all the way into the room, close the curtains and stand near the bed. He had a strange look on his face. It didn't seem to be a look of concern; no . . . it appeared to be one of satisfaction.

Frank cautiously moved closer to the bed and hovered over her, a twisted smile now on his face. He eyed the two pillows that were propped beneath her head which lent support to her motionless, limp frame. Removing one of them, he gathered it in his hands grasping it on both sides and began to slowly position it over her face, slowly lowering it.

Clarence thought for a split second and then used the

best falsetto voice of his life, "Alright Miss Freedman! I'm just tidying up in here and I'll be there in a split second, don't you worry dear, a police officer is already on his way up here to watch over you, paid for by your boss!"

Frank Lindbloom was so startled that he stopped and held the pillow in mid-air for a nanosecond and then returned it under Janice's head. It had never occurred to him to check the bathroom. He had just assumed he was alone with his victim. If he tried to do anything now he would risk being discovered and that was a risk he couldn't take.

He leaned down close to her ears and whispered "I'm leaving now but I'll be back and I want you to know that you've used up the last of your nine lives, bitch. When you're dead you'll finally have the death mark that you, and *all* Jews, deserve; only yours will be securely fastened when you arrive at the morgue . . . right on your big toe!"

Chapter Forty Six

O nce the phone stopped ringing and several things had been accomplished on her to-do list, Michelle had another long conversation with her attorney about some ideas she had for her future professional growth and, at his suggestion, she made updates in her estate planning with special provisions for Travis in case of her untimely death. Sometimes after she had talked with him, she felt as though she had been to a therapy session, renewed, revived and refreshed.

Michelle settled down, kicked off her shoes and massaged her aching feet. "Damn! What I frickin go through to look good." she complained out loud.

Shopping for an exact duplicate of the black satchel that she had discovered, was not as easy a task as she thought it would be and she was disappointed with herself that she had miscalculated just how long it would take. She had to have the cab drop her off at her house, empty out the contents of the satchel and then take it with her in her own car to several office supply stores. After three stores, she had lost count but she knew she couldn't trust this job to anyone but herself. Now her feet were sore and throbbing, but it was well worth it.

Picking up her cup and saucer, she walked barefoot

into one of the spare bedrooms that she temporarily had set up as a makeshift library of sorts and then poured herself another cup of the orange spice herbal tea that had been brewing in the nearby teapot for a few minutes now.

She stood in the doorway and eyed the vast amount of paperwork on the floor. It was a little crude but she was actually pleased with how she had sorted out all the documents into categories. She smiled and let out a long sigh of relief because she knew she had quite a collection before her.

Taking several small sips of tea, she knew that Lucinda had been a godsend and was thankful that she had been able to come over to her house on a moments notice and clean today since she was too busy. It was also a real blessing that she could not read English. She was definitely giving the woman a hefty bonus on her next paycheck.

Now she would have to let Michael know that this phase of the operation was complete but for it to be a success, she would have to return everything to its original place, in the duplicate black satchel she had purchased. Her ex would probably shit in his pants when she told him that SR stood for Salvatore Rizzo, a true enigmatic figure if ever there was one. Everyone in Chicago knew who Rizzo was and to think, he had been her attorney for years. She trusted him and had confided in him. *Now that was a real man*, she thought, *and sexy as all hell with his worldliness and all that thick white hair.*

She wiggled her toes in the carpet getting a little relief from the soreness, and finished her cup of tea when the doorbell chime sounded, bringing her back to reality and the task at hand. Looking at her watch, she muttered "Right on time," knowing full well it was Michael at the front door.

"Come on in!"

Michael arrived wearing jeans that were so tight they looked as though they had been spray painted on and his shirt was an army green color that really showed off his sexy physique. He always looked so good every time she saw him, good enough to eat actually, but she knew that they had both given it their best shot when they were married and that it would never work. Now he was with Ashley, her almost-identical twin and who was she to stand in someone else's way? It just wasn't her style.

"Here come look," she said leading him to the make-shift library.

"It's a bit do-it-yourself, but as long as it works. When are you returning everything?"

"Tonight. I found out from the security guard that Lindbloom's going to be out from eight thirty until nine thirty so I'll make sure it's done when he's gone."

"So why the face?"

"Because I know something you don't know. For starters, the SR stands for Salvatore Rizzo."

"Shut the fuck up! Are you serious?" he asked dumbfounded.

"As serious as a heart attack," she said grinning.

"I've seen him everywhere," Michael responded, "on the news, in magazines, in the newspapers. You know, I think I've actually seen him at some high-end charity balls but most of the ones he attends are way out of *my* league."

"Yeah? Well everybody in Chicago *knows* of him. And your piece-of-shit business partner, Lindbloom is involved in child porn, drugs, human trafficking and a lot of other stuff; it seems he's been a bad boy."

"I had no idea it was on that level of criminal activity, none."

"So is Rizzo involved in the drugs and all the child porn shit too?"

"Nope, just your piece-of-shit partner. You wanted proof, I got you proof. Now you've got some ammunition and can kick that sleaze ball out on his ass and send him to prison where his ass needs to be rotting."

She shut the door to the spare bedroom and picked up her purse along with the overnight bag that she placed over her shoulder. "I've got a duplicate black satchel in here but I've replaced the contents of the white pouches with plain white paper. He'll never know the difference and by the time he realizes what's happened, he'll be out on the street. Now what?"

"Now we go pick out a brand new red mustang for our son as a graduation present and then you're going to promise me that you'll be extra careful when you return that stuff," Michael chuckled and looked at her beautiful face. "You're too much."

"No, not too much," she said as they walked out of her front door. "Just too much for you!"

Chapter Forty Seven

"Here ya go, sir," the men said as they handed over the paperwork and envelopes to Frank Lindbloom. "A truck load of new girls coming in tonight just like the ones last time. Scared little runaways that are all hooked on one form of drug or another."

"That certainly makes it easier when you know you can get a blow job as long you keep them supplied. I like' um hungry like that," Lindbloom replied patting his zipper. "Such small, pouty moist mouths just right for sucking."

"A few may have some black eyes but that was only done on the more vocal and defiant ones as a show of force. That way, the others will be too afraid to speak up or resist."

"Next time just give them an injection of heroine," he said partially opening one of the envelopes. We don't want to damage the merchandise."

"Yeah, yeah, I dunno what got into me, sorry sir."

"Alright Melvin, you can take the guys and meet me tonight at the same place we unloaded our cargo last time. I'll have a few buyers waiting so make sure they're all cleaned up and ready to go. Any bitch on her stinking period qualifies, as *not* ready to go! Hope we're clear on that, not like last time!"

"Alright Mr. Lindbloom, I'll make sure that some of

the boys check them out first. Oh yeah," he said, snapping his finger, "I know we're all set for six o'clock tonight for that doctor to check them out to see that they don't have any shit you can catch. What was the doctor's name?"

"His name is Dr. Whitman. He's aware of our operation so we won't have any problems; but don't be surprised if he wants to sample one of the girls in exchange for a smaller fee. If that happens, you might want to get there around five thirty, just in case."

"I'll put all this paperwork in a safe place, by the way, how old are they this time?"

"The average age is fourteen but this time we have two twelve-year olds in the bunch, just to spice it up."

Lindbloom finished opening the envelope that contained several photos of the twelve year old girls, all smiling in spread-eagle poses. "Yes, I see what you mean; variety *is* the spice of life."

Michelle entered the forty-fourth floor with her overnight bag on her shoulder and a large vase of fresh-cut flowers in her hands. "Hi, I'm not doing any service today," she said to the security guard who was once again involved in his crossword puzzles. "I'm just dropping these off to one of my other clients and I'll be out in two seconds. And these are for you," she said winking at him as she placed four box seat tickets to the next Cubs baseball game on the counter.

"Gee, thanks! Go on up."

Smiling and confident, she walked right past the guard and pressed the appropriate button inside the elevator without ever signing in on the visitor log.

Donning a pair of surgical gloves inside the elevator, she was now ready to complete her mission. Nervous and excited, she knew what she had to do. *You can do this Miss Michelle . . . you will do this Miss Michelle,* she thought to herself multiple times as she was breathing in and out.

When the elevator door opened, she bolted out like a prize thoroughbred out of the starting gate and wasted no time in placing the vase of flowers near the first fire exit she came across before she continued on her way.

The master key that she had borrowed from Lucinda was already in her hand as she arrived at her destination. Once inside unit seventy nine forty two, she wasted no time in heading for the master bedroom, finding the floorboards and lifting them up. "Good, still dusty," she whispered. "That's a good sign. It means he hasn't noticed he's one short." Then she reached inside her overnight bag that was absolutely killing her shoulder and removed the duplicate black satchel.

Just seeing the black satchel again made her heart quicken its pace and she was torn between the idea of trying to obtain more incriminating evidence by taking items from the first satchel or simply returning this fake one.

As she heard a loud pinging sound, she realized that someone was getting off of the elevator. "Shit!" Her heart began pounding so loudly in her ears that for a moment she couldn't think straight. Her muscles froze and her entire body was filled with terror as the footsteps drew nearer and then . . . . slowly faded. That was all it took for her better judgment to win out and she returned the second satchel to its original location. She just couldn't afford to take any more chances.

Now there was just the matter of getting the floor-boards back into their original position. With one small click of the thumbs it was all done!

Checking her watch, it was just past 9:30 so she knew she had to haul ass. Lindbloom knew her car and there was always that possibility that he may come back early. Her brow was slightly damp now so she finished up, gave everything a last look and left the closet. With her eyes now glued to the front door, she made a speedy exit from his condo and headed straight for the elevator.

"Finally, the elevator and not a moment too soon!"

She leaned back on the wall once the doors closed allowing the cool metal to touch the back of her neck and cool her sweaty palms as she waited for her heart and breathing to return to a normal rate.

She stepped out cautiously and noticed the security guard and a group of men were being entertained by a small television set he had under the counter. Not only was his back to her but the television was on some sort of sports channel and there was cheering and laughter coming from the group. Using that opportunity, she removed her heels and ran as fast as she could, barefoot into the parking lot. When she got in her car she was visibly shaken but she grabbed the steering wheel, took a slow deep breath and floored the accelerator in her bare feet. "Time to get the hell out of Dodge!" she chuckled.

Within seconds after she drove off, Frank Lindbloom pulled in and he wasted no time in pressing the seventy-ninth floor button on the elevator. He knew he had to get his documents and pornographic photographs into the secret compartment of his closet as soon as possible.

Although he had never been arrested, there was no sense inviting trouble. Frank liked where he was and that was flying just under the radar. He had his men who were loyal to him and his ventures. It really didn't matter about the trade he was dealing in, what mattered to him was that they were lucrative business enterprises that paid very well and well worth the risk.

He opened the door to his unit and made a beeline for his master bedroom closet. Unlike Salvatore Rizzo, he knew that the fast money was in child porn and drugs and to him it just simply wasn't worth it to develop these so-called relationships with his clients as Rizzo had always said. They were like chickens to him, pluck 'em and fuck 'em!

Manipulating the floorboards, he lifted the first satchel and inserted his paperwork inside but it wasn't until he went to return it to the hidden chamber that he noticed something on the floor, something he swore was not there before but he couldn't determine what it was. He got down on the floor, his nose almost touching the dark Brazilian walnut wood and, in astonishment, found a . . . what the hell was it? A hair! He blinked several times, trying to soak in what he was looking at and then he picked it up and held it against the egress lighting on the floor. It was a long silky singular black strand. The cleaning service wasn't allowed in his closet however it was obvious that someone had been inside this area.

Frank wondered about the second satchel and then dismissed it; but it was there, he had seen it; or *had* he? He stared at the handle on the first satchel and then on the second one, his eyes imitating a tennis match as they moved back and forth. Yes, it was the same satchel, there was no difference.

He lifted it up to check if it had the same weight as before, and it did. Then he unfastened it. The contents looked undisturbed but when he carefully opened the two white pouches he discovered that there was blank white paper inside. He knelt down, unable to move for a moment as though he had been punched in the stomach. The cash, cd's and record books were gone!

Realizing the situation, he replaced the floorboards to their original position and wondered if Rizzo was following him or knew about the information he had on him. No, of course not, now he was just being paranoid.

He got up from his knees and sat in the nearby chair. *Couldn't have been Rizzo, could it?* he thought. Perhaps it was one of Rizzo's flunkies. Let's see now, there was Antonio; he had long black hair that he kept in a ponytail and then there was Alfredo. No. Alfredo had short hair. He had never met the one they call Emilio, or had he?

Disturbed and puzzled, he left his condo and hastily made his way to the elevator to go down to the forty-fourth floor. *That's odd,* he thought. *Why would someone place a perfectly good vase full of flowers here by the emergency exit?*

"Hey, I didn't have any new visitors today did I? Someone not on the list?"

"Like who?"

"Oh, I don't know."

"No, just the regular dry cleaning guy and all the regulars according to this," the guard answered as he showed him the visitor's log. "But while I was gone someone could have come in while my lunch replacement was here. And then there are the guards on the other shifts that have their own way of doing things too. It's not supposed to happen like that Mr. Lindbloom, but it does, sometimes sir."

"Do you mind if I look at the security footage?" he said handing the guard a fifty dollar bill. "You look as though you need a break anyway."

"Thanks, I am due for one. Do you need me to . . ."

"Nope, I already know how to run it."

Sitting down at the console, he proceeded to operate the master control panel with its vast array of buttons, dials and knobs, fast-forwarding through the security footage until he saw something. Staring intently at the screen, he hit the button with the arrows displayed backwards, stopped it and then pressed play. There! He zoomed in for a magnified view. Plain as day, it was that Black bitch! What the hell was *she* doing here? Then he thought for a minute. She did own *The Invisible Butler* so she had reason to be in the building for her other clients. Still, a pensive feeling gnawed at his gut.

He typed in something on the keyboard and the screen switched to the recent elevator footage of the day where he saw Michelle place a vase of flowers near the fire exit sign and then proceed right inside *his* condo! Now he wondered if it had been Michelle acting alone or if Michael had put her up to this.

He got up from the console and pushed the down arrow for the elevator. He wanted to kill that bitch but he knew he still had to be there for his meeting tonight. The buyers wanted top of the line merchandise and he aimed to deliver.

When the elevator doors opened, he stepped inside and popped two oxycontin into his mouth before the doors opened again. *I've got to focus, got to maintain,* he thought. Nothing on earth was going to keep him from collecting some well-earned cash and having a long-awaited sexual encounter with one of the ripe twelve-year olds. "Pluck 'em and fuck 'em!" he whispered to himself. Just thinking about what lay ahead tonight made him more than a bit aroused.

Speeding away, the speedometer's numbers grew higher, but he had a gut feeling that Michael and his lovely ex-wife were both in cahoots together and trying to ruin him.

At least he was certain that Rizzo wasn't involved in *any* way. After all, if it had been Rizzo, he would have been dead by now.

Chapter Forty Eight

"Come on Bianca, I've *only* got a little over an hour before I have to get back to the studio," Ashley complained to her friend.

Ashley couldn't wait to sit back in the cozy booth of her favorite Mexican restaurant, *Pancho's Siesta,* kick off her shoes, and take a much needed break from the daily grind at the studio. *Now is Forever,* the soap opera job that she had managed to secure, was now the number one-rated soap in the country and she was a shoe-in for having her contract renewed. Who knows, there was even talk of her being nominated for a daytime Emmy Award.

"Sorry I took so long," Bianca said, finally joining her. "See that guy over there? He just asked me for my number and he *did* drive up in a Mercedes. My bet is he's out on the old pp, the pussy patrol, and you know me, I can't miss out on an opportunity. After all, a girl has got to think about her options. I can't just settle on being an associate editor as my dream job."

The warm chips and salsa were placed on the table and they were well received by both women. "You knew the whole time didn't you?" Ashley asked with just a hint of playfulness in her voice.

"Honey *everybody* knew that Michael had found perfection in Michelle, his hot heavenly little piece of brown sugar. And you have to admit, the girl *is* absolutely stunning. But now that Michael's older he obviously wants the same thing but gift wrapped in a lighter shade. Guess he craves *white* sugar now, and that's apparently where *you* come in," Bianca said munching on the chips. "I guess there's no truth to the rumor that once you go Black, you never go back! Yeah, you two could be identical twins alright. Hmmm, I wonder what the odds are of finding your own identical twin in this world are and then finding them in a different race. Hell, talk about a Twilight Zone moment!"

"Well, I think that all of that is bullshit Bianca. I do know one thing though."

"What's that?"

"I know that our food is here. Let's eat."

With the arrival of lunch, they unfolded their napkins, placed them in their laps and began to dine on the sizzling hot chicken quesadillas setting before them on the table.

"Umm, smells good," Ashley mentioned, "and they're sizzling too."

"So have you fucked him yet?"

"Bianca!" Ashley said as she almost choked on her mouthful of food, "keep your voice down!" She looked from side to side and demurely smiled. "Yes, we've done the deed and he's absolutely amazing! Best guy I've *ever* had!"

"Guess I'll have to take your word for it even though

your *ever had* isn't exactly like mine. Let's face it sweetie, we both know you don't exactly have a scorecard in the triple digits like me, I mean," she said pointing to herself. "So that would actually imply that you're not really that experienced and knowledgeable like I am." Wiping her mouth, she paused, looked down at her plate and then continued. "Well, maybe I should give him a call so I can get some of *that*. He must be around forty right? And from the way his clothes fit its obvious he works out so he definitely has some staying power, plus a smokin' hot body. I've heard through the grapevine he's at least a full nine inches, not bad for a *White* guy, huh? Would you mind *sharing?*"

"I most certainly do!"

"You know I have it on authority that he likes to butt fuck and he's into that whole tie-you-up-and-blindfold-you-shit too, among *other* things."

"I've been able to accept him just the way he is and as long as it just involves the two of us . . . well I really don't think we'll have a problem."

"Oh, so it's serious then? I mean, with him?"

"Jesus, Bianca!" Ashley leaned in closer to the table "Do you think every man on the planet is out on the, what do you call it, the pussy patrol?"

"No, I suppose they're not. Just the ones able to achieve an erection!" she said laughing while slapping the table rapidly.

Ashley and Bianca continued on with their lunchtime conversation, completely unaware of the unnaturally thin female patron who was seated in the adjoining booth which faced the opposite direction.

It was a woman who had a slight nervous twitch who scratched skin ulcers that were hidden underneath her long sleeves. She had watched them arrive, overheard the bulk of their conversation, paid her bill with cash and then left.

It was only sometime later when the busboy came to clear both tables that the staff discovered the seat cushions had been repeatedly slashed and their stuffing had been pulled out!

Chapter Forty Nine

The Tollway-Arlington Bank seemed like a natural choice as a resting place for the black satchel she had discovered in Lindbloom's condo. Michelle felt secure in the knowledge that the goods on that scumbag, Frank Lindbloom, were now locked up and hidden away in a bank vault and it would take a hell of a lot more than the popping out of a few floorboards to get at it. As she left the bank, she placed the key to the safety deposit box in her purse and continued walking towards her car.

Placing a call to UBMI, she was told that Michael would not be available for quite some time. Still, she left a message. *Why am I not surprised?* she thought.

Taking the long way, she was headed home after a full morning of phone calls and appointments. She needed the extra travel time to clear her mind even though she knew that today was the day she was going full speed ahead with her newest project, *The Cracked Pot.*

The idea had come to her when Travis had mentioned how bare some of the balconies and front porches had appeared when he looked out of the bus windows and saw the various neighborhoods. He was right. Plain and unadorned, she knew there might be a need for a service to actually bring an assortment of flowers to clients with a multitude of colorful pots to choose from. The flowers would be completely maintained by her staff and because they were seasonal, they would be changed at regular intervals providing bursts of color and fragrance to indoor and outdoor spaces. All the client had to do was enjoy them and accept all the compliments for having such good taste. In the winter months, the flowers could be switched out to a variety of small shrubs in the evergreen family and even decorated to coincide with holidays. It was so simple and yet, no one had thought of it.

When she had pitched her idea to her attorney, he practically had all the research done and the incorporation papers drawn up in record time for her. And to add icing to the cake, he had signed up for a year long service at the regular price instead of the special introductory offer, just to help her along.

She didn't know how other people felt but she felt good knowing she had accomplished so much in her life in just thirty one years. Yes, a true success story by anyone's definition, but at what price? True, she didn't have the humble beginnings that Michael had had. Her father had been the first Black Chief of Surgery to be appointed at Provident Hospital, a position that commanded an enormously large six-figure salary and her mother was an English professor who offered piano lessons to the neighborhood children three times a week.

It was no wonder that Michelle had turned out to be sophisticated, well-versed and determined not to let herself or her family down. Even though she was absolutely

beautiful, she had a fire in her belly that drove her to succeed and she constantly pushed herself.

She had received her Bachelor's Degree from the
University of Chicago and then went on to earn her
Master's from Princeton. Along the way, there were gym-
nastic classes, French lessons, martial arts classes, chess
club memberships and charm school which pretty much
guaranteed a passport to life's finer things and placed her
smack dab in the middle of the social elite.

With a failed marriage under her belt, she wondered if
she would ever find a man that would not only understand
her but be able to match wits with her on *any* level, without
a constant power struggle or any of the insecurities her ex-
husband had occasionally exhibited. Hell! She just wanted
someone to *care* for her . . . not *take care* of her. After all, it
should be obvious to most men that she had done alright
for herself, *by herself!*

Pulling up to the curb, she got out and walked slowly to
her front door, smiling as she noticed a beautifully wrapped
present on her doorstep. *Probably from the company where I recently ordered my new stationery,* she thought. She opened her
front door and set her keys down in their specified place,
letting out a deep sigh of relief at finally being home.

Once the high-heels came off, it was straight for the
kitchen to get things set up for her usual cup of orange
spice herbal tea.

Michelle smiled and nervously bit her lower lip in anticipation of what she might find inside the gift box. Would
it be a thank you gift from Michael? Or perhaps it was a

thank you gift from somewhere else. And let's not forget that there were a group of lawyers down at City Hall who were always telling her how pretty she was. But as soon as she opened it, the smile vanished from her face and she froze. She picked up the note, read it and then stared blankly at the note again. There inside the small box was a note that read:

> *Dear Miss Pierson:*
>
> *I would strongly advise you to return my property to me at your earliest possible convenience. Otherwise, I promise you that you will curse the day that you were ever born.*

Chapter Fifty

The secretary answered this call in the same manner that she did the two previous times that they had called before. This was now the third time.

"No sir, he's not in the office right now. I was told that he would be back much later in the day. I'm sorry sir but I'm only a temp and I don't have any other information to give you. Perhaps you could leave your name and number and I can text Mr. Dickerson or call him directly on his private cell phone if it's an emergency."

Again the rough and raspy voice made an unintelligible remark and paused.

Frank Lindbloom was on the other end of the phone, about to go ballistic as he closed his eyes and thought about the turn of events that had happened the previous night. . . . .

He had gone to the office late last night after everyone had left just as he had done hundreds of other times. But this time his access card to the executive elevators didn't work. He tried it several more times but the card reader continued to display *Security Access Denied* in bold red letters.

When he deemed it was pointless, he took the public elevator to the reception area of the UBMI offices, frustrated that it was automatically programmed, it seemed, to stop on every floor.

The cleaning crew was just entering so as luck would have it, the glass doors were opened. Frank went inside and purposely stared at the Latino man, who was sitting in one of the office chairs. He wasn't cleaning, mind you, just sitting there.

With an expression of complete disbelief as if he had just walked by a cockroach, Lindbloom's face openly showed his disgust.

"Is anything wrong señor?"

"You look scared Juan." He stood near the man, looking down at him with a menacing stare. It was obvious that the mere sight of this man left him irritated.

"My name is Ramiro. Ramiro Martinez, sir," he said looking downward. Ramiro recognized the voice of the man who was harassing him and realized that it was the same man who had gotten into the elevator with him when Isabella was inside his linen cart. Now this man was here again, and didn't even recognize him.

"Well Ramiro, you had better start cleaning better and faster or with one word from me you'll be out of a job. So you need to be *Juan Up* on your competition and that means not sitting your funky jalapeño-smelling ass down in *any* of these chairs, ever! Do you understand hombre?"

"Yes señor, I understand."

"What!" he said pointing his finger towards the man's face, "you are to answer me as Mister Lindbloom, do you hear me?"

"Yes sir, Mister Lindbloom, sir."

"Good, because more than anything else in this world you need to understand and never forget that I'm your superior and as such you need to answer me, and all other White people, with some goddamn respect!"

The worker immediately stood up, visibly shaken and took the rag out of his rear pocket and began cleaning, careful not to make eye contact with this man who towered above him and exuded a great deal of racial hatred.

"And I'm glad if your scared shitless because let's face it," he said looking at all the other workers, "after all it's not *My Panic* we're talking about here is it? It's *His Panic* . . . which means it's all of you! Get it? *His Panic!* Shit, even the name of your poor fucking race says how worthless and scared you people *should* be."

Feeling as though he had put the workers in their place, he left the reception area but not before shouting, "Now make this place Spic and Span, and go heavy on the Spic!"

As he went down the hall, he had a funny feeling and wondered where he had seen the Latino man but he shrugged it off. After all, didn't they *all* look alike?

Still walking at a leisurely pace, he noticed something wasn't quite right with the way the light was being reflected off his office door. As he got a few steps closer he found out why. Lindbloom stopped dead in his tracks when he got even closer to his office. There, in plain sight, he was able to see that his office door appeared open. No, it wasn't left completely open; the door had been completely removed!

He quickened his pace and stood directly in the

doorway, hands on his hips with his head askew, before taking a split second to realize that his name had been removed from the glass. Except for the lone desk and chair, his office was empty. He walked inside and looked at the vacant room, swearing under his breath and its starkness left him cold and even angrier. His behavior gage jumped from irritated to aggravated in a twenty second time frame.

Studying the room's layout, he made his way over to one of the only pieces of furniture in the room, the desk, and pulled at the middle drawer that was slightly ajar. To his surprise, there was a single sealed envelope inside the top middle drawer. He recognized the handwriting, which was unmistakably Michael's, and he opened it.

There was a letter inside which revealed how Michael knew about the five hundred thousand dollar check Lindbloom had received under fraudulent pretenses, the poisoning of his son and the gift box dropped off at his ex-wife's home. Additionally, it stated that their partnership was now dissolved and as far as Michael was concerned, he had interpreted the five hundred thousand dollar check as Lindbloom's payment according to the buyout clause.

Reading further, the letter went on to inform him that he could collect his personal belongings at the security desk on the first floor and that all his electronic cards had been deactivated, effective immediately.

Lastly, it revealed that if he made any attempt at retribution, Michael would act on the information he had received about him and prosecute to the full extent of the law.

Almost in a trancelike state, his mind kept thinking about the previous night until he heard the secretary continuing to call his name and he was snapped back to the present reality.

"Are you there sir? Mr. Lindbloom, is there a message you want me to deliver, sir?"

And so the benevolent Michael Dickerson has laid all his cards on the table, he thought.

"Yes, here's the message and I want this sent as a text message, word for word. Do you understand?"

"Yes Mr. Lindbloom, sir."

"You know how to contact me so I would strongly advise you to do so because I'll be expecting my package delivered to me within the next forty-eight hours."

Chapter Fifty One

It was early on a Saturday morning and Michael had arrived just in time. Today was the long-awaited day of the final tournament and the Windy City Gymnasium was packed with fans from the opposing teams, friends who lent their support and parents who strained to capture perfect angles and lighting with their camcorders, cell phones and other assorted recording devices.

The staff had done a marvelous job of decorating and promoting the event because the buzz had been all over town, so much so, that Michelle had contributed heavily and was listed as a corporate sponsor.

Michael looked around, observing there was no seating anywhere. He then noticed Michelle waving her hands above her head, and wandered through the crowd to reach her.

"Christ Almighty Michael, where were you? I've been fighting off people for this seat for the past twenty minutes!" she said rubbing the top of the chair.

"Sorry. Work, you know how it is," he said apologetically. "Is he up yet?"

"Almost. The Sidekicks just finished their vault routines and the Dust Busters are up next." She handed him a program and noticed how nice he smelled and her pulse quickened. "Hey, check out page twenty-eight, I've got a full-page color ad for *The Cracked Pot*," she said, tilting her head.

He opened his program to page twenty-eight and chuckled. "Always working it aren't you?"

"Always, just like *you*."

"Any scouts here?"

"Yes, right over there," she said pointing. "And yes, some are from Ithaca College."

They both sat side by side and watched as Travis performed his exercise on the high bar. Michelle was mesmerized by the twists and turns in his routine and when he executed a difficult dismount from the equipment, she felt a sense of pride. The crowd had been rooting for him all along and when he was finally finished with his routine, they called out the name Oreo, stood up and cheered ecstatically. The noise in the gymnasium was absolutely deafening.

Michael stood up and applauded as well but he had to admit to himself that he had a small sense of guilt at seeing what his son had accomplished because he and he alone knew that he had been too preoccupied to take this journey with his son. It was only now, at the finish line, that he could clearly define himself as an absentee father, and the label stung because the truth hurt. It always does.

And so it went throughout the tournament, one team pitted against the other as the battle played out. The rings, the vault, the uneven bars, the pommel horse and the high bar had all been done. Now all that was left was the floor exercise.

The Sidekicks team watched with baited breath as their last team member performed. He was down to his last tumbling run, which was executed perfectly except when he landed, he accidentally placed his right heel out of bounds for a split second before he recovered; the disappoint in his face was apparent and heartbreaking.

His numbers were posted on the digital scoreboard and the fans, moaned at first but applauded loudly afterwards, some for effort and some for sympathy.

"And the final contestant of the day representing the Dust Busters team is Travis Dickerson, number ten from Mercer High School!"

The crowd roared but gradually grew silent when Travis raised his arm, nodded at the judges, and began.

Michael couldn't count the number of somersaults, handstands and jumps that Travis executed. There were just too many. It was simply amazing and even though it had taken years of training and sacrifice, Travis made it all appear effortless. When he was on the floor his suppleness showcased just how limber he actually was and his risk-taking stunts were off the charts. Travis' chest heaved up and down and he knew that his second tumbling run was much more difficult but he had only seconds to collect himself and get his second wind.

He carried out the final steps in his exercise with fluid movements and ended with a full-twisting double back somersault, his seventy seconds passing in the blink of an eye.

His team ran out onto the floor to congratulate him on

an outstanding, unflawed performance. They knew as well as the judges that his degree of difficulty was unsurpassed so it came as no surprise when he received a perfect mark on the scoreboard.

The crowd went hysterical and again chanted the name Oreo over and over while Michael and Michelle instinctively hugged each other, both smitten with pride at their son's win for the Dust Buster's team.

With the trophy ceremony over, Michael watched Michelle jump up and head down from the stands to meet the college scouts that now had Travis' attention. He was sure to be under serious consideration for the gymnastics team and in his freshman year too, an unprecedented move by any standard.

He thought about all the things that had been on his mind of late; how he was going to make an effort to spend more time with his son, how he was seriously considering the possibility of marriage again, how he had abruptly ended his partnership and seen the last of Frank Lindbloom and sending more flowers to Janice Freedman, who was still in the hospital.

He finally stood up when the crowd had dispersed a bit more and thought about approaching the subject of Ashley with Michelle but he wasn't sure how well it would be received. He realized that he couldn't put it off forever though.

Stretching his legs, he reached into his sports jacket

and viewed the text message on his cell phone that his temporary secretary had left for him. Sighing, he also knew he would have to discuss this with Michelle but he felt the timing wasn't quite right; not with the winning team celebration and all. So as a result, Michael made the decision to wait until later in the day to discuss Lindbloom's text message with Michelle. But it was a decision they would both soon live to regret.

Chapter Fifty Two

Some moments earlier, Antonio had given his daily oral briefing to Salvatore and was now anxiously awaiting further instructions. His eyes glanced over to the corner of the desk where an open decanter along with three tall crystal wine glasses rested upon a sterling silver tray. He looked at his friends, Alfredo and Emilio, who were seated next to him, and wondered who Mr. Rizzo was on the phone with in the other room. Although there were questions he wanted to ask his friends, he knew that their being silent was the better and far safer choice. There would be plenty of time for talk with them later.

The side door made a clicking sound and slowly opened as Salvatore quietly walked to re-enter the office and once again sit down at his desk. His hand automatically reached for the familiar cigarette holder that had already been prepared for him and Antonio, acknowledging the cue, lit the tip as his boss brought the device to his lips.

He smiled at the men and inhaled deeply. "I trust you will forgive my exit a few moments ago but it was necessary to receive confirmation from my sources at the John Hancock Center. Ah, Antonio I see you are admiring this one today," he said lifting up his newest bronze cigarette holder. "I actually bought this one at a private auction arranged by a friend at Sotheby's. It is of Italian origin so of course it is the very best," he said with complete conviction. "Then I had it adorned with tanzanite in the center with my initials."

Clearing his throat, he looked at each man and nodded his head slowly, staring not only into their eyes but into their very souls, before he began again.

"And now for the business at hand. It appears that our old friend Frank Lindbloom has plans of his own that he has put into motion. It is most unfortunate that his plans have now forced him to take drastic measures, causing harm to whoever is in his path whether that is an older woman, a guiltless boy or confused teenaged girls."

The three men sat upright in their chairs, listening to every word with eagerness to do his bidding.

"According to my sources, he now threatens my reputation and my future plans. He has become vile like a cancer and his businesses are contemptible. It is for that reason that I have decided he has meddled in my affairs for the *very* last time." Salvatore inhaled deeply on the bronze cigarette holder, set it down and then folded his hands in front of him placing them on his desk and each of these men, his most trusted men, waited for the plan to be revealed.

"He wants everyone to bow down and give him a sense of power but he never gives ... he only takes, and his taking is at a cost to the innocent! His drug dealers are at the schools and his monkeys peddle girls the way a vendor at a circus peddles peanuts. It ends *now!*" he said pounding his fist on the desk. "Little does he realize that true power is never measured by what you can give but by what you can actually take!"

Salvatore continued on for several more minutes revealing how Lindbloom had collected incriminating evidence from individuals who felt that loyalty could be purchased for one price on one day and for another on the next. How he loathed disloyal people and their double standard of ethics. "Two-faced or as we say in the old country, *aggettivo falso!"*

Reaching into his desk drawer, he retrieved three large envelopes that were sealed. He handed an envelope to each man and sat back in his chair, taking a long drag on his cigarette holder, the smoke creating an eerie effect in the filtered light creeping in through the plantation shutters. Then he continued.

"Inside you will find an extremely generous amount of cash which represents a payment in advance for the services that I trust and know you will all perform. Additionally, each of you have lists in the envelopes, each one being different, of the names of those individuals who have forgotten where their loyalty *should* lie and have made the grave decision to betray me. That is where the three of you come in," he said clasping his hands together in a prayer-like gesture, "it is *crucial* that each individual on your list be exterminated and it is *essential* that it be within the next forty-eight hours!"

Nodding his head, Antonio leaned forward and waited for Salvatore to acknowledge him before he spoke, "Is Frank Lindbloom's name on one of our lists sir?"

"Yes, it is but I'm delegating that task to Emilio."

The men raised their eyebrows in unison and nodded for they knew that Emilio's nickname on the street was 'The Executioner.'

"We all know about the recent incident with his seventeen year-old daughter when she was on a field trip to the Museum of Natural History. Unfortunately, she was abducted by Lindbloom himself. Then he allowed her to be shamed and disgraced."

"Is she going to be alright?" the two other men asked Salvatore.

"She's at home now recovering and that is why it is only fitting that Emilio have Lindbloom's name, and Emilio alone!"

Salvatore now turned to the corner of the desk and picked up the silver tray, moving it closer to him. He began pouring the liquid from the decanter into the tall wine glasses with exceptional care.

"This is a *Nerello Mascalese* blended wine, a red grape variety from the Sicilian region of Southern Italy, a place very dear to my heart," he said as he pursed his lips. "There, I believe it has had enough time to breathe. You know, according to the Greek author, Homer, this type of wine was used by Ulysses to intoxicate the Cyclops. There are even some that are bold enough to say that this wine actually originated in Greece." He paused and looked at the three men hanging on his every word, "but being of pure Sicilian descent, we all know better. So this plan is in agreement with all of you, no?" he said, as he waited for an answer.

All three men raised their tall glasses in a toast with Salvatore and when their glasses softly clinked, Antonio made direct eye contact and answered, "Mr. Rizzo, sir, I know I speak for all of us when I say that this task will not only be a pleasure . . . it will be an honor."

Chapter Fifty Three

"Yes, I used it last night Candace and girl let me tell you, that damn thing was *really* something, practically knocked my socks off! It works in a pinch. And girl, that reverse feature is unbelievable! I felt like I was having one of my kung fu workouts! Whew! Girl, that thing really *is* a tornado! The only thing I'm sorry about is that I can't host a *Simple Pleasures* party but with my work schedule . . . damn I wish I wasn't so swamped."

Hearing a beeping noise, Michelle immediately knew that another incoming call was trying to come through. "Oh, that's probably my son wanting me to pick him up from his friend's house. They've been celebrating their tournament win all day. I'll call you later, have to run, bye!"

She pressed the flash button on her cordless telephone and waited to hear how her son was going to try to have his pick up time extended.

"Hello?"

The voice on the other end was rough and raspy; with its disdain for her coming through loud and clear.

"Having a good day Miss Pierson?"

She instantly recognized the individual who possessed the voice and it sickened her. "As a matter of fact I am, you asshole. Don't call my home and don't you *ever* try to threaten me again!"

"And I thought we were such good friends, you being the former wife of my *former* partner and all. Hmmm, what a shame. You know, I have many friends and I'd like very much for you to talk to my newest friend so don't hang up on me bitch! Here he is, you may have heard of him before, his name is Travis!"

Michelle went numb. The next thing she heard was the unmistakable sound of her son's voice.

"Mom? . . . is that you? . . . Mom? . . ." the voice on the other end asked. Then his voice was suddenly cut off.

"Travis? . . . . Travis? . . . . Travis!" she screamed into the receiver. "Oh God, my baby, what have you done?"

"There, there now Miss Michelle. *Miss honey child,* did I say that right? Well, it appears that you and your ex-husband haven't been very good parents. Seems you forgot to tell your child not to get into cars with people. But its okay, it's all good," he calmly continued, "I'll be teaching him *that* lesson and a few more of my own choosing before the end of the night," he said with sinister undertones in his voice.

He listened as he heard the terror in her voice and in her breathing and it stirred something deep within him to the point where he had to actually adjust himself in his underwear, which was now quite moist.

"True, you don't have the typical low I.Q. and steel wool for hair. In fact, your hair is *very* different, it's long, black and silky, isn't it? I trust that the violation you feel now is equal to the one that I felt when I noticed your long, black silky hair in the closet of *my* bedroom, the sanctuary of *my* home! Not yours, *mine!*"

"Let's see now, you went through your rebellious stage at Ingleside High School where you met your future husband but then you got your act together at the University of Chicago and then it was on to Princeton for your Master's wasn't it? Always wanting to do things your own way right? Perhaps that's why you were a catalog model, huh? Didn't want to feel obligated to your family for using their fortune to put you through school, right? My, my, Miss Michelle, that was positively noble of you. Yes, the Black American Princess who holds court so all us common folk can look at her astounding beauty and be in awe. Only, I'm not good enough to be in your presence am I? No. You didn't even realize that I also went to Princeton, just like you," he said slowly and with emphasis.

"Yes, the best that life has to offer is all yours, money, education, independence, brains and even incredible beauty, a pivotal achievement for anyone . . . comparable to being the ace in a deck of playing cards. But don't you *ever* forget, honey . . . . child . . . that you are still just a Queen of Spades!" he screamed to the top of his lungs.

"Frank, please . . . just don't hurt my son!" she pleaded, "just don't hurt my son, oh God, my baby! Please! Please don't hurt him!"

"Oh, so now its *Frank* is it? That sounds a lot better than, what was that you referred to me as? Asshole, right?"

Michelle's body was shaking uncontrollably as she sat on her sofa holding herself and openly sobbing. "Oh God!" she moaned, shaking her head back and forth. "God help me!" she said, closing her eyes.

"God isn't going to help your tight, hot, beautiful ass this time, my dear. Remember you may have started this shit but I'm going to finish it and I guarantee you, bitch; you won't like the ending!

At midnight tonight be at the elevated train platform on the Green Line. That's at the Randolph and Wabash stop. Have my black satchel with you and don't involve the police or you'll never see your son again!"

Chapter Fifty Four

Michael could hardly get a word in edgewise as Clarence continued to apologize and voice his remorse for not revealing to Michael what he had seen in Janice's hospital room.

"It's alright Casey. I wish you had told me earlier but at least you told me."

"What do you want me to do?"

"Absolutely nothing. I'll handle it. By the way, Casey?"

"Yes?"

"I went by the hospital and visited her today and she's off the respirator and breathing on her own. Now, get some sleep!"

Within seconds, the phone rang again and the thought of having to calm Casey down once more made him weary. *Why can't he just take a valium and chill out like everybody else?* Michael thought.

"Yes, what is it *now?*"

"Oh God Michael, thank God I got a hold of you," Michelle said with relief in her voice. "First off, I'm calm so *don't* tell me to calm down and second, I'm *not* going to panic." She waited a few seconds and then she came out with it, "Lindbloom found out about the switch in the satchels and he wants the original one back. And . . . and he's got Travis," she finally revealed.

"What! Fuck, this is worse than I thought," Michael said rubbing his hand repeatedly over his forehead. "Okay, okay first of all where *is* the satchel and can you get it?"

"I'm on my way to the Tollway-Arlington Bank now, it's in a safety deposit box but I need you to call the bank manager there right away because he knows you from the commercials you did and he'll let me in."

"You got it. What do you want me to say to him?"

"Tell him that I'm on my way and that even though the bank is closing in an hour, I've got to get in there and get that satchel."

"Consider it done. Were you able to see or talk to Travis?"

"Yes, I spoke to him but only for a second or two. It was his voice so I know he's still alive."

"We'll do what he says. We'll get the satchel, give it to him and be done with it. Remember, he doesn't want Travis; all he really wants is the satchel. Keep

telling yourself that and be strong," he said trying to comfort her. "Where are you now?"

"In the car driving to the bank's downtown branch but traffic is a bitch!"

"Why didn't you use a bank close to your house?"

"Because they don't have a safety deposit box big enough for the satchel!"

"Where's the drop off?" he asked, a little irritated that she was not forthcoming with any of the information he needed. Not waiting for an answer, he continued, "why did you have to take the satchel, why not just empty out the contents and leave it there?"

"Because I needed to see everything and then put it back in order and..." she hesitated, "I don't know."

"Well, what the hell *do* you know?"

"Michael, get off the fucking phone and call the bank manager!"

The line went dead and he knew she had ended the call.

Deeply troubled, Michael went straight to the bar and poured himself a drink. *I need a dose of liquid courage,* he thought. This time it was not the familiar Courvoisier that he reached for, it was bourbon. He sat down on the sofa and felt the perspiration dripping down his armpits and hated the thought of that sonofabitch making him sweat.

He took a small sip and felt responsible for even getting Michelle pumped up enough where she felt it vital to go on a reconnaissance mission and search for clues regarding Travis' poisoning. He should have known that her impetuous nature would have caused some sort of spontaneous action on her behalf, and it had.

He decided that he would wait and hope and do something else he hadn't done in a long time; he would pray. After all, Travis was his son, his *only* son and if he was hurt in any way whatsoever he swore he would gladly spend the rest of his life in prison for killing Lindbloom in cold blood!

He put down his glass and searched through the crowded directory in his cell phone, found the bank manager's private phone number and called him.

Chapter Fifty Five

Thanks to Michael's phone call, Michelle had retrieved the original black satchel from the bank even after they had closed but before the vault was locked up for the day.

She glanced down at the floor on the passenger side of her car and ensured it was safe and sound at every traffic light or stop sign she encountered as she drove back to her house.

Her son was the only thing on her mind right now and he encompassed not only her every thought but her very being. He had become her life and all her money, successful ventures, beauty and achievements meant nothing unless her son would be there, in the future, to share them with her.

Arriving at her home, she was exhausted, nerves on edge and mentally weary. Still she had the ability to center her energy and do a number of breathing techniques that she had learned in her martial arts classes. It seemed to be the only thing that helped her compose herself. In and out and then again, in and out, until she was convinced she had cleared her mind of all the negative energy around her. She had to keep herself busy because according to the time-frame that Frank Lindbloom had set, she knew it was going to be a long wait.

Time passed slowly and the minutes felt long and pronounced as every movement of the second hand on the kitchen clock brought her closer to the inevitable, getting to the train platform, facing Frank Lindbloom and getting her son back, *alive.*

The wait was not only torture, it was agonizing.

The kitchen cabinet was absently left open and the orange spice herbal teabag was now steeping in her favorite mug as she made her way back into the kitchen after taking a quick hot shower. As strange as it may have seemed to someone else, the shower made her feel better and a bit more alert since she knew that her body needed rest; rest that she would not give it knowing her son's life was at stake. How she yearned to hold him in her arms, feel the warmth of his body, smell his scent and feel him breathe. How she yearned to tell him . . . that she loved him. Instead all she had done on the phone was call out his name, and in hindsight she realized it may have been a wasted opportunity to tell him how she truly felt.

What a fool she had been to think she could outsmart Frank Lindbloom, after all, he was a bona fide criminal and completely ruthless.

Got to remember that I'd better call Michael before he calls me back, she thought as she picked up her mug and took a sip of the hot brew before setting it down on the nearby beverage coaster. Adjusting her bathrobe, she meditated in a yoga position, and she waited.

THE SYMBIOTIC SECTION

Every bit of Michelle's inner strength was used as she channeled it into the pen, assortment of papers and large envelopes on the kitchen table. This task had been extremely difficult, emotionally draining, and had taken a great deal of time.

The first envelope was made out to Travis in case she did not come out of this alive, the second was to Michael in the event that he survived and she did not, and the third was to her attorney with a list of very detailed instructions which included a key to her safety deposit box, a copy of her will and a copy of her revocable trust.

When finished, she looked at the kitchen clock and realized it was finally nine fifteen and time to get dressed. Her mind was now refocused and she took the phone into the bedroom with her, engaging the hands-free speaker feature so she could talk to Michael at the same time.

"Hey, it's me. Sorry I took so long to call you back but I had to get my head together and make sure that all the paperwork in the satchel was all there and in order. How are you doing?"

"Alright, I guess. I hate being helpless like this, not being able to do anything and not being there with you."

"I told you, I really think its best if we go separately. Besides, I think there's that annual Blue's Festival or something like that going on and I don't want either of us to get stuck in traffic."

"Right. Alright . . . where is this supposed to happen?" he asked with a touch of trepidation in his voice.

"He told me that at midnight tonight I need to be at the elevated train platform at the Randolph and Wabash stop."

"Why there?"

"Jesus, Michael I don't *know* why! Listen, I've got the satchel and now I'm dressed so I'm hanging up."

"Michelle?"

"Yes?"

"Be careful."

She took a deep breath and went through the motions of turning out the lights. Then she gathered the three large envelopes and placed them on the foyer table near the front door. Pausing, she took out her cell phone and called her attorney's number. Shit! He wasn't picking up, but at least she could leave a message. In the past he had always returned her messages. *Yes, he was very good about that*, she thought.

Hearing the voice on the other end made her mind wander for a few seconds to something else completely different but she refocused and was brought back to reality when she heard the beep on the other end.

"Hey listen its Michelle and I've gotten myself involved in something bad, *really* bad and I don't have time to explain it right now. All I can tell you is I may not come out of this alive," she said as her voice was cracking. "Tonight I'll be at the elevated train platform that's at the Randolph and Wabash stop at midnight and if I don't make it, I want you to go to my house and take the spare house key that I keep under the birdbath and look on the table in the foyer area. There will be three envelopes on the table. I think you can take it from there."

Putting the phone back in her purse, she looked at the envelopes she had placed on the small table. "Shit! I forgot this one," she muttered as she realized she had not written on the third large envelope. Running into the kitchen, she quickly grabbed the pen off of the table and wrote the name onto the third envelope, locked her front door and drove away.

The large third envelope she had addressed at the last minute was to the one person in the world that she knew she could completely trust; the person who would have her back. She didn't even have to give it a second thought because it was the logical choice to make it.

The large third envelope, which was placed on the table, was to her attorney, and it was addressed to Salvatore Rizzo.

Chapter Fifty Six

It was close to ten thirty p.m. when Elizabeth arrived home feeling tired, wound up and a bit queasy. Not knowing if it was from a night of partying or from her illness, she knew she needed a shower like nobody's business. An overpowering stench and strong musky odor clung to her body from having engaged in sexual relations with multiple partners, four to be exact, on *this* night. *And why not?* she thought as she turned on the water. *After all, who really gives a fuck?* Well aware that her recent behavior had probably spread the HIV-virus, she felt totally justified in having sex, feeling alive and feeling wanted again. Besides, she was just doing to men what they had *always* done to her. No, she had no regrets. And now, thanks to Dr. Whitman's most recent report, she discovered that she was now in Stage Four of the disease and that meant only one thing; that it was steadily progressing on a one-way course.

Yes, thanks to her HIV-positive diagnosis, she knew how she was going out but she had made a conscious choice to go out *her* way, on *her* terms and if that meant infecting tons of men in the process, then so be it.

"Let's face it," she said aloud, "there are only a handful of people in this entire world even worth *caring* about!"

She watched the suds slide off of her body and go

down the drain, down the drain like the men she had just screwed; only they didn't know it yet. "Oh no," she whined, as she held her stomach. But the pain and queasiness wasn't just in her stomach this time, it was throughout her entire body. She exhaled a few times, dried off and slipped into a pair of old hospital scrubs, her street-legal pajamas, as she referred to them. Turning on the television, she waited for the uncomfortable feeling to pass.

And then she saw the commercial for the Tollway-Arlington Bank and was unable to change the channel. She sat there, mesmerized and appalled, all at the same time. It was like watching a bad car wreck that you knew was horrific but you just couldn't force yourself to turn away. Fixated on the star of the commercial, it brought everything back home; all the bad feelings, the doubts and the anger towards Michael for having destroyed her life.

Her physical pain was much worse now and she knew she would have to phone someone, not just anyone, but someone who could hook her up with some *real* drugs to take away her hurt.

What the hell, was everybody out on a Saturday night? she thought, as she heard countless rings from making countless calls with no answer to each number she tried… and then, finally, someone picked up.

"What," a monotone voice answered, without any emotion in it whatsoever.

"E.T., it's me, Elizabeth Lindbloom, and I need something . . . just enough to get me through for a couple of days until I can see my doctor on Monday. I've got money," she said, looking at the wad of cash she had earned for tonight's sexual favors. "Can you come over here to my house and hook me up?"

The man on the other end spoke with an inner-city accent and was obviously angry, "What the hell is da matter wicha bitch! Don'tcha know I run a bizness? Ya know what I'm sayin'? I'm a biznessman so lookey here, if you had a bizness and Saturday night wuz *yo* buziest night would ya leave yo' place a bizness and go service one client or would you stay where yo clients iz so dey don't go elsewhere? Ya know what I'm sayin'?"

"I'll do anything, I just don't think I'm going to be able to make it through to Monday. I'll pay extra and I'll do anything . . . anything for it really," she promised.

Convinced that he could not only have extra profit but get a blow job out of it too, the man on the other end of the phone made her a proposition. "Alright now sweet thang, here's what I'm a gonna do fo' you. I ain't comin' up there to where you stay but if you can get your ass down here, where *my* bizness iz in about an hour, I'll sho' nuf hook you up with some good shit and we can always negotiate the price for everything else baby. Ya know what I'm sayin'?"

"Alright, that sounds fair. Where *is* your office?" she asked, feeling a sense of relief.

"Well lookey here, tonight my office is under the elevated train tracks at Randolph and Wabash. I'll be walkin' back and forth 'tween the garbage dumpsters and the vacant lot. But don't you worry bout that, I knows what you look like and I'll find you."

"Is that a safe area? I mean, I've heard things about that part of town on the news," she said hesitantly.

"Bitch! Do you want dis' shit or not?" he said with annoyance.

"Yes, I'm sorry. I'll be there. What time E.T.?"

"Be there around ten thirty and don't be late bitch!"

Chapter Fifty Seven

Elizabeth arrived at the meeting place she had agreed upon with E.T. but upon seeing the type of area she was in, she chose to keep her doors and windows locked and not to get out of her car. Sighing, she was thankful she had decided to bring the twenty-two caliber handgun she had recently bought from a friend of a friend with her. Christ, talk about bad areas!

Looking around for E.T., she thought about leaving, but knew if she stood him up, she would lose an important source for her drugs, her lifeline. These days they put all kinds of shit in stuff and you couldn't be sure if you were getting a partially diluted product or part rat poison! Even coming down here was worth it for two clear reasons. One, she knew that E.T. could be completely trusted, and two, he definitely had a high-quality product. She checked her car's clock again, "ten thirty three," she muttered. "Perhaps some music would make me feel better," she said absent-mindedly.

A station that played seventies tunes was selected and Elizabeth began to tap her fingers on the dashboard hoping her supplier would arrive shortly.

She grew frustrated when E.T. didn't show. The noise from the elevated trains overhead was deafening, their steel wheels clattering and squealing along the metal tracks. *They must be reaching speeds of sixty miles per hour!* she thought.

Having lived in Chicago her entire life, she had never even ridden a bus or so much as been on a subway train. Now, here she was in this bottomless pit and E.T. would probably want the transaction to take place on the train itself. Overhead, she saw an enormous amount of bluish sparks fly off the wheels as she looked upward, through her windshield, and it frightened her even more.

"Whazup Miss 'Lizbeth!"

"Oh, Jesus! You scared me half to death E.T.," she said placing her hand over her heart.

"You alone baby?" he asked, peering into her vehicle.

"Yes . . . yes," she stuttered, "it's just me. That's what you wanted isn't it?"

"Yeah. Hey this is a nice ride, one a doz suv's, huh?" he said nodding his head slowly. "Das good baby, das real good. You'll have plenty of room to do yo thang in the back," he commented.

"Do you have anything you can give me, like last time, but stronger?"

Not answering her, he pulled out a small baggie that contained a darkish-colored rock, showed it to her, and had her unlock her rear door. Now inside the rear compartment of her vehicle, he continued. "This will fix you up real nice 'cept fo one thing you gots ta' know," he said, looking puzzled at her outfit."

"What's that?"

"Dis here is black tar heroine. It ain't like some of the

other shit on the street you done tried. Da first hit, well, it'll give you da high you crave and da next is ta well, keep you from gettin' sick. So babygirl if you get dis, there ain't no going back cuz you can best be sho that yo ass will be chasing the ultimate high and you may *never* catch it." He chuckled and made some sniffing sounds and then continued. "You may catch the tail, but you ain't never gone get that monkey off yo back. But you ain't gots ta worry, cuz I'll be here. Das why they call me E.T. I do what I needs to do by the elevated tracks. Das what the initials stand for, E.T., but like in the movie . . . you can jus phone home and I'll have yo shit for you. You know what I'm sayin?"

"I'm just doing it this once so all that other stuff you're saying doesn't really matter to me," she said eyeing the baggie in his hand.

"Alright 'den, now we gotta go over the payment," he said, as he took a spoon, needle, small rubber cord and other items out of a small zippered bag. "Tricks of the trade, sweet thang," he said, winking at her.

"I told you I can pay, I have three hundred dollars," she said emphatically.

Opening her purse, Elizabeth revealed three hundred dollars worth of paper money in different denominations, which was crumpled up. "Is this enough?" she asked, putting it closer to him.

"Tell you what I'm a gonna do. I'm only gonna ask fo' fifty this time and you can work the rest off by doing me a favor. See those men standing behind the garbage dumpster over there?" he said pointing in the general direction.

"Yes," she said nodding.

"Well, dem dare are my bizness associates and I'd like you to make them feel good tonight. Can you do that fo' me sweet thang?" he asked dangling the packet in front of her.

"That wasn't part of the deal E.T." she said nervously biting her lower lip.

Her body was racked with pain but moreover she was afraid to say no to him. "Alright," she agreed. "What do I have to do?" she asked, already having a good idea.

The man smiled to reveal a gold front tooth and motioned for his two friends to come over to the vehicle. Running across the street, they glanced at Elizabeth and then got inside the rear of the vehicle as E.T. opened the door for them.

"This here is 'Lizabeth man and she gonna do ya'll a favor man, you know what I'm sayin? Come here sweet thang," he said, indicating for her to move into the rear portion of her vehicle. "Dis here is my man number one and dis here is my man number two. What you is gonna do is take off just yo pants and get on all fours, you know, doggie style. My man number one here is gonna be underneath you and you is gonna suck his dick like there ain't no tomorrow and while you is doin' that, my man number two here is gonna do his bizness 'wich ya from behind at the *exact* same time. So when you is done suckin' off my man number one I wantcha to go ahead and then fuck him. And when my man number two is done fuckin' you from behind, I wantcha ta go ahead and suck him off when he's ready. Ya know what I'm sayin'?"

Elizabeth, felt repulsed at the idea of performing these lewd acts with these men who reeked of body odor and were obviously high on something. *Hell, I just showered and this could probably go on for quite some time with the amount of the controlled substances in their systems!* she thought.

With her options running out and the pain in her joints increasing to an almost intolerable level, she agreed as she got up on all fours with her pants and underwear off. "I have two requests E.T.," she said looking into his eyes and smiling.

"Go 'head sweet thang," he said grinning as he saw his buddies admiring her ass.

Smiling widely, she said, "I want your friends to have a true experience, a reeeeeeally good time, the *natural* way and be able to completely and fully relieve themselves inside of me. Just like in the good ole' days. You can have some too E.T," she said slyly.

"Goddamn! You's the real deal sweet thang!"

"Naw man, she's the bomb!" one of his associates said.

"It'll be more enjoyable that way for *all* of us. Besides, I'm clean! So, number one, I would like you to give me the heroine first, and number two," she said as she held out her right arm for the injection, "it's all good, so I don't want any of you guys to wear condoms."

Chapter Fifty Eight

The first bandana that had been formed into a ball and shoved in Travis' mouth was soaked in saliva; the second was tied securely around his mouth, and together they prevented him from making any kind of sound, hell it was all he could do to breathe! He was scared shitless out of his mind but knew he would have to keep his wits about him just to keep from hyperventilating or choking from the bandana partially obstructing his airway.

He had heard his mother's voice, if only for a few seconds, but he had heard her. That meant she knew he had been kidnapped and that she was going to try to get him back. He also knew that his mom would tell his dad, and just the thought of that gave him hope.

This was like some horrible nightmare except that he knew it wasn't a nightmare. If things didn't go according to the way that Mr. Lindbloom wanted them to go, he might not *ever* wake up.

Travis had also been handcuffed and blindfolded, which gave him plenty of time to think about why Mr. Lindbloom was doing this and, more significantly, how he could get away. He held himself stiffly as the car went over several potholes and bumps in the road, causing his body to sway and bounce in the seat.

The five men rode in silence down narrow streets, driving through alleyways and what seemed to be unnecessary detours, until they finally arrived at the planned destination.

On one hand he was glad the car had stopped but on the other he didn't know if it meant the end of his life was drawing near. He heard the car doors open and was led out, elbow first, and told to sit on the bumper of the car and not move.

The next few minutes were sheer agony as he did nothing but listen to the sound of the elevated trains above his head. After several minutes passed, he heard another vehicle drive up and then there were footsteps that came closer and closer still until they stopped where he was sitting.

"Ughhhhh!" he said as the bandanas were untied and removed. Appreciative that he could finally move his tongue, his mouth felt dry and his throat was parched almost to the point of being raw. Suddenly and without warning, the blindfold was yanked off of from his face, the thick elastic band snapping his ear. "Ow!" he cried out.

"Good evening Travis," came the voice from behind him. He already knew it was the voice of Frank Lindbloom, his kidnapper. "I trust that your accommodations, although not at the level you are used to, still fulfilled the basics. Hopefully, this will all be over soon and you'll be sitting at home with a bottle of the newest five-hour energy drink or whatever the hell it is you kids drink nowadays. In the meantime, is there anything I can get for you?"

"Yes, I'd just like some water and to be able to go to the

bathroom, Mr. Lindbloom, sir."

Melvin, Lindbloom's right hand man, shoved a bottle of water to Travis' lips since he was still handcuffed, "here you go kid, drink away."

His thirst satisfied, Travis asked, "and the bathroom?"

Lindbloom looked around and scoped out the area. "Of course, of course, follow me Travis, you can go right over there behind that dumpster," he said escorting him.

Once they were behind the dumpster, Travis remembered that because he was still handcuffed, he wouldn't be able to urinate properly unless his pants were unzipped and his penis was held away from his body. He looked at Lindbloom and swallowed but was silent.

"Oh, I guess you'll be needing some assistance," Lindbloom said as he understood and quickly provided this much-needed service.

Travis urinated with a forceful stream and in all his life it had never felt so good to pee. "Ahhhh," he said, "thank you very much, sir."

Frank Lindbloom looked at Travis. He was tall for his age, almost *his* height and the racial mixture he possessed did him justice. His jawline, deep set brown eyes, broad shoulders from doing gymnastics and tight buttocks, made him very attractive. He thought about how he had watched him grow up into this good-looking, muscular young man. Forgetting himself, he began to tuck Travis' genitals back into his underwear, only his hand lingered on the spongy, soft mushroom-shaped head of the boy's penis and he began to gently stroke it, his hand knowing just how much pressure to apply and where.

"Come on Travis, we've known each other for years now, we're practically family, you and I. It's dark here and we're behind this dumpster," he continued. "No one, not a soul has to know boy, I promise you. I know what you're thinking . . . that's its wrong or even bad but it's not Travis. It's alright to want to experiment at your age. Hell, I experimented when I was your age. I promise you that you'll want it once you've done it. I'm experienced so I can teach you things. All you have to do is relax, trust me, and let it happen, because it's *natural*. You see, I can make you feel exactly how *you* want because I'm a man too and I already *know* what you want. You and I," he said, breathing deeply and rapidly, "*We are exactly the same, but different.*"

Travis looked at him, his heart beating out of his chest in fear, and in his calmest voice he managed to say, "I'm done urinating now Mr. Lindbloom. Can we please go back sir?" he asked, crossing his fingers even though he was still handcuffed.

His moment denied him; Frank clumsily situated the boy back into his clothes and walked behind him as they made their way slowly back across the street.

Frank looked up and noticed that this particular train platform was completely dark, not even so much as one light was working. At least there were no patrons waiting. Must be some sort of a power outage with the lights again. *That's Chicago for you, a piece-of-shit-city!* he thought.

When they were back at the car he grew agitated. "What time is it?" he asked one of his men.

"It's eleven forty five."

"Good it won't be long now," Lindbloom said.

"Hey, what about that car over there?"

"That was here when we pulled up you idiot and you can see from here that there's no one in the driver's seat!"

"Focus guys, focus," Lindbloom warned his men. "Here comes someone driving down the street. Ah ha, there are two cars coming within minutes of each other actually. Take the boy upstairs to the train platform, its time; and watch him!" he said with a menacing tone of voice.

"We'll watch him, Mr. Lindbloom, don't worry," Eric said.

Michael drove up first, turned off his lights and stepped out of his car. Hearing the sound of the train go by, he automatically looked up but couldn't see anything on the train platform. It was too dark and, thanks to the trains, loud as hell. He sighed with a bit of relief just knowing that Travis was still alive. Making his way up the platform, he took two steps at a time until he reached the top. His heart raced as he stood there looking across the sets of tracks that separated him from his son. "Travis, its dad, are you alright?"

"I'm fine dad. Really I am, don't worry."

"Unless you have what Mr. Lindbloom is waiting for, you had better have a seat over there," Melvin gestured from across the tracks.

Michael did what he was told to do since he knew he was not in a position to bargain. Not yet anyway.

Then another vehicle pulled up. Michael was still seated on the bench but he turned his head and looked down the stairs. *Thank God, it was Michelle,* he thought and not a moment too soon.

She turned off her lights and drove up to an empty parking space then she killed the engine and stepped out. Opening the passenger door, she removed a large black satchel from the floor of her vehicle and slammed the car door shut. She had a foreboding sense about this place and wanted to get this over with as soon as possible. She just wanted her son.

Walking up the stairs to the train platform, she held onto the worn stairwell carefully with one hand, her fingernails practically scrapping off the chipped paint flakes. The other hand had a steadfast grip on the satchel. At first she saw Michael sitting down on the bench and then she saw her son on the opposite side of the tracks and her heart skipped a beat.

When she arrived at the very top, Michael stood up and put his arms around her but she never let go of the satchel.

"And so we have the proud parents of this young lad. I give to you Michael and Michelle Dickerson. Oh, that's right; you refused to change your last name didn't you? I beg your pardon, Miss Pierson. Do you have the satchel?" Lindbloom asked, from across the platform.

"Yes, now please Frank, give us back our son. We don't want any trouble, we just want our son."

Lindbloom selected one of his men to go up the steps on the opposite side of the platform and bring back the satchel.

"Wait! Michael said, "what about Travis?"

"Yes, you promised . . . . ." Michelle reaffirmed.

"I promised you that if you didn't have the satchel you would never see your son again. And that is *all* I promised. Nothing more and nothing less," he reminded them both.

It was tense as one of Lindbloom's goons went around to the other side of the platform and took the steps to the side which they were on. He reached the top of the platform, had them in his sights, and then walked closer towards Michelle, ordering Michael to remain seated on the bench and to stay that way. He came closer to her but she moved away walking backwards, the satchel still gripped tightly in her hand.

And then the platform began to vibrate, a little at first and then more as a train drew nearer. Michelle continued to back up as the man approached her, his eyes focused on what was in her hand.

"Don't let her get on that train!" Lindbloom screamed.

As the train increased its speed, the clacking and banging sound of the wheels was overwhelming and Michelle stopped suddenly and turned sideways with the man practically on her heels and in one swift motion, Michael pushed him onto the tracks, and his foot touched the dreaded third rail as he struggled to get up, instantly electrocuting him!

Michelle steadied herself and ran to the bench with Michael close behind, offering his arms to shield her face from the body that lie smoldering on the tracks.

"You should not have done that Michael!" Lindbloom bellowed.

"Maybe he should've looked at the schedule a bit more closely and then he would have known that the trains don't stop here after midnight," Michelle said breathing heavily.

"Touché, Miss Pierson." Lindbloom said, bowing to her. "Now, I believe there is still the matter of the satchel."

"We want to go over on the opposite side to be with our son and hold him. If you're going to kill us then I want us to die while we're all holding each other, and together! Those are my terms Frank and they are *not* open to negotiation."

Lindbloom looked over at the boy and the three men who were now holding him and nodded. "Uncuff his hands," he ordered. "If the boy tries to run I want you to throw him onto the tracks so we'll have ourselves a little barbecue as well."

It didn't take Michelle and Michael long to run down the steps and then run back up the other stairwell to the other side of the platform, the side where Travis was being held.

"Travis!" Michelle whispered as she held him in her arms as tight as she possibly could. Michael was right at the rear, hugging them both from behind.

"Sorry to break up this touching family affair but I have other plans for this evening. The satchel, Miss Pierson," he said as one of his thugs pulled out a switchblade, opened it with one button, and put it to her throat, leading her a few yards away from her son and Michael.

Once again, the platform began to vibrate and this time they were all aware that the train was not going to stop at the platform.

Then she made eye contact with Michael and Travis and looked down at the train tracks and then back up at Michael and then Travis.

The platform was vibrating more now and the sound of the approaching train was growing louder.

Michelle slowly set down the satchel and a second later, she quickly threw it over to where Michael was. "Run!" she screamed as she kicked the thug's leg, catching him off balance momentarily. "He probably can't shoot straight anyway!"

Then she made a split-second decision to kick him in the solar plexus, knocking the wind out of him. Once he was down she went for the throat, performing a swift punching motion on it, crushing his windpipe.

Michael grabbed the satchel and took Travis' hand as they ran out onto the live tracks, not just away from the platform but towards the next stop. "For God's sake Travis, don't step on the third rail!" Michael screamed.

"Melvin! Eric! . . . . bring me back that satchel!" Lindbloom shouted. "Get them but don't shoot, I've got disks in there that I can't replace!"

As Lindbloom ran to capture Michelle, he realized that if she got away she was going to be too fast for him and he knew what he had to do next. He saw how she was making her way to the end of the platform where she could easily jump onto the tracks to follow Michael and her son, so it was then that he made his move, and just as Michelle was about to bolt onto the tracks, she instantly froze. There standing only ten feet away from her was Lindbloom and he had a gun pointed directly at her head.

"Touché asshole. I didn't know you even *carried* a gun," she said, trying to catch her breath.

"Well it appears I do but since we've become such good friends, I have something to tell you. Yes, I have a confession." He walked only a few inches closer to her, careful to keep a substantial distance between them and not give her the opportunity to remove his weapon using her martial arts training.

"I have to confess that I'm not the best shot in the world Michelle but I don't think I'll miss at this range, do you?"

Chapter Fifty Nine

"Oh shit! Where the fuck am I?" Elizabeth moaned, as she sat halfway up in the back seat of her vehicle. *They're gone,* she thought. Finally. She blinked a few times and belched as she brought her hand up to her cheek and removed the strands of hair that were plastered to it. She felt slightly dizzy and her lips were dry with a white crusted substance, but other than those minor irritations, she felt okay. No, better than okay, she wasn't hurting anymore. After all, wasn't that her goal?

Reaching behind her, she felt for the bottom half of her scrubs and realized that she had been urinated on. Yawning, she grabbed her scrubs and using them as a towel, wiped herself off.

Hell, those guys really knew how to party. And what a party it was. There was shouting, grunting, swearing and the sound of hands slapping her with cocks thrusting at full force into her. Shit! her SUV was rocking back and forth *and* from side to side! And then there was E.T. who insisted on squeezing and biting her nipples through her clothes and ramming his huge cock into her, first from the front and then straight into her already used and tired ass. It was a no-holds-barred Fuck-Fest and although parts of it were a blur, it was all good. She felt the moistness that was still between her legs and grimaced at how she had gotten that way but then a devious smile slowly crept onto her crusted lips. A feeling of not being sore and a feeling of knowing she had turned the tables on the low life pricks that had convinced her to fuck them, gave her deep satisfaction. She had fucked them all right. Yeah, they were sucked *and* fucked; only they didn't know it yet!

A bit steadier now, she leaned her head up against the rear window and peered out. The sound of the trains must have awakened her. "Hell, I need a cup of coffee," she muttered, but then she knew she didn't really want the coffee, she just wanted to enjoy the euphoria she was feeling, she wanted to be in the moment; and she was doing just that.

Looking up at the train platform, she tried to focus on what seemed to be a familiar figure. "Am I dreaming?" she asked herself, looking out of the window again. "No, it couldn't be. Is that Frank? Is that my brother? Is that my brother's voice?"

Her mind was still foggy as she floated in and out of consciousness, unable to tell fantasy from reality. "There," she said, putting on her panties, "I've got to have a look for myself but this is a bad area so I may need this," she whispered reaching for her purse. She opened it and noticed right away there was two hundred and fifty dollars remaining inside her purse and a tiny baggie with a note that read:

Thanks sweet thang. Thought you might like an extra taste of what is to come and I'm open twenty four / seven just for you baby.

THE SYMBIOTIC SECTION

Remember that yo' everythang can be anythang!
E.T.

She picked up the baggie and smiled when she noticed the small black rock inside. So, E.T. had scruples after all. Elizabeth grinned. "And he can even read and write," she said, giggling.

Still searching in her purse, she shoved the crumpled money aside, and continued searching for the pouch near the bottom and finding it; she took out the twenty-two caliber handgun.

Frank will be so surprised to see me and maybe we can even go out for a bite to eat, she thought. Even though her legs were weak, she got out of her vehicle and wobbled over to where she thought she had last heard her brother. It was hard to confirm anything visually with only a few working street lights illuminating the area, but she was sure she had heard her brother's voice. In her condition, she knew she would never be able to make it up the stairs so she called out to him.

"Frank . . . hey Frank, its Elizabeth. Was that you I saw? Are you up there?"

Everything was as quiet as one could expect on a Saturday night for this part of town and the occasional train actually seemed to desensitize the situation. There was music from the Blues Festival playing in the background from the concert taking place miles away and Michelle was glad because it gave her something to at least listen to.

Lindbloom hadn't spoken to Michelle and she had barely moved. It was pretty intense and for that reason, the yelling from down below was actually a welcome relief for her but Lindbloom was stunned beyond belief.

"Elizabeth!" he yelled. "What are you doing here?"

"Frank, I can't come up the stairs. I'm too fucked up! But you still love me don't you?"

Frank continued to keep his gun directed at Michelle's head as he moved backwards and looked down over the railing and then back at his victim. It was his sister alright, no doubt about it. What the fuck was she doing *here?* He saw the condition she was in and knew he would have to deal with her later after all this was over and hopefully, it wouldn't be too much longer now. Looking at her hand, he instantly zoomed in on the small caliber gun that she held in it and this worried him.

"Wait there for me Elizabeth. Sit down if you have to but wait for me."

"Things not going as planned?" Michelle insinuated with a hint of a smile.

"Nothing that I can't handle. Always trying to get the last word in edgewise, aren't you? Just remember that when Melvin gets back here with your precious Michael and your half-breed son that all the kung fu shit in the world won't help you outrun a bullet or save your ass you meddling bitch."

"It's *Black* bitch to you!" she said defiantly as she saw her captor walking in her direction.

That was all he could take; why did niggers like her refuse to stay in their place? Fed up with her backtalk, he cocked his pistol and pointed it in her direction. "I can see

Melvin now and he's got them both. So if you don't shut that full, pouty mouth of yours, than I promise you that this will be the day that you'll see your son's head blown off right in front of you!"

Chapter Sixty

Michael and Travis could be seen walking back to where Michelle was being held and her heart sank when she saw their faces. She tried not to stare but she also noticed that her ex-husband was limping.

Michael had run so fast that his foot had become caught in-between the wooden planks that provided the spacing for the tracks. With his ankle twisted, he knew he was defeated and ordered Travis to leave him and take off with the satchel. But Travis had refused to leave his father. Whatever happens will happen to both of us dad, he had said.

Melvin was careful to direct them back onto the platform when he had heard the sound of *any* approaching train. No use having the train engineer alert the Chicago Transit Authority that there were passengers *actually* walking in-between the tracks! They didn't get very far and Melvin was grateful for that.

"Well, I can see there won't be any more running from you," Lindbloom said with amusement looking at Michael. "It must really hurt having to humble yourself before your *former* partner."

Michael limped to the platform and hobbled up, with Travis' help to where Michelle was sitting, his ankle visibly swollen.

Lindbloom now had possession of the satchel and finally let out a sigh of relief. "All three of you, get down on your knees with your hands locked behind your heads and turn away from me!" he ordered. "You've all meddled in my affairs for the last time!"

"Where the hell is Eric?" Lindbloom finally asked.

"Oh, he didn't watch his footing with his bad leg and all and he lost his balance. It's a shame he stepped on the third rail," Melvin answered. "Guess he didn't focus enough, hey Mr. Lindbloom?" he said chuckling.

"Tough break but you know what they say Melvin, fecal occurs."

"Frank are you still there?" Elizabeth asked, waking up from her drug-induced stupor. "Is that Michael? Do you have Michael with you up there? I hate him! No, I still love him you know," she confessed, hardly able to stand up straight.

"Frank, I don't want you to hurt him!" she yelled from the bottom of the stairs, as she tried to steady herself and aim her gun.

Everything was moving, not too fast but fast enough to make it difficult for her to get a clean shot off as she attempted to aim the weapon at her brother's head, even though it was dark on the platform. Squeezing the trigger had no effect so she pointed the gun at herself, trying to figure out what had just happened and looked down the barrel of the gun to determine if she could correct the device's problem herself. "What's going on? What's happening?" *I've got to stop Frank from killing Michael,* is all she could think about. She tried to stand up and climb up to the platform but it was too much for her and she lost her grip becoming dizzy again, falling down a cluster of stairs and was knocked unconscious, her gun that had failed to fire, still tightly gripped in her hand.

"Elizabeth, I told you to stay downstairs! Get back in your car and shut the fuck up! I told you I'll be there shortly!"

"Oh really? I wouldn't count on that," a distant voice said as a cigarette lighter flashed for an instant and lit up a completely darkened corner. "Good evening!" the voice resonated in the distance as a puff of smoke was seen.

The smoothness and delivery along with the Italian accent left no doubt that it was none other than Salvatore Rizzo.

He stepped out of the dark shadows and made his presence known with a golden cigarette holder in his relaxed hand. "Frank, my friend, it appears you did not prepare the work area and, as such, you overlooked my presence in the darkness of night. But then you have always been a bit laissez-faire when it comes to business matters. You agree, no?"

Melvin, stunned and frozen in his expression, almost urinated on himself, as he watched the tall figure walk forward out of the shadows.

The music from the Blues Festival was playing the song *The Thrill is Gone,* in the background, and Travis thought the song was so appropriate for the moment. He didn't know who this mysterious man was, but he felt a lot better just seeing the reaction this man had on his assailants.

Michelle stopped breathing for a moment when she heard his voice. She knew that her attorney was here because of the message she had left on his answering machine but she didn't know why he had come. *Perhaps he was in with Lindbloom,* she thought. *No, he was here to help her.*

She kept her head crouched down determined not to look behind her, not with Lindbloom so close to where they were all kneeling. God, she prayed that the hour of deliverance was near.

"Mr. Rizzo, uh, how long have you . . . uh . . . been there?" Lindbloom nervously asked.

There was a weight and confidence to his voice as Salvatore answered, "Long enough. What is in the satchel Frank?" he asked, as he studied Lindbloom's body language. Salvatore's eyes grew cold and they did not blink as he waited for an answer.

"Just some papers that were stolen from me. It's nothing really."

"It would appear it was more than nothing since you now have this family before you on their knees, execution style."

Rizzo walked a step closer although he was still quite a distance away from the group, and his eyes now focused on Travis. "You look much better now; I was wondering have you recovered from the arsenic poisoning?"

Travis looked back at Frank Lindbloom but was too frightened to answer.

Seeing this trepidation, Rizzo's voice took on a slightly different tone, "Let the boy speak!"

"Yes, the doctor said I'm going to make a full recovery."

"Grazie."

"I want to know what is in the satchel Frank and I will not ask again," he said, a bit irritated.

"Files! Files that this bitch stole from me out of my own home and now she has to pay . . . they *all* have to pay!" he said angrily.

"I'm afraid that won't be possible. You see there is one small problem," he said walking over to a nearby bench and sitting down. "The satchel you seek happens to contain information . . . a great deal of information about me, therefore it is *my* property, you agree, no?"

"I was o-o-o only keeping that information in a safe p-p-place in case I needed it. I would never think of using it against you Mr. Rizzo. It was just for insurance purposes that's all," he said with a nervous stutter. "Rizzo you know I bust my ass all over this town, you can ask anybody. *Anybody,* do you hear! And you've had my goddamn balls in a fucking sling so many times I can't even begin to keep count! You squeeze and squeeze," he said clenching his open fist repeatedly, "until you squeeze a person like *me,* dry. I know they call you *The Orange,* except I don't have anything left!" he screamed, with saliva flying out of his mouth. "Did you ever think that maybe the *juice* isn't worth the squeeze?"

As calm as before, Salvatore responded, "That is because you are still not yet a real man, you only possess the *shell* of a man," he said, as his bluish-gray eyes narrowed. "A *real* man," he said, tilting his head towards the kneeling victims, "would a *real* man do this?"

"If that's true then it's because you won't fucking *let* me be a real man! What, with your stooges and informants all over the goddamn place, you might as well be the mayor. You already act as though you're running the whole goddamn city!" he seethed.

Rizzo was unperturbed by Lindbloom's outburst and took a long drag as he put his golden cigarette holder to his lips before he spoke. "Not the whole goddamn city . . . just the parts of the city that interest me Frank . . . just the parts that interest me . . . like that satchel," he reiterated.

"If you want the satchel then you'll have to goddamn take it," he said with a look of seriousness in his face. "Let's face it not even *you*, the Great Salvatore Rizzo is dumb enough to try and take it. See?" he continued sarcastically, "you're not so powerful without your well-paid flunkies around are you? "Feeling all alone, are we Rizzo?"

"Not exactly," Salvatore, calmly answered.

Rizzo snapped his fingers and out of several pitch black corners on the platform, a large multitude of men stepped out, one by one, each one saying "I'm ready!" as they made their presence known. And in the midst of the multitude were Alfredo, Antonio and Emilio, who took their places and stood next to Salvatore, their arms boldly crossed. The remaining brigade on the platform spread out and didn't conceal the fact that they were all heavily armed and at the ready.

"Antonio, take Mr. Dickerson and his family to safety at once. I have a van waiting for them downstairs."

Antonio nodded and did as he was told, helping

Michelle up from her knees along with Travis and Michael who was limping and in discomfort. Before Michelle walked down the steps she looked back and mouthed the words *thank you* to Salvatore.

"You see, my friend," Salvatore said, as he was slowly standing up, "it appears you have come full circle. That is why you have chosen this place to meet. Or did you ever think that this place chose *you*? Look around you Frank. What do you see? Even under the cover of total darkness there is much that remains to be seen! Look over there," he said, tilting his head to the right, "somewhere out there is a fourteen year-old girl who is about to give birth and become a mother for the *second* time. Someone else, very soon from now will go home tonight and beat their one-year old child to death. It will end up in a trash bag and thrown into the dumpster but the mother will claim the child was taken and receive gifts and money from her church and the community and probably end up being television's newest reality star. And over here," he said tilting his head towards the left, "there's probably a junkie shooting up, even though he knows the poison he's putting in his veins will someday kill him, and then there is his dealer, who rejoices in the fact that he's going to have money in his pocket for another day even though he is destroying other people's lives in the process too.

Make no mistake about it Frank, these are all parasites that prey upon everyone and use them as much-needed hosts . . . from the diseased prostitutes to the salt of the earth."

He inhaled deeply on his golden cigarette holder and then he continued. "Can you smell it Frank? Can you smell the hopelessness and despair that this place reeks of? You know in biology there is a name for such a thing. It is something known as symbiosis. Yes, it is the close association of animals of different species that is often, but not always, of mutual benefit to each other.

Take the Egyptian plover bird. It doesn't have to look far for its next meal because it picks the teeth of the crocodile. Even though the crocodile could easily kill it and have a tasty meal, it chooses to allow this bird into its mouth because the bird is providing a simple but much-needed service.

Look around you Frank . . . why this whole goddamn city is just part of *The Symbiotic Section,* waiting for people like you . . . and for people like me. The only problem is that you have committed, as we say back in the old country, an *Un peccato terribile,* a terrible sin. You have destroyed the lives of children and ensured that your drug dealers sell *exclusively* at the schools. You have taken advantage of young girls who are confused and drowning in a sea of trouble and instead of giving them a hand to save them, you have instead given them a few quick jabs with a needle to ensure their paths will be set in a downward spiral and they will lose their souls *forever."*

Now the train was coming, closer and faster as all the others had done before.

Salvatore turned, looked at Alfredo, and nodded.

Alfredo heeded his cue, ran over to Melvin, and with

pinpoint accuracy, he shot Melvin right between the eyes just as the loud roar of the train was going by, stifling the sound of his gunshot.

Frank Lindbloom was visibly shaken as he saw Melvin's bloody, lifeless body slump onto the platform. He looked down to see that he had once again defecated on himself, the stain and the smell was obvious, and he was beyond terrified.

"Please, please Rizzo!" he cried, as he turned around to discover the exits were all blocked by Rizzo's loyal defense force. A broken shell of a man, Frank got down on his knees and pleaded. He did the only thing he *could* do; he sobbed and begged Rizzo for his life.

Alfredo stood next to Rizzo entirely devoid of all emotion and removed his gloves. Then with a pristine white handkerchief, Rizzo took the gun from Alfredo and held it out for Emilio, who was now donning his own pair of gloves.

Once his gloves were on, Emilio wasted no time in taking the gun and he walked, matter-of-factly, over to Lindbloom and stood at attention, waiting to do his master's bidding.

Frank was still on his knees but was now holding on to Emilio's pants leg and weeping, but Emilio was statuesque and waited, at the ready, for his cue.

After several minutes, the train platform started to rumble just a bit, and then a bit more, until it began to noticeably vibrate from the sound of the approaching train.

Salvatore turned and faced the traitor who was now

off his knees and down on his belly, continuing to sob and plead for mercy. Mercy that Rizzo knew he could not give him.

And then, with the train drawing nearer, Rizzo spoke, "There is a saying we have in Sicily called *Giustizia Assoluta*. It means absolute justice! Arrivederci Frank!"

With Salvatore's nod, Emilio stood directly behind Lindbloom and shot him once in the back of the head at close range. The sound was almost deafening.

"Grazie," Emilio said, breathing heavily, "that was for my daughter, Isabella, who he kidnapped and then allowed to be raped and ruined."

"As we say in the old country Emilio, *Siete Benvenuto,* you are welcome," Rizzo commented. "But do not worry my friend, she is not ruined. I will personally see to that."

Chapter Sixty One

Although the shot that had killed Frank Lindbloom had been camouflaged by the roaring sound of the train, it was still necessary for Rizzo and his brigade to leave the area quickly. If they were lucky, it would be just another Saturday night with the usual sounds of gunshots in the background from the numerous firecrackers and drive-by shootings in the area. There would be no need to call the authorities, as they would be routinely frequenting this area in fifteen minutes. Still, they had only minutes to make their departure according to Rizzo's precise timeframe.

When Emilio reached the bottom of the stairs, he looked at Elizabeth's still unconscious body. Then he carefully removed her twenty-two caliber handgun from her hand that had misfired, replacing it with the same gun that had just been used to execute both Melvin and Frank. He meticulously positioned her fingers on the murder weapon and then squeezed her hand closed to ensure the gunshot residue would be transferred onto her hands as well as to her clothing. Next he motioned several of his comrades to carry her up to the train platform and place her next to where her brother lie, in a pool of blood, before they also left the area.

The satchel was now with Rizzo, its rightful owner,

and although the members of his crew did not know his whereabouts, who he was with or what he was doing, all they needed to know was that each person who had played a part in this epic was filled with jubilation as their adventure culminated because on *this* night, this incredibly special night, his loyal defense force knew that justice, *absolute justice* had indeed been served.

Chapter Sixty Two

Four Weeks Later . . . .

The University of Chicago Medical Center was once again bustling with the sounds of activity from patient admittances, announcements over the public address system, and of course, the drama.

Today, the sounds coming from room four twelve could be heard down the hall as the two visitors in Janice's room didn't try to hold down their noise level on this visit, their final one.

Clarence, true to form, was nearing the end of one of his raunchy jokes.

"So after the bartender kisses her hand and sucks each individual finger, she smiles and says . . . thanks for caring, but all I really wanted to tell you is that I need a soapy rag for my hands because the ladies room is out of toilet paper!" Casey said laughing hysterically, as he slapped the nightstand and almost fell over in the chair he was in.

"Whew! Ha, ha, ha, ha, ha!" Ashley laughed and squealed, "that was one of your most gross jokes," she said, wiping tears from her eyes.

"Oh Ashley, honey!" Janice chimed in, "I can see you

don't know Casey that well. That was one of his more tame jokes!" she said slapping her bed.

"Oh boy, my side hurts from laughing so hard," Ashley chuckled.

"So are you stunned about the story in the paper? I mean about Frank Lindbloom being murdered?" Janice asked.

"I just can't believe it," Ashley answered, shaking her head back and forth, "but I can't say that I'll miss him. He was such an evil and contemptible human being that I, for one, will be sleeping a hell of a lot better! "So did you see who was behind the wheel when you were hit?"

"As a matter of fact, I don't even remember being hit. The doctor said it was something about a suppressed memory. And you know what? I'm *glad* I can't remember. But I'd like to think it was Lindbloom. That way, I feel he got his just rewards," Janice remarked.

"Ashley, what was Michael's reaction to Lindbloom's murder?" Clarence asked.

"Well," she said, "he seems to be taking it all in stride. You know there was bad blood between them for years but he's working it out."

"Speaking of working it out, I'll be working on getting out of here tomorrow and I don't want to see a hospital room again for a very, very long time!" Janice said.

Clarence began yet another joke, this one was really disgusting but hilarious but it held the attention of both women. Janice paid so much attention that she even managed to forget about all the pain she was still in.

And so the time went by and the day passed without incident, except for a great deal more of Clarence's sick jokes, Ashley's tears of joy and Janice's laughter on this visit, their final visit to room four twelve.

Chapter Sixty Three

The cab ride was just what Michelle needed to help her sort things out today. She smoothed out the new outfit she had just purchased from Lord & Taylor, checked for any runs in her super sheer hosiery and then leaned back in the cab, closing her eyes.

It was Wednesday and she had had a lot to think about these past four weeks. She had come within inches of not only losing her own life but that of Michael's and her son's. Her newest business venture, *The Cracked Pot,* had gone from six high-end clients to well over one hundred, and was still growing, and let's not forget that she was just putting the finishing touches on a cookbook titled *The Cajun Invasion.* Certainly a lot for anyone to think about!

She let out a sigh and then thought about the evening she had been driven home on that fateful night, the last night that she had seen Frank Lindbloom alive and was thankful that private security had been provided for her, Michael and Travis. And then there was the driver, Antonio wasn't it? Who flat out told them never, under *any* circumstances, were they to ever mention anything about the events that had led up to their almost becoming murder victims and how they were set free. *Really?* That was a given!

And this entire time, her attorney, her very own attorney, Salvatore Rizzo was at the center of everything, there was no escaping that. He had generously paid for the expensive therapy sessions that she, Michael and Travis had attended two times per week followed by lavish spa treatments exclusively for her to ensure her relaxation. Each time sending a driver to take her to and from each appointment and twice a week there was always a package on her doorstep containing the orange spice herbal tea she loved and the imported chocolates she enjoyed munching on during previous visits to his office some months ago. She was indeed very grateful, but she wondered, if gratitude was *all* that she was feeling. Or was it something *more*?

Once she exited the vehicle, she smiled when she saw Michael, however she was quick to pick up on the pensive look on his face. Perhaps it was because Ashley was with him.

"Ashley, how are you girl!" she said, as she walked up to her. They touched cheek-to-cheek with puckered mouths, their lips never *really* actually touching the skin of one another.

"I'm great," she answered.

"Why the cab? What happened to your car?"

"It's in the shop again, you know how it is."

"You look so beautiful, is that new?"

"Yes, just thought I'd treat myself."

Michael looked stunned as the two women walked arm in arm towards the entrance of the *Good Luck Cultural Center*. "I didn't know you two knew each other," he commented.

"Oh Michael," Michelle said, "we've already passed go and collected our two hundred dollars!" she said laughing. "Come on or we'll be late for Travis' graduation."

Michael shook his head in disbelief and chuckled as he followed the two women. *And I was sweating over nothing,* he thought.

Once inside, they all found their assigned seating, something that was normal for a concert but unheard of for a graduation. Michael, Michelle and Ashley were seated directly in the front row. *Wow, we really lucked out,* Michelle thought, *these seats are perfect. I wonder how we got placed here?* she wondered.

With the programs handed out, and all the friends, faculty and family seated, the Mercer High School graduation began. Everyone looked around, in amazement, at how elegant and tasteful the new venue was.

Michael looked behind him to see Clarence Casey wheeling Janice Freedman to a special section that had been reserved just for them and he nodded, acknowledging their arrival.

Clarence was wearing a light beige suit that was tailored to perfection along with a soft pink shirt, pink socks and pink handkerchief. Yes, it was quite the showstopper. Janice had on simple white slacks along with a melon-colored chiffon top. Her gray hair was colored, her makeup had been updated and she had been given a trendy haircut, all courtesy of Clarence. Amazingly, she looked ten years younger.

Michelle also looked behind her, blew kisses at Clarence and Janice and then she noticed how Michael's eyes lit up when he looked at Ashley, his masculine features, softening under her spell and she wondered if anyone would *ever* look at her in that manner. One day perhaps, but who was she kidding? Wasn't she being a tad bit silly?

She was way too busy, way too successful and married to her career. What man in his right mind would be able to deal with that without feeling insecure after a while? It would definitely take more than an average man to be able to cope with her, on *any* level. She thought about it for a moment and realized that it might take one of Travis' superhero comic book characters, someone with real power who had a secret identity and would love her with reckless abandon. Now she smiled . . . she *was* being silly.

Feeling a little melancholy, she excused herself and went to the ladies room to regroup her thoughts. *Got to get a hold of yourself Michelle! After all, you're a self-made millionaire for Christ's sake! So what if you don't have a man . . . get over it!*

She entered the ladies room and sat down at one of the empty vanities and took it all in. The expensive fixtures, ornate but tasteful decor, choices of creamy pump soaps, lotions and embossed, disposable hand towels. Wow, she could get used to this type of luxury!

A quick lipstick touchup and she felt better. As she made her exit and walked briskly back to the main auditorium, a man approached her, handing her an embossed white envelope, practically shoving it in her hand, and then he walked away. She knew this man . . . it was Antonio! The same man who had taken them to safety the night Frank Lindbloom was killed.

While the microphone was being checked one last time for sound, Michelle made a quick entrance, sat down, and with utter curiosity and hands slightly shaking, she slowly opened the envelope and read its contents. She was stunned.

After the dull announcements and dismal speeches, the curtains parted and the special guest was introduced. Looking his absolute best, it was none other than Salvatore Rizzo.

There was total silence until he made his way to the microphone where he received a standing ovation.

"Graduating class, honored guests, parents, friends, our hard-working faculty and distinguished members of the Board of the Chinese Cultural Center, we have come here today to meet in this new place, this wonderful center," he said pausing, "that has brought us *all* together. . . . . "

He continued with his speech and he effortlessly had the attention of every single person in the audience, especially Michelle's. She looked at him as he stood there, speaking with such a command of the room, and she felt herself starting to smile. She wouldn't be alive today if it wasn't for this man. He appeared to be such a mystery and yet she wondered and had to admit to herself that she already knew a great deal about him. After all, even though she hadn't copied every file that Lindbloom had taken, she was able to remember a great deal of what they had proved or implied in relation to him. Then she thought to herself; *Was it so immoral to try to make a right out of a wrong? Was it horrible to have someone on your side that could pull a few strings for you? Didn't ordinary people deserve a second chance? . . . . . Didn't she?*

His speech was winding down now, " . . . . And so we are doomed to become a generation without a cause, but it's not too late if we adopt a purpose now, today . . . and resolve to not only fulfill our dreams, but surpass them. Let us not just yearn for the future, let us take hold and form it!"

The crowd was on its feet applauding loudly as he dipped his head in a slight bow, however when he did so, he made it a point to make direct eye contact with Michelle and for a split second, their eyes met and she smiled.

The graduates made their way across the stage, one by one until, sometime later, Travis had his turn and walked across as the others had done. Even though it was advised to hold your applause, no one held back. At this moment in her life, Michelle felt exhilarated, almost to the point of being invincible, until the ceremony finally ended.

After the customary photos, kisses and barrage of joyful tears, Michelle said her goodbyes to her son, hugging him tightly and then to Michael and Ashley but not before handing Travis the keys to his new red Mustang that was parked and waiting for him outside the Cultural Center. "Travis, I'm so proud of you! These are for you, you've earned it. Now be careful and obey the speed limit and remember to wear your seatbelt . . ." she said tearing up.

"It's okay Mom," Travis cut her off, "you and dad have taught me well, grasshopper!" he said bowing. "Look at my car everybody, it's so rad!"

Then she turned to Michael and Ashley, who were holding hands and to Janice and Clarence, "You guys enjoy yourselves, but don't forget we're having a huge victory dinner Saturday night at my place and I want you all there at eight o'clock sharp."

"Do you need a ride Michelle?" Michael asked, after he made certain it was okay with Ashley.

"Oh that's alright. Thanks anyway, but I'll be okay. Don't you worry about me, I realized today that I'm going to be just fine," she answered, with brightness in her eyes. She kept walking past the families that were issuing their congratulations to their children until she was eventually unnoticeable, blending into the crowd.

"Where did she go?" Ashley asked, "I wanted to know if I can bring something on Saturday."

Michael had a slight smile on his face, as he had watched her enter a stretch limousine and be driven away. A limousine he had seen several times before at only the most exclusive of charity events. "She's going home Ashley and I believe she's finally on her way."

The day had been long, but *her* journey had been longer, so much longer, in fact, it had taken an entire lifetime.

Upon her arrival, she looked around the arboretum

eyeing a silver tray which was placed in a far corner of the room with a package of her favorite orange spice herbal tea upon it along with the expensive chocolates she always treated herself to, and she couldn't help but appreciate the attention to detail. The champagne was already perfectly chilled near the Jacuzzi and the special floor-to-ceiling windows had been treated to see out but not see in. She had been to only one other home in Lake Forest for a women's conference but unfortunately, she had had to make an early departure. Even so, she never forgot the magnificent homes which looked like something out of Beverly Hills, most having over six thousand square feet.

This tasteful and luxurious home had everything she had ever wanted, and at almost sixteen thousand square feet, it was beyond any mansion she had ever seen in all her travels, and it overlooked Lake Michigan to boot!

Of course from the documents she had seen she knew that there were other homes; a two-hundred acre country estate in the South of France, an enormous seaside villa in Capri, Italy, a hillside home on the island of Maui and the fabulous three-story penthouse in Manhattan. All his and all completely paid for. And yet, with all his wealth and unmatched success, she had seen how compassionate and humble he was. The years had not hardened his heart and for that she was glad.

She walked over to the tray and slowly removed the handwritten note from her purse which she had received at the graduation, reading it again. Its message was simple, but the choice had to be hers and hers alone. It was then that she saw the chair, the chair with the bikini and pink robe upon it. Still boxed with the letter *M* embroidered on the cuffs in delicate white peonies, her favorite flower.

She knew from her meetings with Salvatore that indecision was a weakness. This was her moment, she would have to choose here and now or depart. Michelle closed her eyes, sucked in her breath and gently smiled.

Decision finally made, she leaned back in the Jacuzzi and enjoyed another glass of the finest champagne she had ever had in her life, her cares seemingly melting away in the swirling waters that surrounded her weary body.

"The temperature is to your liking, no?"

"Oh, yes, very much so. A perfect 102 degrees, right?"

"Absolutely!"

She turned sideways and decided that this was as good a time as any and loosened her bikini top, arched her back and smiled, "all this time you were my attorney. I've come to you with all my business deals, shared my dreams and hopes and failures with you, and for so many years . . ."

"One can reflect on the past and learn," he said, as he removed the clip from her hair, watching it cascade down her soft, bronzed shoulders. "One can even grow from it, but to dwell on is a waste of the present *and* the future."

"And the future?" she asked, "does it hold anything of importance for you now?"

His bluish-gray eyes looked deeply into hers as he leaned over and gently removed her top. "Everything I am and everything I want is right here, right now, in *this* room."

She set the half-empty glass of champagne down and returned his gaze. No words were spoken for several moments but then, there were none needed.

Finally, Michelle dear, finally, she thought to herself. *Can this really be happening? Is it really true?*

Removing his robe, he revealed a still slender body with firm muscle tone and a taut, flat belly, as he joined her inside the Jacuzzi, his eyes never leaving hers.

"You see, my love, it was meant to be this way because of all the things you have shared with me over the years, I can't get you out of my mind and because of all that I feel for you, God in heaven knows that I don't want to have you out of my heart, not now, not *ever!* Whether you realize it or not, my love," he paused and then slowly and sensuously kissed her, taking her breath away . . . . .

"We are exactly the same, but different!"

Epilogue

One Year Later . . . . . .

*J*anice Freedman made a full recovery and realized a few things about herself. First of all, she wanted to give back to the community, so she volunteered her time at the University of Chicago Medical Center, every other weekend; Second, she knew she couldn't retire and whole-heartedly accepted the promotion Michael gave her to Vice President of Contracts; Thirdly, she finally came out of the closet, because if Lindbloom, who wasn't the brightest star in the sky, knew she was gay, then there would probably be others who also knew or would find out soon enough; Finally, she kept her new makeover look that Clarence had customized for her, just because it made her feel better. The grapevine says she met someone at the *Miss Lay-Dees Bar* and is very happy.

Bianca Lapicola, always on the lookout for wealthy mid-dle-aged men on the PP, finally hit the jackpot and hooked up with Daniel Livingston, the Executive Producer of the segment, *Made in Chicago*. He adored her and allowed her free creative rein of it. Within a few months, she single-handedly transformed the segment into a one hour television show that was a ratings success.

As for her personal life, she was no longer on the prowl for men on the PP, kept in touch with Ashley, seeing her as often as her schedule allowed, and made certain that Daniel knew she wore the pants in their relationship, just the way that Daniel liked it.

Debra Morris, alas, the perpetual victim of sexual assaults, decided she might as well get paid for what she was doing anyway . . . getting screwed! On a dare, she answered an ad for an adult production company and became one of the biggest adult film stars that (S.A.P.) Starlight Adult Productions had ever had the pleasure of working with. Debra became very wealthy, thoroughly enjoyed her work and never looked back. It's said that every year, she sends Michael Dickerson a copy of her latest release and her specialty in films was anal sex!

Steven Powell, the Assistant District Attorney, went on to win an extremely large number of cases for the State in a calendar year, although many judges were constantly irritated by his requests for unnecessary subpoenas and his obsessive attention to detail.

THE SYMBIOTIC SECTION

Darryl Black continued working as a defense attorney and sustained an excellent working relationship with Salvatore, being a link to prominent cases that needed that special touch, for an outrageous fee, of course, but thanks to Salvatore, he never lost a case.

Tyrone Robinson continued to play professional football for the Chicago Bears, but in the off-season he set up a foundation to help inner-city kids take trips to China in a sort of cultural exchange program. His wife, Jazmine, kept closer tabs on her husband, monitoring his e-mails and becoming more involved in his off-season activities. Word has it that they are happy and expecting twins. Yes, I guess you could say that five hundred thousand dollars is a small price to pay for happiness and freedom.

Candace Hernandez resigned from her job at *Simply Pleasures* and with generous financial backing from Michelle, opened her own highly successful adult toy business. She named it *The Candy Store*.

Marc Greenberg continued working at UBMI in his own little world of numbers, oblivious to everything else going on in the firm. At Michael's request, he helped create an iron-clad checks and balance system so that there would never be any more check requests that slipped by him again. As for his brother, his charges were mysteriously dropped.

Dr. Reginald Fulton took some much needed time off and successfully completed a drug rehab program at a respected facility in Desert Hills, Arizona. As a token of his appreciation for the information he always provided, Salvatore paid for all the costs involved. Unfortunately, once he was completely drug free, his wife no longer felt needed and left him for someone who had a bad substance abuse problem. In court she said that she finally felt wanted again.

Saddened but not deterred, Dr. Fulton recovered emotionally and had no problem winning full physical and legal custody of his children because, after all, they were his life.

Dr. James Whitman eventually retired and went to live in the lap of luxury, just as he had planned in the Caribbean on the island of St. Barts. Unfortunately, because of his close association with Frank Lindbloom by performing examinations on under-age girls and sampling his fair share of the merchandise, he was secretly paid a visit by Emilio one night, and mysteriously disappeared, never to be seen again.

Antonio and Alfredo, wanting to secure long-term employment, had no trouble continuing to work for Salvatore

Rizzo. Their loyalty and devotion to him remained unwavering and steadfast.

Antonio considered himself to be very similar to his boss, and began his own collection of pocket knives and, when the situation presented itself, he was more than willing to test them out in the field, so to speak, at the behest of his boss.

Emilio took some time off to be with his family but was welcomed back with open arms. He worked constantly to sharpen his craft and maintain his reputation as *The Executioner* in certain circles, proudly adding num chucks to his repertoire of offensive weapons. He maintained a low profile but always made it a point to be at-the-ready should his special skills be needed.

The Stanford Court of Arms Hotel was raided by Rizzo's loyal defense force releasing forty young girls from the shame and degradation of human slavery and each was given counseling and drug addiction treatment as needed. Soon afterwards, the hotel suspiciously caught fire and was burnt to the ground.

Wolfthings continued to win numerous races at the Arlington Park Race Track and was eventually put out to stud by a mysterious new owner with the initials S.R.

Isabella was treated at the hospital and was relieved when she tested negative for pregnancy and all other sexually transmitted diseases. Additionally, she attended therapy sessions from the counseling of a well-respected psychiatrist, who just happened to be of Italian descent. Under his nurturing and with the ever-present supervision of Emilio, she recovered from her ordeal and eventually learned to have trust and enjoy life again. Eventually she met a young man who was a journalist for the *Chicago Tribune Newspaper* and they fell in love. They had Emilio's blessing right from the start and were engaged six months after their initial introductions.

Ramiro Martinez was at home with his family on his one day off when he was taken away from his favorite television show to answer a knock at the door. He was shocked to see two people standing in front of him, señorita Isabella and a man she introduced as her father, Emilio. After talking with Ramiro and meeting his family, Emilio drove them to a nice area that had a laundromat and dry-cleaning store for sell, thanked him again for his help and handed him an envelope. The envelope contained the keys to the store, fifty-thousand dollars in cash, and a note stating that he would *always* be protected at this location.

Ramiro wept tears of joy because he knew that now he could not only continue to work hard but that now he could provide a better life for his family. It is said that Ramiro never misses a single Sunday worship service because not only does he now believe in God, he truly believes in miracles.

Herbert and Paige MacNamera returned from their trip to China but the entire ordeal proved too much for Herbert and, being unable to overcome his bouts of distrust and jealousy when it came to his wife, they divorced shortly afterwards.

Paige kept in touch with Mr. Quan Lee over the internet and continued practicing her Tai Chi exercises every morning. After a few months, Mr. Lee made the decision to join her in the United States and together they opened an Asian-Themed Bed and Breakfast, the first of its kind, called *The Lotus House*. Rumor has it that they are much more than business partners.

Henry Lee, owner of *The Black Pearl Restaurant,* was so fascinated with the Baccarat crystal that he received as a gift from Salvatore Rizzo, that he had custom glass cabinets installed in his restaurant's gift shop to showcase all the crystal he had since purchased and could hardly keep enough in stock due to his customer demand.

Elizabeth Lindbloom was found guilty of discharging a weapon in a residential area, having a firearm without a gun permit, drunk and disorderly conduct, being under the influence of a controlled substance, and of a double homicide. With the gunshot residue on her hands, having a motive because she wanted drugs, drugs that her brother would not supply her with, and being placed at the scene of the crime, she was convicted of all the charges. For some time, there was talk that she might even be sentenced to death, however during her trial when it was revealed that she was HIV-positive and under extreme emotional stress, she was sentenced and taken to a Maximum Security Women's Correctional Facility for the criminally insane and lived her life in a special section for patients there with infectious diseases.

By day, she pays special attention to her grooming, asking the guards if someone by the name of E.T. is listed on the visitor's log for her. At night, she is heard to moan and call out for her brother because she claims to see him roaming the hallways in search of her.

Travis drove his new red Mustang, with a custom license plate that read *Oreo,* to Ithaca College and chose to reside in a co-ed dorm instead of a fraternity. Number one, he felt it would be quieter and number two; it was where Kimberly, the girl he always winked at in Mrs. Young's class, was residing.

Making the *Ithaca Bombers'* gymnastics team was no problem for him and he made friends easily. He wrote to his parents twice a month and applied himself to his studies when he wasn't involved in gymnastics. He maintained a 4.0 grade point average and he was quite confident in his decision to major in Biology, with a focus on symbiosis.

Eldrick Travell, or E.T. as he was known on the street, finally decided to get off the streets after getting yet *another* woman pregnant. Through some of his user friends which just happened to be guards, he secured a full-time position as a medical orderly in a Maximum Security Women's Correctional Facility. Because, after all, it was a job where he didn't have to work or think too hard about with many fringe benefits, including unlimited access to powerful, mind-altering drugs.

One day, he had to deliver some paperwork to a different section of the facility and that's when he saw Elizabeth Lindbloom. Shocked that she was even a patient and repulsed by her appearance, he questioned why she was there. Informed that she was in the psyche ward and was now at Stage IV with an HIV-positive diagnosis, he quit without giving notice.

It was a few months later when E.T. was chronically ill, that he was finally checked out and told he had tested positive for the HIV virus. Distraught and extremely depressed, it was no coincidence that he was found in a run down motel, dead of an intentional drug overdose!

My Man Number One and My Man Number Two continued to get high and do what they had to do to get by without any remorse for the people they got hooked on drugs or any regard for their lifestyle choices.

E. T.'s suicide, although unexpected, made it easier for them to divide up his territory underneath the elevated tracks with more profits realized than ever before. Neither one of them had the slightest inkling of what they were *actually* passing on to their female customers when they accepted sexual favors as trade in lieu of money. To them it was just business as usual. You know what I'm sayin'?

Ashley Taylor, renewed her contract on the hit soap opera, *Now is Forever,* for a large unprecedented sum, but still managed to shoot an occasional commercial for the Tollway-Arlington Bank. When Michael finally asked her how she could afford to live in the Marina City Towers when she was working at the coffee shop, she simply informed him that it was her parents' condo and she was allowed to rent it from them for a reduced rate. It was something so simple that he had never thought of it as an option.

She and Michael followed the charity circuit, attending balls and fund raisers for worthy causes and he loved that she enjoyed the limelight. Additionally, she hosted lavish parties at his two homes but put her foot down when it came to cooking and cleaning, something Michael wasn't quite prepared for but adjusted to. Nonetheless, they enjoyed a stable, healthy, super hot sexual relationship and Michael found out, in due time, that she was as outlandish in the bedroom as he was. Shit! This girl was into *everything!*

THE SYMBIOTIC SECTION

Michael Dickerson took Ashley to the *Windy City Balloon Airport* in the small Village of Fox River Grove and proposed to her aboard an early morning hot air balloon ride.

It was obvious to Bianca that her friend had accepted even before she saw the four-carat diamond ring on her finger. Michael had never been happier but this time he was mature enough to find just the right balance between business and pleasure, making time for Ashley *and* Travis. Between work and personal time, he even managed to occasionally work on his golf swing. He actually assisted Ashley with some of the plans for their upcoming nuptials and, with the help of Salvatore Rizzo, was planning to take United Bank Marketing Incorporated public.

Clarence Casey never revealed to Janice about the incident with Lindbloom in her hospital room. To him, it was a chapter that should remain closed.

He continued to work as Creative Director at UBMI but also branched out to co-produce small independent films and act as an occasional Creative Consultant for the soap, *Now is Forever.* It seems he just couldn't get enough of being around Ashley, on and off camera.

On the set of *Now is Forever,* he met the male star, Jerry Leonard, who was the most gorgeous man Clarence Casey had ever seen.

One evening, Jerry dropped by Clarence's home to pick

up a script he had tweaked and after a few drinks too many, Jerry confessed to Clarence that he was hopelessly gay, still in the closet and completely smitten with him. Clarence couldn't have been happier, but of course it was all hush - - hush. Because, baby girl, it's always about the drama!

Michelle Pierson continued to delve into her various projects but now she learned to pace herself. *The Invisible Butler's* day to day operations were now handled by Lucinda, who excelled in housekeeping duties. As promised, Michelle gave her a large bonus, promoted her to a supervisory position and paid a private tutor to help her become skilled at reading and writing in English.

The Cracked Pot became so exclusive that she had to hire a staff of ten, just to keep up with the demand, but it was worth it.

Her cookbook, *The Cajun Invasion,* made the New York Times Bestseller List and she was trying out recipes, here and there, for a follow-up cookbook, *The Cajun Persuasion.*

She looked forward to receiving Travis' letters twice a month and was always ready to put everything on hold for her beloved Salvatore, if that's what was needed or what he wanted because all the success in the world couldn't do for her what this man had done. How she adored him! With talk of marriage on the horizon, she knew she had found a superhero after all!

THE SYMBIOTIC SECTION

Salvatore Rizzo continued to cultivate his business relationships because, as he had always said, relationships are a key element in life and the most valuable commodity one can have is information. He was persistent in influencing the parts of the city that interested him, accepted his share of high-end legal cases, gave millions to charity and, along with his loyal defense force, ensured that the average working man, got justice too. In short, he was in complete control of a goddamn empire!

As for his personal life, he had once said that -- Regardless, we all have our vices and we all have our, shall we say, pleasures. Michelle Pierson was a shining star, the feather in his cap and the crowned jewel he had been searching for. The incomparable Salvatore Rizzo had finally met his match with a woman who could sustain his interests in *and* out of the bedroom and his deep love, commitment and devotion to her never waivered, not even once.

Yes, she was indeed a rare treasure that he alone possessed!

And so the two of them continued . . . . . a force to be reckoned with.

They lived, they laughed and God, how they loved!

THE END

CPSIA information can be obtained at www.ICGtesting.com
Printed in the USA
LVOW08s1740070913

351187LV00006B/6/P